# TARGETED

## TO KILL

### A MEN OF THE BADGE NOVEL

# RILEY
# McKISSACK

TARGETED TO KILL

For more information on the author and her works, please see www.RileyMcKissack.com

ISBN: 978-0-9913299-0-8

Published in the United States of America.

# ABOUT THE AUTHOR

**Riley McKissack** is an award-winning journalist. Cornered gunmen, cop killers, a bomb going off in a domestic terrorism incident, Riley's covered them all. Riley spent years chasing stories involving every type of bad guy and cop imaginable, including FBI, Homeland Security, homicide detectives and arson investigators.

Riley sponged up the drama, tension and danger on SWAT operations, hostage negotiations, drug busts and countless other dangerous situations.

That passion and drama spills out onto the pages of Riley's novels, along with the personal stories behind the men and women who stand between danger and the people they love.

Riley can be found at:
*https://facebook.com/riley.mckissack*
*http://rileymckissack.com*
*https://twitter .com/RileyMckissack*

JOIN THE RILEY MCKISSACK NEWSLETTER
*http://www.rileymckissack.com/contact*

# CHAPTER ONE

Mick's hand curled around Becca's neck, pulling her mouth closer to his. Her sapphire blue eyes shone in the dark, pulsing with need for him.

He read the desire and answered it, leaning in to take her mouth, that mouth that knew how to drive him crazy, a destination he wanted to visit as often as possible.

Long, hot moments later, they slid along the bench seat of the old pickup truck, ending up lying along the worn out, leather seats, their bodies entwined.

Mick had worked long and hard to own the pickup, though it was nothing compared to some of the vehicles other guys in school drove. But, that was okay. As soon as he'd seen that comfy bench seat, he'd known he had to have it. So, he'd worked as many hours as he could get just so he and Becca could have private moments like this.

He fit his body to hers, his hands pulling her hips into his, wanting, needing her body against his own.

Steam clouded the windshield and the windows, giving an extra added intimacy to the truck's cab. Mick lived for these moments with Becca, her soft skin against his.

He nuzzled into her neck, inhaling her scent, sucking softly against the pulse point that beat in rhythm with his own.

A soft moan slipped from Becca's lips just before he took her mouth once again, tasting her, connecting with her. God, he wanted her, wanted all that she so willingly offered.

1

"Take me," she whispered. "Make me yours."

A heat rose up in him, singeing his mind, firing it with impulses that were ancient, pounding drums of desire.

****

*Ten Years Later*

The dark prison yard shimmered with the sloughed off desperation of men who'd lost the right to determine their own existence, men who lived in cages, locked away when the sun went down like dangerous animals.

Mick Hampton crouched in the shadows, prepared to help three of the feral beasts escape. What their associates planned to do was inhuman. Agonizing death or maiming injuries awaited many if Mick was unsuccessful in traveling with the pack back to their lair.

He sucked in a deep breath and hoped he was up to the job this time.

"Go, go, go," Rowdy's voice punched out in a machine gun staccato. "Now, now, now."

And Mick did. He charged across the dark prison yard between the circling slashes of light from the guard tower. Even with a baseball player's sliding finish, he barely made it to cover before another pulse of light illuminated the hard-packed ground he'd just crossed.

The finger of light circled around the prison yard, searching for anything out of place. In the following moment of blackness, another beast bolted across the dirt, then another, then another, until three felons lurked in the night with him.

Mick held his breath, waiting for a screaming siren to alert the entire compound a breakout was in progress. But, only an owl hooted from the woods surrounding the prison fences.

"Where is that damn ambulance?" Rowdy muttered.

Sean Jackson, aka Rowdy, had gotten his nickname long

ago because he was notoriously short on patience, ready to start a fight at the drop of a dirty baseball cap.

Within seconds that seemed like hours, an ambulance rolled out of the covered back entrance to the prison. With perfect timing, the ambulance slid to a short stop, hiding behind the out building before the light could circle back around to note it stopping.

Rowdy jerked open the back of the ambulance. A guard lay on the floor, his hands and feet secured with zip ties, duct tape over his mouth. Another couple of zip ties attached him to a low, cabinet door so he couldn't get up. The guy was secured as tightly as a deer on the hood of a pickup truck.

The man's eyes widened like a cornered animal ready for butchering as Rowdy leaned in and jeered into his face, "Heh, heh, heh. Who's laughing now?" Rowdy hauled off and slugged the bound man. The guard's head hit the hard floor with a metallic sound that spoke of concussion, then his eyes rolled back in his head.

Mick cringed at the force of the blow. There wasn't supposed to be a guard in the back. The guy should have gone inside to file paperwork, giving the driver, who'd been carefully placed by the militia group for tonight's escape, just long enough to take off with the ambulance.

The driver was one of the many secret supporters of the North Georgia militia, known as Homegrown. The group planned to take down the federal government with a series of attacks designed to systematically break its will.

How many people lived normal lives, working jobs that would give them access, such as this ambulance driver, laying in wait for just the right moment to be of service to this terrorist cell?

The driver was using a fake identity. He'd be picked up later even though he'd ditch this identity after tonight.

The unconscious guard was the first of their victims on this mission.

And the first thing that could go wrong on an undercover operation such as this. Nothing ever went exactly as any cop planned.

Quickly, efficiently, Rowdy went into action, all business, as if he hadn't just taken out a personal vendetta against one of his least favorite guards.

A large hunting knife lay on the ambulance floor, probably placed there by the ambulance driver. Rowdy picked up the knife and leaned over the guard. Mick tensed, his eyes following the knife, ready to pounce. Was Rowdy going to slit the guard's throat with that knife?

If Rowdy went for the man's throat, it would be an all-out fight to the death between Mick and Rowdy who'd taken every opportunity to lift weights in the months he'd been imprisoned. Rowdy's snake tattoo slithered across the rippling muscles of his bulging biceps, the evil head with open jaws and extended fangs, ending on a large forearm that pulsed with power, making it clear Mick wouldn't fare well in that fight.

Not to mention White, Rowdy's second in command, who would probably wrap his meaty hands around Mick's throat, choking him easily with those muscles he'd honed using the weights that taxpayer dollars provided him in prison.

But, he'd have to try. Mick knew for a fact the guard had three little girls under ten at home, and a wife.

Rowdy turned the jagged, serrated edge of the knife toward the guard. But, he just sliced the zip ties with a popping sound.

Air escaped Mick's lungs with the same feeling of sudden release.

Quickly, Rowdy stripped the guard of his uniform and shoved him out onto the ground. Then, just for fun, White pulled the guy's boxer shorts and undershirt off, leaving the man naked in the cold, night air.

"Nice touch." Rowdy chuckled. "Should'a thought of it myself."

Then, he looked at Mick with eyes that seemed to be calculating whether to finish Mick off now or wait till they got outside the earshot of the prison guards. "Get in," he growled at Mick.

Mick followed White and Stan into the ambulance as

4

Rowdy slipped on the uniform, an unsuspecting police officer's worse nightmare-an armed convict with the perfect disguise.

And a bad attitude.

Rowdy reached into a cabinet and pulled out three semiautomatic pistols, handing them around. "They're ready to go, like I expect you to be if anything goes down at the gate." Rowdy's dirty, yellowed teeth clipped off each word with precision.

The guy seemed to take pride in his lack of personal grooming, enjoying the affront his untrimmed beard and stained teeth had on other prisoners when he got up in their faces, spitting out his foul breath.

Mick checked his gun. "Empty. There's no bullets in this gun."

Rowdy slid Mick a sly look. "We'll get you some at the next stop. Just wave it around if anything happens and they'll duck."

The empty gun said clearer than words that Mick wasn't considered completely trustworthy by the group. They'd taken him cause he was Stan's cellmate but also because an associate of Rowdy's had vouched for Mick, saying he was a true "homegrown" patriot.

The associate had gotten a reduced sentence in exchange for the cooperation. But, Mick couldn't help but wonder, had something else been whispered to Rowdy by the associate?

Undercover was hell cause you just never really knew. He'd talked up the same bull as these guys about bringing down the federal government.

Had he convinced them?

Or did they plan to get Mick killed if the cops stopped the group, buying time to gun down whoever had shot Mick?

At first glance, these guys didn't seem all that smart. Big and mean, their development seemed to have stopped at the neck. When Mick had first met them, he'd thought if they were the head of the snake, a BB gun could finish them off.

But, the longer he was around them, the more he began to

think that evil touches, like the empty gun, could take these guys a long way.

This "breakout" had taken some organizing and cooperation from the Feds to happen. In placing Mick in the middle of this cell, they'd hoped he would report back to the real organizers of the plot. Cause no one figured these guys could ever pull off the operation that was planned.

They'd figured Homegrown was just taking care of their own, not letting financers of their operation languish in jail. Figured if their people thought they'd be forgotten and abandoned once they went to prison, they'd be more likely to roll over and give the Feds information.

The big bang was theorized to happen in three days. Buzz had been growing, according to the lawyer who'd conveyed information to Mick when they met in prison. The lawyer carried notes from Hernandez, his FBI contact on the operation. And Mick sent information back to Hernandez the same way.

Mick had to find out what was supposed to happen and where. The world was a big place with many targets.

He had to stop these guys from hurting innocent Americans. If he were killed, there was no telling if the group could be stopped before they killed many people.

The knife Rowdy had used to cut the zip ties lay discarded on the ground. Mick picked it up, turning it in his hands so he'd be ready to gut anyone who tried to hurt him. The metal gleamed, reflecting light in a clear message that someone would pay if they took him on.

Gutting? Not a nice way to die, your innards spilling out as you quickly bleed to death.

Rowdy's face even paled a little bit as he eyed the knife in Mick's hands. He leaned away slightly. Then he sucked in a deep breath and stepped back into his relished role as boss.

"White, you lay on the gurney, ready to go if anything happens." White slid onto the gurney, his gun held tightly in his hand, and Rowdy tossed a blanket over him.

"Stan, you get into this compartment. And Atlanta, you get

into that one over there."

Mick looked at the tiny compartment he was supposed to squeeze into, then at the large one indicated for Stan.

"I'll get in this one with Stan."

"No." Stan shook his head. "I don't like being that close to no man." He reached for the compartment door and lifted it.

"Too bad. I'm too tall for that one," Mick said and stepped into the larger, bench-like compartment and lay down in the comfortably sized space. He turned the knife so that it caught the light, glinting back a message to Stan.

Stan was already a bit afraid of Mick to start with, not as physically strong as White or Rowdy. He spent more time brushing his teeth than lifting weights, his teeth dentist clean.

Mick had appreciated the lack of bad breath in a cellmate.

"Dang it." Stan bared those pearly whites in a grimace at the space where he would have to lay beside Mick, then dropped the compartment door with a heavy thud that echoed in Mick's ears. Mick could only assume Stan got into the smaller compartment where he'd have to curl up, cause Mick couldn't hear anything for several seconds.

Screw it. He wasn't going to be so disabled by not having a gun as well as being in a position where he couldn't jump up, ready to go. These guys would be out of the ambulance and gone before he could even unwind from that small space.

He'd felt comfortable going up against Stan cause in the two months they'd been cellmates, Stan had developed an affection for Mick, Atlanta as he was known in jail. Besides, Stan was the least likely to gun down anybody without needing to defend himself.

Which is why Mick was placed in his cell instead of with White or Rowdy.

White's slash of white hair over his ear, thus his nickname, made him look older, but he was still physically able to have strangled Mick in his sleep had they been cellmates.

The ambulance jerked forward, and minutes later, they passed through the gate. When they left the prison behind, the

7

vehicle picked up speed until it raced through the dark Georgia countryside.

With a screech, the vehicle made a hard left turn and began bumping along a lonely, dirt road that cut away from the main road.

Mick figured he knew which road, cause the area surrounding the prison was as familiar to him as the small cell he'd been locked into every night for two months. He'd grown up in this county and had driven every dark road in the area during high school, looking for a place to park.

Biting memories attacked him with sharp stings. Images of Becca Jefferson flooded his mind. Dark hair, pale skin, blue eyes that could convince him of anything, and a body to kill for. Small, tight, and made just for him.

He and Becca's favorite pastime had been searching for hidden away places to park, where they could press their bodies against each other in the dark. Hot, high school moments of passion seared his mind with memories that could still singe his mind if he let it go there.

He seldom let it go there anymore.

Rowdy knocked on his compartment. "Get out. We're almost at the SUV." Mick gripped the knife and lifted the lid slowly, checking for any guns aimed his way. The knife would be an object of revenge, because he could still be dead easily or on his way there before he got the blade into anyone's gut.

Everyone seemed intent on exiting the ambulance. White threw the blanket off and stood. Stan unwound himself from the small compartment, with a glare at Mick. Mick shrugged.

The ambulance screeched to a stop, dust swirling around it like smoke from the fires of hell.

Rowdy pushed the back door open and dust poured into the ambulance. Rowdy coughed like a tuberculosis patient as Mick pulled his T-shirt up over his nose and mouth to form a mask against the heavy cloud and squinted his eyes to keep dirt out.

"Damn it," Rowdy cursed in a strangled voice as he jumped out and swung his gun in a wide circle, ready for any law enforcement that happened along.

The four escapees and the driver all ran in a pack toward the SUV. The cool night air of freedom felt good after the dank smells of prison, scented with the body odor of other men. Mick had breathed that stench for the last two months.

He'd willingly agreed to this mission because it was critical to ferret out details of the attack.

It had coincidently tied into a second agenda of his. He'd already been studying these guys and their connection to a drug ring that was pumping poison into the area. Homegrown justified the drug trafficking as just a means to an end to finance their domestic terrorism.

Mick's life mission was to reach up the ladder of drug trafficking, pulling down men from each rung. If he reached the top dog, good, but anyone he could take out of the business signified countless lives saved.

But, now, his only concern was the attack that was set to happen in three days.

"Here." Rowdy tossed a plastic grocery store bag of clothes at each prisoner. "Change into these, then toss your prison crap in the bushes."

They all stripped down to their skivvies.

"Yowser, that'll wake you up," Stan said with a laugh.

The cold breeze blew across Mick's skin like a disinfectant, scrubbing away some of the stink of the prison.

He quickly pulled on the street clothes, then tossed his prison jumpsuit into the dark woods beyond the road, careful to keep an eye on the guys.

They could easily jump in the car and leave him out here. Then the last few months of deep undercover, hanging out in a prison with these delightful folks and a few hundred of their best friends would have been for nothing.

Or they could just kill him, shooting him before he could get a jump on them with the knife.

"Everybody get in the back and lay low!" Rowdy yelled. "Buck, up front. You can say you're going home from your shift or for some personal reason if we get stopped." The ambulance driver got in the front.

"If some nosey cop don't buy the story, we all roll out the back of this SUV, loaded for bear, and shoot up Smokey the Bear." Rowdy giggled like he kinda hoped they got that chance.

Stan and White crawled into the back of the SUV, but Rowdy turned toward Mick.

"Atlanta." Rowdy's expression turned to a full-on glare, and his gun pointed at Mick's gut. "I need that knife." He tilted his head, like he was measuring the distance the bullet would have to travel.

At this distance, Mick probably wouldn't even live long enough to take revenge on Rowdy. He tossed the knife down in the dirt near Rowdy's feet.

Rowdy leaned down, his gun still trained on Mick, picked up the knife, wiping it on his pants leg. Then, he indicated with a head bob toward the car that Mick should get in.

Damn it. He needed that knife. But, you had to just let things go on a moment-by-moment basis when you were on an operation like this.

Play with the hand you got dealt.

As Mick squeezed down in the back of the SUV, the familiar scent of other men's body odor wafted through the air. Two months of smelling that stink in prison had probably shaved years off his life. Now, he craved the smell of fresh air as much as his freedom.

Through the window, the night sky shone down on him, stars, a sliver of a moon, and wide-open space, all that he'd missed. He couldn't count how many nights it had been since he'd seen more of the night sky than the two inches visible through the little slit window in his cell.

How had he ever thought it a good idea to volunteer to be the one who went inside, deep into the belly of this beast?

This unwashed, odorous beast.

"Hunker down good," Rowdy ordered. He always ordered, never just asked or told. His tone always insinuated he'd hurt you if you didn't.

They drove through the dark for a bit, Mick somewhat disoriented from being inside the compartment as well as now being unable to see out the windows of the SUV.

He'd tried to keep up with the direction of turns since they'd left the prison, but distance was playing a game with his mind. Their travel seemed wrong. They should have been on the freeway by now.

Flashes of streetlights shimmered through the window, and a traffic light beamed green as they went under it, confirming they'd headed away from the highway. What the hell were these guys playing at?

Did they have a safe house somewhere to lay low until the heat died down? He leaned up to peer out the window.

"Get down," Rowdy bellowed. "Don't get up till I say you can. Wanta get us all thrown back in the big house?"

"I thought we'd 'a stayed away from the towns, stayed on the back roads," Mick said as non-threateningly as possible, not wanting to get Rowdy's ire up.

"That's why we ain't paying you to think. We got us a little unfinished business detail to tie up." Rowdy shot a jackal's smile at White.

White grinned maliciously at Rowdy, their evil expressions joining into one ungodly hint at their plans. "Got us a little unfinished business," White snickered.

White's gun subtly shifted toward Mick's direction. One bullet or two at this close range and he'd be just another thing gone wrong on the mission.

He'd be a learning lesson at the Bureau. "Don't ever do like that stupid Mick Hampton, and get yourself all alone with the bad guys."

How stupid was he? This scenario went against every lesson learned at Quantico. And on the streets of Atlanta as a cop.

Don't get alone with the bad guys.

Too late.

But, somebody had to do it. They couldn't wait to line up a confidential informant like another prisoner, or someone local in the mountains facing criminal charges.

There just wasn't enough time. Three days until the bomb didn't give him a lot of time to figure out where and how to stop it.

The SUV slowed, then stopped on what felt like a back alley or side road. No streetlights bounced through the windows of the SUV and a cushiony silence surrounded them, with the sensory deprivation of a closed coffin.

A sick feeling boiled in Mick's gut. But, his empty gun didn't give him much leverage to change the group's plans.

"Stay here, Atlanta," Rowdy said to Mick. "We'll be right back with the detail."

Nausea roiled in Mick's stomach as White and Rowdy piled out, leaving him with the ambulance driver and Stan.

"We ought to be pushing this car toward the North Georgia Mountains as fast as possible," Mick whispered.

Stan nodded. "You got that right."

They should be heading toward folk who would help them, hide them, cover for them.

Why were they stopping now, in a populated area? This had to be Manning's Crossing, the only town anywhere near the prison. Questions beat through his brain and he tried to rise up to peer over the back wheel well.

"Get down," Stan hissed. His gun in Mick's face added an exclamation point.

The goodwill of his cellmate apparently only carried up to a point.

# CHAPTER TWO

Becca Jefferson steered her car along a dark stretch of country road outside the city limits of Manning's Crossing. Out here, no streetlights lit the way, and weeds and overgrown woods crowded the sides of the road.

She peered ahead, watching for dogs wandering around in the dark.

"There's another dog, Miss Becca!" hollered Mitzi, one of her sixth grade students.

Becca took her foot off the gas of the almost-silent Prius. The skinny dog turned, his eyes flashing wide, only just then seeming to realize a vehicle was coming at him.

"Why they keep running out in front of cars for?" The little girl gave a dismissive laugh as if the dogs were stupid.

"These cars are pretty quiet," Becca started the explanation she'd given countless times about the car since she'd gotten it.

"You'd think that would be a good thing, but people, and obviously dogs," she said with a wave of her hand toward the body skulking off into the bushes, "can't hear it coming, so I just have to watch out for anybody getting in the way. Not to mention other cars, since half the time the driver doesn't even notice I'm there."

She rolled down the windows so that Mitzi could listen as they drove on.

"I like this car. It's cool." The little blonde flipped her straggly, unkempt hair over her shoulder as she looked around the new vehicle's interior. "I bet it cost a lot. How much did it cost?"

Becca just laughed. "I figure I'll save money in the long run, cause I'll save on the cost of gas."

Mitzi nodded knowingly. "My step daddy says your daddy's a judge, says you guys have lots of money."

Not that Becca had accepted any of it since she'd started teaching school. Even when things did get a little tight toward the end of the month.

Her father might have co-signed on the mortgage for her house, but Becca made the payments.

"I also can feel good about this car, telling myself I'm saving the environment." She tilted her head and smiled at Mitzi. "Global warming, climate change, all that."

The girl's eyes narrowed. She looked away then back at Becca, pursing her mouth. "My step daddy says that's a load of bull."

By the way Mitzi cut off the last word, Becca figured bull wasn't the exact word he used.

Mitzi tilted her head. "Do you believe in that stuff?"

Becca shrugged. It was never good to directly contradict a kid's parents. "I can't say for certain, but it seems like I ought to do whatever I can to prevent it just in case all the bad scenarios they talk about are true."

"What is *scenarios*?" Mitzi said quietly.

"Possibilities."

She liked that Mitzi had a lot of questions. In class, she often waited till everyone else had left before sidling up to Becca's desk to ask what most of the students could look up at home on the Internet.

She already figured Mitzi didn't have a computer or the Internet at home cause the little girl had skipped lunch several times, staying in the library to use a computer to work on papers, caring more about knowledge than her hunger. The girl usually showed up at school with a hungry look about her.

Becca always brought her lunch to her anyway. It was

already paid for in the disadvantaged lunch program Becca had registered her for.

The librarian arched an eyebrow at the food tray the first time Becca had brought it into the library. But, she meticulously pretended not to notice later trays since she'd seen how hungrily Mitzi had gobbled down the food.

Mitzi never asked for anything. You just had to figure out a way to get her what she needed, what any child had a right to expect. Food, the same learning opportunities as other students.

And self respect, the reason she'd encouraged Mitzi to join the group of girls that met after school once a week in the gym for pizza and soft drinks.

The girls talked about all sorts of stuff, and Becca brought in guest speakers to help these girls who'd been shortchanged in life for various reasons.

Some by losing a parent, or being tossed into the foster care system when both parents failed them. Others, like Mitzi, didn't even have the necessary basics to survive in the world of preteens who wore the designer brands that Mitzi could never afford.

A haircut and clothes that fit seemed beyond her grasp.

The rusty, noisy beat up pickup truck her stepfather drove said her family wasn't wasting money on luxuries. Long after the other girls had left to walk home or had been picked up, Mitzi's stepfather or mother would swing by the school for Mitzi, never even apologizing to Becca as she waited in the dark parking lot for them.

Becca wanted to give them the benefit of the doubt. Maybe they were working late, finding it hard to put food on the table like so many of the parents of her students these days. But, tonight nobody had shown up and no one answered the phone when Mitzi tried to call them.

So, Becca had offered to drive her home. The discomfort on the girl's face when she'd finally had to accept the ride said something about what waited at the other end of that trip.

"Here it is, Miss Becca." Mitzi pointed to the entrance to a mobile home park that was the address for many of the suspects that appeared in her father's courtroom. As the head judge of the county superior court, he'd mentioned the trailer park often enough.

"You can drop me off here. I can walk the rest of the way," Mitzi said, not meeting Becca's eyes as she reached for the door handle.

"Hold on." Becca touched Mitzi's hand as the girl reached to unbuckle the seatbelt.

The road winding through the trailers was dark. *Mobile home* was the politically correct term, but there was nothing mobile looking about these things.

Certainly not upwardly mobile. She knew there had to be some residents who had aspirations, forced to live here short-term for economic reasons.

But the broken-down look of so many of the trailers said most of the residents had just given up, tired out by life, by trying to survive, or they just couldn't be bothered.

Trash littered the front yards, seemingly tossed down whenever someone finished a beer, a soda or a bag of chips.

Cardboard covered up missing windows in several of the trailers. Broken-down looking cars and skinny, scavenging dogs poking at the trash on the ground filled out the picture.

People here probably bought a lot of lottery tickets.

"Where's your home?" Becca looked at Mitzi, who still didn't make eye contact.

"At the back," she said, with a vague point.

"No, I don't want you walking home in the dark."

Mitzi shrugged. "I do it all the time. I walk to my friend Jenny's house. She lives down that way." She pointed somewhere down the lonely road outside of the trailer park. "And Mama has me walk to the store."

Becca had seen a convenience store about two miles back the way they'd come. Any female walking along that road at night would be easy prey if the wrong person came by.

A shudder ran through her, thinking of "her Mitzi" being

16

snatched up by a child predator.

She turned into the trailer park and slowly drove, waiting for Mitzi to direct her.

Finally, Mitzi vaguely pointed at a trailer that looked low rent even compared to the rest of these trailers. Cardboard replaced missing glass in three out of five windows that Becca could see from her car.

Loud noise from a television racketed through the slightly open front door, along with arguing. A man and a woman yelled at the top of their lungs, liberally tossing out curse words.

As Becca's headlights flashed on the front door, the yelling stopped and a woman stuck her head out to look. Then, she pushed the door back and stumbled onto the rickety front porch.

"Mitzi, get your ass in the house. We was wondering where you was at."

Neon bright, platinum blonde hair covered half the woman's face. The other half looked drunk, and her slurred words confirmed the impression.

Her dazed eyes caught sight of Becca and she glared, then turned her full-on hatred back toward Mitzi. "I don't got time to be running you all over town to no meetings," she hissed, spittle gathering at the corners of her mouth.

"So don't be asking me next week if you can go to that meeting. Don't know why you can't get all your talking done during school hours, no how. Next week, you get on the bus after school with all them other kids."

The woman didn't even acknowledge Becca's wave. Just burped and stumbled back into the house.

Mitzi trembled in her seat, reaching for the door but only fumbling ineffectively with the handle.

"It's okay, Mitzi," Becca said in a soothing tone and reached for Mitzi's hand.

The little girl allowed Becca to take her hand, and even gave her a squeeze back. "I can give you a ride out here anytime you need."

"I don't think she gone let me. You heard her. My step daddy already says I get funny ideas at that meeting."

Like that she deserved to be treated with respect by men. And that her body was her own.

Becca had a sixth sense feeling about that man though she didn't have any hard evidence. The social worker who'd visited the house this past week at Becca's request might have something to do with her parents' sudden reluctance to let Mitzi attend the group.

But, Becca had a legal obligation to report any suspected abuse, not to mention a moral obligation.

Even if it meant the girl lost the one means of emotional support that might help her stand up against unwanted advances?

Damn, it was a rock and a hard place.

"Thank you, Miss Becca." Mitzi's voice sounded strangled as she ducked her head to hide the tears shimmering in her eyes. Becca had to fight heated tears that pushed up into her own eyes.

"Hey, I've got something for you." Becca pulled a bag from the back seat. "I bought these for my cousin's girl but they were the wrong size. I don't want to have to bother with taking them back. Thought they might fit you."

Mitzi eyed the bag hungrily, then shook her head. "My mama won't let me take charity."

"You're doing me a favor, so I don't have to go back to the store. I was just gonna drop the bag off at the Salvation Army drop box on the way back to town."

Mitzi chewed on her bottom lip, then nodded quickly. "I'll bring them back to school tomorrow if she don't let me keep 'em."

Then, she gave a knowing smile. "My step daddy will probably just say you're so rich you won't even miss that money."

Becca laughed at the sly expression in the girl's eyes as she reached for the bag. Mitzi's stepfather's resentment toward

Becca's father might actually work to their advantage.

Had the man been in her father's courtroom, been sentenced by the judge? Was that the real basis of his anger toward Becca, a simmering resentment she felt every time he didn't make eye contact with her?

Mitzi left the car and scurried into the trailer to the sounds of a loud television and loud voices before the door slammed behind her.

Would she show up tomorrow wearing one of the cute outfits Becca had bought with her own money? She'd had so much fun shopping, imagining the kick of pride the tween would get wearing the new clothes.

Mitzi was such a pretty little thing, despite her long, untrimmed hair and her almost-ragged clothes. Her mother could have dressed her better for just a few dollars at the Salvation Army Store. Many of the local churches also had a grab box of outgrown clothes that anyone could choose from.

Becca turned her car around and headed home, wondering which of the outfits Mitzi might choose first. If allowed.

"Oh, man, it's getting late. I hope Barley isn't too upset with me." She'd had her neighbor check in on her little dog and even take him out in the back yard. But, Barley seemed upset whenever Becca got off her usual schedule.

As if he worried that she might not come home.

Like Tess and Mick had failed to do. Tess couldn't help it. Dead people couldn't walk dogs.

But, Mick had chosen to leave her, and thus Barley by association.

She put her foot down on the Prius' gas pedal, hurrying home to the little dog that would be waiting by the door, looking out through the glass side panels. Pacing and worrying she might abandon him the way Becca's twin and Mick had.

# CHAPTER THREE

The crisp night air blew across her face. Barley lifted his face to the sky and barked a welcome to the early fall weather.

"Come on, Barley." Becca gave the leash a tug, urging the little dog to his favorite spot for his personal business. "We're late tonight, I know. You mad at me, getting home late?"

Barley looked up at her as if she were speaking dog. Like he understood everything she said.

She laughed out loud. "Oh, Barley, you are so smart, and so funny." Dogs hadn't made a living surviving off people for no reason. Barley's ability to read her and respond to the clues he picked up bespoke a long history of well-fed dogs.

"You're angling for extra treats, aren't you, pal?"

Treat? Barley cocked his head.

"Yeah, you definitely understand that word. You'll get it when we get home, so finish up."

He complied by lifting his leg, then kicking his heels behind him with a masculine flair, spreading his scent in the wind.

"A little girl I mentor after school didn't have a ride home," she continued to talk to the dog companionably. He seemed to like the running dialogues they shared. Or was it her that liked the conversations?

"So, I volunteered to take her home," she continued.

Barley looked back at her with an "Oh, yeah?" expression, then headed further down the alley behind their house.

She often suspected he cooperated in these conversations as a way to lengthen his walks. But, it didn't really matter if he listened or not. She liked talking to him.

Mick or Tess used to fill the spot of convenient listener. Before . . .

She turned away from that memory and concentrated on today.

"That girl lived way out in the country on the other side of town. The ride was worth the glimpse I got into her life." Barley looked back at her. "Yes, sir," she answered the glance.

Barley lifted his leg covering up the scent of a Lab that lived down the street and liked to walk this alley as well.

Becca walked her little "rescue dog," as everyone called them these days, down the dark alley. Back when she was a kid, they'd just called them dogs, figuring the pound was where everyone got their dogs.

"You can get most any kind of dog at the pound that you want," her dad always said.

If you judged by Barley, he was right. Everyone loved Barley. They couldn't walk a block without someone stopping to coo over her cute dog.

As Barley nosed around, checking for signs of other dogs and covering up any he found with his own scent, she looked up at the sky. "Almost no moon," she said.

A cool breeze feathered her hair back from her face and Barley looked up, woofing toward the end of the dark alley.

She looked down the lane. "Some cat down there, Barley?" She couldn't see much without streetlights, and clouds covered the moon. A storm was coming, according to the local TV weatherman, said it was going to be a big blow.

The glow from back porches or lights placed near trashcans by the homeowners usually provided enough for dog walking.

But, tonight it seemed few people had left their lights on. Barley growled low in his throat and peered into the dark.

No sound carried to her, but she trusted Barley's instincts. Was there a coyote down there? Sometimes they sneaked into the area, looking for stray cats or unsecured garbage.

Or was it a person in the alley? It wasn't garbage day but maybe someone was taking out the garbage to the cans that lined the backsides of the yards.

A sixth sense of her own kicked in, with a funny feeling skittering down her spine. She started backing toward her yard, not sure exactly what felt odd about the situation.

This was her neighborhood, and she'd walked Barley back here hundreds of times in the dark.

But, something definitely felt off. She backed away, as she warned all her female students to do in the self-protection seminars she gave along with female police officers from the local police department. "Listen to your instincts," the cops always warned.

Her cell phone rang and she pulled it out of her pocket, checking the incoming number. "Hey, Daddy."

"Becca." Just the sound of his voice was reassuring. "There's been a breakout at the prison." Not reassuring.

"Be careful, kid." Uncharacteristically strained and breathy, his voice sparked with an alarm that she hardly ever heard from him. He was a seen-it-all type of a guy.

Seen-it-all and sentenced-the-guilty type of a guy, her daddy the judge.

If he was worried . . .

The noise down the alley. She turned to look back down the dark lane. Was it possible?

Before she turned fully, a large hand gripped her around the mouth, yanking away her phone and tossing it down.

A spurt of terror shot through her, instantly galvanizing her to fight, fight for her life. Fight against the strong, male hands that clamped onto her like the Jaws of Life, trying to force her into compliance with the steely grip.

Barley erupted into a crazed frenzy, barking as Becca felt herself lifted off her feet, one hand around her waist, the other jerking her head back against a chest that reeked of sweat and dirt, the body odor so strong she almost gagged.

She arched her back like a toddler and kicked against his knees, struggling, trying not to be taken to a second location. "Whatever happens to you at a second location is going to be much worse than what happens to you at the first," her father had drilled into her and Tess' heads.

"Shut up, missy, or I'll break your neck now," the man hissed into her ear, his breath rancid to the point that she almost threw up into his hand. His rough mitt gripped her head like he could twist it off like a twist top beer.

A growling came from below her. Barley ravaged the man's ankle, doing all the damage a Pekingese-Terrier mutt could do. The man held her off the ground as he kicked at the little dog, connecting with his rib cage.

Barley yelped. Then, came back, lunging for the man's feet as he walked, carrying Becca.

The man stumbled, almost falling onto Becca. When his hand loosened from his death grip on her head, she began to fight again. This was her only chance. Now or never. Now or death, instinct told her.

She rolled away from the man, kicking and clawing, shrieking one long cat-like squall of a feline being snatched by coyotes. But he grabbed her by the hair and yanked her back, his hand fastening on her mouth again. The terror of that hand around her head caused her to still instantly.

She could imagine the snap her neck would make, that cracking sound the last thing she might remember on earth.

It was useless to struggle now, her gut told her. Maybe she'd get a second chance to run.

"What's going on out there?" a voice yelled. "Get my gun, Shirley. I think there's coyotes in the alley. Is Snickers in the house?"

"Sorry," the man holding her yelled toward Becca's neighbor from three doors down. "Just my dog going after a cat."

"Oh, okay," Becca's neighbor called back. She could hear the question in his voice, wondering who was out there in his alley. They all knew everyone who walked dogs back here.

Maybe he'd call the cops. A pulse of hope flickered in her. But, the screen door snapped closed.

They were all conditioned to feel safe here.

Her neighbor's inside door closed also and a quick pulse of tears rose to Becca's eyes. She'd thought she might have been saved.

"Get that dog," the man holding her whispered.

Becca shot a glance to the side. Who was he talking to?

A second man came from behind them and stomped on Barley's leash.

"Gotcha, little guy," he said in an almost-gentle tone. Then, he was in front of them, holding Barley, opening the back of an SUV and placing him inside, just before the large man tossed Becca in after Barley.

Rolling into the back of the SUV, she was instantly grabbed by hands.

Terror and desperation pulsed through her. She screamed, kicked and writhed, trying to escape the male hands, clawing at them before she was pinned in place.

She was being taken to a second location.

For what purpose? Rape? Then murder?

A hand clamped onto her mouth.

"What are you doing?" a male voice protested.

Or that's what she thought he said because she was still struggling against the hands that clamped onto her.

A steel gun barrel flashed in the light from the street lamps. Pointing toward her?

No. It pointed in the general direction of the argumentative voice.

"Get in the front, Atlanta. There's not enough room for all of us back here. And shut your trap, trying to run the show," snarled a man, venom pouring out with his words.

She couldn't see the man who crawled over her, but as he did so, he patted her on the back in an almost- reassuring manner. But that had to be wishful thinking.

Because she wanted so badly to believe she wasn't alone in

this horrific situation, kidnapped in the back of a car.

But the pat had felt better than the rough hands that secured her to the floor of the car. Funny, how in such a moment of trauma and terror, a person could latch onto the least little thing as a sign of hope. Hope that she might live through the night.

Hope that she wouldn't be raped and strangled to death.

"I got her cell phone," one man crowed. "Her dog and her cell phone."

A flicker of hope sparked within her. Her father had to have heard what was happening to her. Her cell phone would be a direct link for the police to follow.

"Turn that damned thing off," snarled a voice, a voice that crushed hope. "They can follow those damn things. Take the battery out, too."

Crushed hope and rubbed it into the dirt.

\*\*\*\*

Mick looked straight ahead, while trying to pretend he wasn't listening to every sound from the back of the SUV.

He'd be damned if he let them hurt Becca.

His gut clenched as he listened for any sounds of real abuse. So far, she'd just been manhandled into the car and terrorized.

But, who knew what they had in store for her.

Were they planning to rape her, just grabbing any woman, after so long in prison?

No, they'd have grabbed a convenience store clerk or some woman gassing up her car, if that were true.

The daughter of the county's Superior Court Head Judge? That was no coincidence.

Mick hadn't asked who put these boys in jail.

Who would have thought they'd be so petty as to try to get revenge against the judge at the possible price of being caught and sent back to prison?

But, they rebelled at any authority outside of their own little circle of social rejects and degenerates.

Details. Obviously, he ought to have thought of that one. It was always the details that screwed you.

A growling roar from Becca's little dog caused the men to laugh. "Here, take the mutt," Rowdy said, hurling the pup toward the front seat.

Mick instinctively grabbed at the flying ball of fur, stopping it just inches away from slamming into the dashboard.

"Hey," White yelled. "Careful with the dog. You don't hurt dogs."

That was the most indignant tone he'd ever heard from White.

"Yeah," Mick growled. "Roughing up human bitches is fine. But canine bitches are off limits." Even as he snarled, trying to sound like a badass, he felt remorse for every word.

Stan and White howled their approval. Their laughter almost covered up the small feminine gasp that sounded from the depths of the back area. Damn. Had she recognized his voice?

Adrenalin raced through him. He wanted to grab for the driver's gun, which was lying beside him on the seat, and try putting a few bullets into these guys before Becca accidentally gave away his cover and the whole gang turned on him.

But, he was seriously outgunned. If he died, who would protect Becca? And the thousands of people these guys and their buddies planned on killing?

"You got that right, for once, Atlanta. Can't trust them human bitches," Rowdy growled in a good imitation of Barley just moments ago. The difference was that Rowdy had the goods to back up his threat. And Rowdy's patience was pushed every day just by waking up.

If he hadn't focused his anger on the federal government, he'd have turned it somewhere else. The man was a fight waiting for a place to happen.

His long rap sheet before this recent drug arrest included assault and battery, simple assault, aggravated battery.

If there was some type of a legal term for a fight, Rowdy

had it tagged onto him.

Mick wanted to pull Becca out of the car by any means possible. But, if he did, who would find the head of this snake that threatened to swallow countless victims?

Mick buttoned it and waited for a chance to free Becca and then put Rowdy back in prison, so he could watch the prison doors slam on the scumbag for life.

He would take pleasure in doing that, saving innocent lives and disrupting drug routes, eating his way up the food chain to the big dogs that ran the drug ring that funded their domestic terrorism agenda. Those guys were the ones he had the vendetta against.

Rowdy had just been a tool in that process. Until he had put his hands on Becca.

Then, it became personal.

# CHAPTER FOUR

Becca heard the voice, with its unique timbre. It sounded a lot like Mick Hampton. Was she crazy? Grabbing at any possible hope that she might not die tonight?

Imagining the voice as that of the man she'd almost married. Would have married, if everything hadn't gone to hell one night on the streets of a bad neighborhood in Atlanta.

That night. Well, that night had become the worse night of her life until now. Even though she'd been nowhere near the shooting scene, she'd been damaged as well.

Bullet casings had lined the street, flashed all over the news for days. She'd been called to Grady Hospital because they thought Mick might not make it.

They hadn't told her about the other victim until she'd gotten there.

Now, she latched onto the voice that had floated across the back seat of the car to give her hope.

Barley quieted in the front seat and that told her more than anything that maybe she was right, because Barley loved Mick and had grieved for him when he'd stopped coming around.

She could imagine Barley nuzzling into the comfort of Mick's arms. Much as she longed to do.

Every cell in her body leaned toward that gravelly, deep voice that was one of the most attractive features of the man.

She loved that voice. Never more than right now, under

these circumstances. It had to be Mick, though what he was doing with these guys was beyond her.

Some type of cop work? Had to be.

Damn that job. Why couldn't he give it up?

Law enforcement had already cost them both so much.

"That dog cottons to ya, Atlanta," White said, with almost a jealous tinge to his voice. He leaned over the back seat, looking forward. "He keeps licking your face. Why's he like you so much? Dogs usually like me."

No reply came back. She listened, wishing for just another syllable from his lips. Just another few words to reassure her that she would survive this night.

"I got a way about me, White," the man said and the voice soothed through Becca's body like a drug.

****

An hour later, they were driving up the freeway, just another SUV traveling north on I-75. Mick had his windshield visor down, using the little mirror attached to it to keep an eye on everything that went on in the rear of the SUV.

He hit the button to lower his window, letting fresh air blow through the vehicle.

The better to cool his temper.

The pine scented air swirled through the car.

"Damn, that smells good," Stan said. "Almost better'n my mama's chicken pot pie."

"Ooohwee, I ain't had me none of that in a long time," Rowdy said from the back of the SUV. "I tell you what else I ain't had me none of."

Mick sucked in a quick lungful of air as Rowdy leered down at Becca, his hands shaped into two large pincers, like a horny crab.

His hands disappeared below the rear seat and almost immediately an elbow flew and Rowdy yelped in pain, jumping back.

"That's what you get," Becca barked.

Barley growled and tried to get over the seat.

"Don't try me, girl," Rowdy yelled. A loud slap followed the words, and Becca cried out as if she'd just been hit.

A roaring anger filled Mick. He turned in his seat. "Hey, this ain't s'posed to be 'bout abusing no girl."

The driver, Chad Ryan, picked up his pistol, which he'd wisely moved away from Mick's side of the car. He drove with one hand, the other hand gripping the pistol.

Mick wanted to lunge for the gun but it was unlikely it'd result in anything beside most everybody in the car ending up dead. If the driver lost it at sixty miles an hour, who knew how many pieces they'd all end up in. A rollover wouldn't be good for anybody.

But, if he went for Rowdy, he'd be dead in a heartbeat at the least and Becca all alone in this situation.

"This girl isn't even supposed to be part of our plan. What part of bringing down the federal government does she play?" Mick said, hoping to evoke the whole "we're noble patriots," emotions they'd all talked about earlier.

"Yeah, she is part of the plan," Chad said. "But, we didn't kidnap her for no tittie-grabbing. That ain't why she's here." He glared at Rowdy in his rearview mirror.

"You shut up," Rowdy said, pointing his gun at Chad's head.

Chad really hadn't taken the Rowdy part of the equation into consideration before he spoke either; it was clear from the look on his face.

"Pull over," Rowdy yelled.

Chad's face paled. The guy had a gun, too, and still he was afraid of Rowdy. He took his foot off the gas, and the car began slowing down.

To hell with that. The large Suburban was outfitted with a bench seat, something that was becoming almost antiquated these days. But, the seat was probably chosen to give more room to hide drugs behind it. Finally, a piece of luck for Mick.

He unbuckled his seat belt, set Barley onto the floor board and slid slightly across the seat, allowing him to put his foot on the gas. It had been a bit of a struggle getting his foot over the middle divider but Chad had just looked at him with a surprised expression. Probably got the drift of what he was doing and appreciated anybody taking Rowdy's attention off him.

Mick pressed down on the gas pedal, sending the car shooting forward.

"What the hell?" Rowdy yelled.

"It ain't me, it's him, got his foot on the pedal," Chad said.

Mick nonchalantly grabbed the steering wheel, down low where Rowdy couldn't see his hand. Chad's eyes widened, apparently realizing he'd just lost all control of the vehicle.

"If you shoot him, this car is gonna flip and we're all gonna be dead." Mick looked back at Rowdy. "Especially people not wearing a seat belt. I think he'll do it, too. He's got a crazy look in his eyes."

Chad looked at Mick with new respect. If Chad shot Mick, Mick could still yank the steering wheel, causing them to crash.

Mick might not have a gun, but he wasn't unarmed.

Though he'd probably be dead if the car flipped. Just the cost of doing business in the undercover world.

Rowdy slid his pistol over to point at Mick. "Yeah, but I shoot you and nothing happens cept'n one less irritation for me. And you know how I hate irritations."

"Yeah," Mick said on a laugh. "Like a bullet hole in the windshield and brain matter splattered all over ain't gonna raise no suspicions. Hell, the windshield might even bust out."

A low animal growl emitted from the back of the SUV. Mick watched in the mirror as Rowdy's common sense struggled to push back his fury. It was gonna be a losing battle cause common sense wasn't Rowdy's strong point.

"Let's just all settle down," Stan said in that joking way he had that Mick had seen him use to defuse bad situations in prison.

"Yeah, I got the girl," White said, in a low, quiet voice. "She ain't going nowhere."

31

Rowdy sucked in a gulp of air, then almost like he flipped a button, he changed his expression back to good ole boy.

"Don't let her get up, White. If she do, hit her with your weapon. And I don't mean the one you keep in your pants. I mean your gun."

Stan and White laughed loudly. Almost like they'd played this role many times before, glossing everything over after Rowdy went crazy. As long as he was back to acting halfway normal, which was the best they could hope for.

Mick sucked in a breath of air, and let up on the gas. But, he kept his hand on the steering wheel, his insurance that Chad didn't put a bullet into the side of his head.

He prayed nothing else happened until they got to these guys' hideout. And he prayed nothing else set off Becca's innate need to stand up to bullies. Cause it could get her killed with these guys.

These weren't the middle school bullies Becca and Tess had encountered as kids.

They'd developed a toughness when their mother had died.

A larger boy at school had laughed that their mother had been stupid, getting herself killed in that bank robbery. Tess and Becca had jumped on him like ninja twins, one grabbing his head under her arm, while the other pummeled his stomach.

Now, that innate feistiness could get Becca killed.

At least, she seemed to instinctively understand the situation with Mick, not saying anything to reveal she knew who he was.

As a daughter of a criminal judge, she'd heard it all, and as the sister of a cop and the girlfriend of a cop, she'd been prepped for this moment all her life.

Suddenly, after his brain calmed down from full fury and fear for his and Becca's life, what Chad had said finally sank in.

They'd purposefully taken Becca. For some reason other than just revenge. Otherwise, it wouldn't matter what they did to her.

Why did they want Becca?

# CHAPTER FIVE

About two hours later, they bumped up a dirt, pothole pocked road, each jostle knocking him around. What sort of havoc had the rough road taken on Becca?

Finally, they ground to a halt in front of an old, wooden cabin that looked like it had grown up out of the earth, it blended so well with the wooded landscape behind it. It sat halfway up a mountain that climbed up into the misty, early morning light.

Trucks and SUVs were parked around the dirt lot in front of the cabin. Mud spattered the sides of most of them, and gun racks in almost all of the rear windows held an assortment of rifles. It was good hunting territory, after all. Who would question the guns?

Mick eyed the guns. Maybe he could get his hands on one of them.

He opened his door, holding Barley in his left arm, and breathed in a deep gulp of mountain air. "That smells good."

"Not nearly as good as this female smells," Rowdy said, shooting a dark look at the driver, almost challenging him.

"Now that you're out o' jail, maybe you can find you a willing woman, Rowdy," White said, stretching and pushing the SUV's back door open.

If there was a woman alive who'd want to kiss that mouth, Mick thought.

A boot to the butt sent White flying out into the dirt behind the car. "Hee, hee hee. Ain't we all just so funny," Rowdy crowed.

Apparently, White had thought since they were on the same bandwagon to bring down the federal government, he could joke at Rowdy's expense.

That probably hadn't been done since Rowdy had gone through puberty and gained the muscle that let him push other men around, intimidating them with his size.

Rowdy got out and stood over White to emphasize his point. Stan swung his legs out the back door, stood up and extended a hand back to Becca, helping her out of the SUV.

She almost stumbled from the lack of use of her legs, and Stan grabbed her around the waist to steady her. Without even sneaking a grope.

Maybe Mick would shoot Stan last, if he had a choice among the three men needing to be shot. If he could get some bullets.

Mick set Barley down. "Go do your business, boy."

But, Barley ran straight to Becca, whimpering and jumping on her leg.

She picked up the little dog, cuddling him against her chest.

Her eyes met Mick's over the dog, giving a kick to his system. The power of her gaze, with those sapphire blue eyes shining with intelligence, sent shock waves pulsing through him. They rolled out, activating every cell in his body, every cell with its memory of touching her, her touching him.

God, the woman was a ferocious beauty.

She was as delicious as she'd ever been, that glossy, chocolate colored hair spilling down over her shoulders, which he knew underneath those clothes would be milky white.

He could just taste her now, her sweetness. The impulse to run his mouth all over her body almost overwhelmed him.

Her compact body was enough to make a man do crazy things just to get the chance to pull her up against him.

He wanted to hold the eye contact longer, to look at her face, her body, her hair. A visual gift he'd denied himself for so long.

Rowdy sauntered up to stand beside Mick. Rowdy looked Becca up and down as if she were naked. "She's something, ain't she?" he said in a tone that implied he and Mick were thinking the same ugly thoughts.

"It's okay, boy. We're fine," Becca said to Barley, nuzzling her face into his fur as if to cover Rowdy's scent, patting him. She looked at the dog as she spoke, but Mick felt the message was intended for him.

She'd just been kidnapped, pawed, and slapped. And she was worried about him. So like her.

"Okay for now," Rowdy said under his breath as he turned and headed toward the cabin

A gnawing need to kill Rowdy ate at Mick's self-restraint, chewing away his ability not to go for the man's jugular. He'd kill Rowdy, if nothing else, if this mission went to hell. No doubt, the world would be a better place without that man.

And Mick's doing so would be anything but professional.

All the men headed toward the cabin's door, smiles on their faces, hitching up their pants and tucking in their shirts. Stan steered Becca toward the cabin with a grip on her arm. She stumbled along beside him as if her legs were still numb from the ride.

Mick followed but Rowdy turned to point a finger at him. "Keep an eye on her."

Stan released Becca. She almost fell and Mick grabbed for her.

Stan looked back, his hand extended as if to catch her, but then when Mick took her arm, Stan followed the other guys through the door.

A loud roar of welcomes erupted from the cabin's front door as each of the men entered. Finally, the door shut.

Mick looked down at Becca. Her face flashed with relief as their eyes met. "Thank God," she murmured, tears filling her eyes. She reached a hand for his face.

He shook his head sharply, stepping back, though he made

sure she had her balance before he let her go.

He couldn't risk more physical contact with her, because of the emotional reaction it could produce from both of them. The urge to clutch her to him was so overpowering, he was afraid he might give in to it.

But, someone could be looking out the window. Or with these guys, there could be cameras everywhere, keeping an eye out for the Feds they so hated and feared.

Mick eyed the surrounding vehicles, looking for an open window through which he could grab a gun. They all seemed shut up tight. Were any of the doors unlocked? He had a funny feeling these guys carried so many weapons that they didn't dare leave their doors unsecured.

He sidled toward the nearest truck, eyeing the cabin for anyone peering out.

Becca sat Barley on the ground and edged closer to Mick, changing her expression to a frown for the benefit of any onlookers, punching a finger toward his chest. "What are you doing with these people, Mick?"

"My name's Atlanta, and don't forget it. We don't know each other." He pushed her hand away, the grasped the nearest door handle. Locked.

Becca's eyes flashed with fear and desperation, glancing down the dirt road they'd come up. "Let's run," she whispered. "Let's go, let's get out of here."

God, that was what he wanted to do, just leave with her. But, he couldn't. "You go," he said in a low voice. "Get out now, while they're all inside." Maybe someone had left their keys in the ignition and Becca could take it and flee.

He moved down the line of vehicles, further away from the cabin.

"Are you insane?" Becca's eyes took on a crazed, desperate tint. She darted looks back toward the cabin. "I'm not leaving you here with these nuts. Nothing is worth this, *Atlanta*," she twisted the name sarcastically.

"I'm on a job. I can't let these guys get away with what

they're planning." He gritted his teeth. He couldn't get sucked into her emotion.

Only two things were important right now, the mission and getting her out safely. He needed to concentrate on those things, despite the raw emotion just seeing her poured through his body.

"Get out of here, Becca," he growled. "Go now." He infused a cop's authority into his voice, the growl he'd used on unruly crowds, drunken boyfriends and men who thought they could physically intimidate their women.

He growled for her own good. This was about her life.

He tried another door handle. No luck.

She stepped closer as if knowing her words would carry more impact if he were distracted from his mission by her nearness. She looked up at him with those eyes that could convince him to do almost anything. "Don't be such a hero. You being dead won't make the world a better place."

God, how could he convince her to run, run for her life? He couldn't concentrate on what he needed to do as long as he had to worry about her.

At any moment, those thugs could come back out and the chance would be lost. He glanced toward the cabin and as if on cue, a blind lifted.

Grabbing Becca by the collar, he jerked her up against the nearest truck. Hurt and betrayal swept across her face. "Get your hands off me." She struggled convincingly against his hold because she wasn't acting.

This was all too real of a situation, and her every action was infused with the anxiety that had to be ripping through her.

"They're watching us. Stop struggling." Slowly, she stilled, and he loosened his hold but kept one handful of her shirt tightly gripped.

Her eyes flashed toward the window where the gap in the blinds indicated they were still being watched. She shoved away from him in a more-than-convincing fashion.

"When that blind closes, I'll say run." He narrowed his eyes

37

at her. "And you run."

Anger boiled in her eyes and he knew he had to give her something more than just that command. "I'd go with you," he softened his voice, seeing the responding softening in her eyes. That gentle expression brought back so many memories with the accompanying urge to pull her up against his body, take her mouth, and transport them to that place that was their natural habitat.

That place of passion, desire . . . , and everything else they'd lost. Everything he'd given up.

Damn it to hell. A countdown to death for hundreds of people, at least, had begun. Three days. He had three days to crack the code, find out where they planned to strike.

He toughened his resolve by reminding himself of all that was at risk, then pushed on. "This mission is too important for me to leave now. It's been months in the making, me getting in with these guys."

"Congratulations," she said in a tone he recognized as her most disgusted. "You've befriended a bunch of mongrels. Even Barley knows he's too good for them."

She leaned down and picked up Barley, then nuzzled her face into his fur, her hands trembling as she clutched at the small dog.

He leaned in, lowering his voice. "I won't let anything happen to you."

"Something's already happened to me." She glared at him. "I've been terrorized, kidnapped, tossed around like a stray, unwanted dog. Hit."

"Where'd he hit you?" His eyes flashed to her face and neck. He'd have already noticed any bruising there.

She shook her head dismissively. "On my arm. I threw it up in time."

He took her wrist, turning it. A purple mark was coming up on her forearm. "I'm gonna kill that bastard."

She nodded. "Get in line." Then, she glanced back at the cabin, her face pale, her eyes wide. "They're going to kill me,

Atlanta," she said the nickname with an ugly twist. "Because I've seen all their faces. They can't let me go. If they had any thought to ever let me go, they would have blindfolded me."

That thought had already occurred to him.

"So, you're the cop now?" He glared at her to cover for the fact that she was right.

"Oh please, don't pull that fake tough guy stuff on me." She nodded knowingly. "I saw you pull that turnaround so many times in high school, it's not funny. Mrs. Green's twelfth grade English class."

She laughed harshly. "Play act all you want for these guys, but don't pull that on me."

He nodded. "I don't know what these guys are thinking, bringing you up here. But, I do know this." He stopped, taking in a deep breath and swallowing. His fists clenched and unclenched with the need to do take action.

He looked into her eyes with the full force of his determination to protect her. "I will kill everyone of these mothers, sacrifice the mission if I have to, to keep them from killing you."

The next, he prayed he was right to tell her. "These guys are part of a militia group that is dead serious about killing people. Word is, it's coming soon, real soon. Lots of people could die if I don't intercept them, find out where they plan to strike."

She glanced away. He knew her tricks, too. She'd always done that when he'd made a point she didn't want to concede, not wanting him to see the impact of his words.

He motioned toward Barley.

"Put him down like you're letting him do his business. Probably not a bad idea anyway since he was in the car so long."

She set Barley on his feet and the little Pekingese-Terrier mix looked up at her questioningly. "I'm fine, Barley," she soothed in a tone that made Mick ache for her to direct the same voice at him.

It had been so long since he'd heard her say his name in

that special tone she used for dogs and kids and people she really loved.

A lifetime.

The little dog turned and began sniffing at a bush before he made use of it for the reason all dogs thought bushes, poles and fire hydrants were intended.

"At least someone's back to normal," he said.

Becca glanced at him, her expression darkening. "You're back to normal. All cop, all the time."

He'd never be back to normal. No amount of life saving would ever make up for the one life he'd lost, the one person who should have been able to depend on him more than anyone. His partner.

He fastened his gaze on Becca, very like Tess in so many ways. They were identical twins but he'd always known who was who. Even when they'd tried to fool him.

One thing was for sure, he'd never kissed Tess. Never wanted to.

But, now Becca's face was a living reminder of his dead partner. And how he'd never let anyone he loved ever get killed again. He looked into Becca's eyes, willing her to believe him.

"I'll get you out of this, no matter what I have to do, no matter what mission I have to sacrifice."

Her eyes met his for a long moment with a sizzling connection that shot through his body, an electric fire that threatened to singe his every nerve ending.

His body clenched with a spasm of want that was preposterous in their current situation. Impossible in any situation.

As if she'd felt the connection too, she glanced away hiding her response. She swallowed hard then met his eyes, her expression shuttered closed once again. She nodded. "I know you mean that, Atlanta. But, I'm not sure it's within your ability to do."

They both knew that not everyone could be saved once

these situations started unraveling.

Damn. What should he have done? Pressed his point when they'd been in that alley? Him, with an unloaded weapon, against four gun-toting "patriots."

He'd have gotten himself and Becca both shot dead right then.

And now? Now was even worse, as outnumbered as they were.

Maybe they should both start running.

# CHAPTER SIX

But the thought of what these guys were planning, supposedly a large bomb to kill God knew how many people.

An Oklahoma City-sized bomb.

The news footage of the Murrah Federal Building was still shown at the FBI Training Academy to remind recruits of the hate that lived on the world. The hate some of those people felt for FBI agents just for wearing the badge. For anyone wearing a badge really.

The images of the Oklahoma bombing flashed through his mind every time he'd questioned the time he'd spent in that prison. Half the building had been blown away. Just drive a truck up to it and what did you get?

Little babies covered in blood.

Mother's screaming in anguish when their babies didn't make it out.

He ground his teeth together. He couldn't let that happen.

And he couldn't let anything happen to Becca.

"I promise you. I will protect you with my life, Becca."

He fastened his gaze on her, intently, willing her to trust him as he'd willed other victims and endangered people before her.

"As long as you're alive," she ground out what he was thinking, cutting her eyes toward the house. "Those guys have the odds in their favor."

He'd give his life for her. But, that might not be enough.

His body wasn't bulletproof. A fact he'd learned on the streets of Atlanta one ugly night.

You couldn't always protect the ones you loved. The memory knifed through his heart.

She glanced at the cabin then touched his arm, her expression soft and gentle, the one used for her students. "It wasn't your fault."

Shock flashed through him. It was the first time they'd spoken about the incident in more than two years. Aching pain filled him.

It had been his fault.

But, there was nothing he could do about that now.

Now, he had to concentrate on all the lives he could still save.

Including Becca's.

The front door opened, spilling out raucous laughter and loud, jovial conversation, much like that at a family picnic. How could they gather to discuss slaughtering people and still laugh like it was nothing?

Mick's stomach turned just thinking that there were people in the world like that.

White walked out, glancing back to someone who was yelling something at him. Mick couldn't quite make out the words. White nodded.

He approached Mick and Becca, looking them up and down, studying them.

"They want you to walk out back behind the building with me." He pointed one finger casually at Becca.

A knot of fear gripped Mick's stomach. Was this it? Was he planning to finish her off now?

Becca's eyes widened.

White shook his head. "Nobody's gonna hurt you, darlin'. They need you." He placed a reassuring hand on her shoulder. "The bigwigs gonna leave out and don't want you eyeballing 'em."

He might not kill White, either.

"Get your jacket," Mick said. "It's cold out here." She must have been carrying the jacket when she'd been kidnapped and had dropped it because Stan had it in his hand when they'd returned to the SUV.

If she had a chance to run, she'd need that jacket. These mountains could get real cold in a heartbeat. Especially with those storm clouds moving in.

She turned toward the truck, leaning in when Mick opened the SUV back. As she grabbed her jacket, Mick scanned the back area for anything he could use as a weapon. Nothing. As if Rowdy had already thought of it.

Of course he had.

Mick turned, fast on White and Becca's heels as they headed toward the back of the cabin. The preferred place to off someone. Drag the body into the woods and be done with it.

Chad had said they needed Becca. For how long?

As White followed Becca, Mick followed White, ready to bash the guy's brain in with his gun butt.

They rounded the back of the cabin to a sweeping vista that unrolled mountain after mountain, smoky in the early morning dawn as the sun crept closer to the horizon.

Mick studied the surroundings, trying to get his bearings. One mountain loomed larger than the surrounding mountains confirming what he'd already believed. They were in the vicinity of the little town of Hawk's Peak where his buddy was the new sheriff.

If he could get Becca to Grant, she'd be safe.

"Ain't it purty?" White waved his hand toward the view. "I'd break out o' jail a hundred times just to get back to this."

Becca looked up, as if roused from sleep, and took in the view.

"Beautiful," she murmured, her voice low and husky. As White gazed toward the horizon, she shot Mick a glance.

Was she also remembering the trip they took together to the North Georgia Mountains one summer weekend?

Remembering when all was still right in their world, when

44

they had a future to look forward to. When they had loved each other.

And didn't know the damage that great loss could do to a relationship.

He might have survived the shooting. But, their relationship hadn't.

He bit back a curse. Don't go there, he ordered himself.

Slamming car doors and yelled good-byes echoed from the front of the cabin, reminders of his immediate concern.

If Becca hadn't been here, he'd have been there, taking notes, memorizing faces.

This was definitely a mission divided. But, he couldn't help that. It was what it was.

Could he sacrifice one innocent civilian for a thousand possible victims?

No. Especially not when the person was Becca.

"Okay," White said when the sound of car engines faded down the mountain. "Let's go inside." He walked onto the back deck and pushed open the sliding glass door.

Inside, there was only Stan and Rowdy.

"You get any more details?" White looked at Rowdy.

"Get her in there." Rowdy jerked his head toward a hallway, with a virulent frown.

"And use this." He tossed a length of rope at White.

White caught it and looked down at it as if he didn't know what it was for.

Yeah, Stan and White were definitely the weaker links in Rowdy's chain of cruelty.

"Wait a minute," Rowdy barked. The man did relish authority. "Come here, missy." He crooked a finger at Becca as he reached into his coat pocket.

Mick stiffened, his muscles tightening in readiness to leap at Rowdy. He waited, preparing for whatever Rowdy pulled out.

Just a cell phone emerged in his hand. He inserted the battery and hit the power button.

The lights flashed on, then he punched a few buttons, listened to it for a moment, and held the phone out toward Becca. "Tell your daddy you're okay," he said then put the phone on speaker.

Becca lunged forward, grabbing at the phone but Rowdy jerked it away from her, not allowing her to take control of the device. He held it near her ear and she yelped, "Dad?"

"Becca? Are you okay?" Her dad's voice was strained, half hoarse.

Tears erupted from her eyes, tearing at Mick's gut like glass. God, he wanted her out of this situation.

"I'm okay. I'm okay," she blurted into the phone. That was all she got out before Rowdy ripped the phone away from her ear.

He hit the disconnect button, then immediately powered the phone down and took out the battery.

"That ain't her phone, is it?" White looked at Rowdy. "The one I picked up in the alley."

"How stupid do you think I am?" Rowdy stared White down. "This one can't be traced. Bought with cash and some minutes put on it over in Gainesville, couple of weeks ago by our buddies. Won't be tracing this phone anytime soon."

His manner of speaking and accent suddenly was much less mountain, much less country. Was his good ole boy talking just a front?

Rowdy nodded at Becca. "Now, take her ass back there and tie her up good." Suddenly, the accent was back.

"I need to use the restroom," Becca said, her tone saying she hated asking permission like one of her students.

"We all need something, baby." Rowdy looked her up and down, as if deciding whether he wanted to take her now or later.

Mick tensed.

Rowdy's expression said he'd definitely be the first of the group. Becca stiffened, tightening her mouth as if fighting not to show her panic.

A shiver ran through Mick at the thought that these guys

planned to use her as a sex toy. They might have an overriding reason for kidnapping her but that might not stop them from having a little fun with her on the side. He needed to distract their attention from her before their "needs" took over the situation.

"How 'bout a restroom break for her?" Mick said. "Been in the car for hours, same as the dog."

Rowdy cut his eyes at Mick, as his hand trailed down to where his gun showed in his waistband. "Figured you for a pussy hound. Got all the sweet words and concerns 'bout the ladies, don't 'cha, Atlanta?"

Stan and White laughed and Rowdy grinned at them. "He wants to be first to have a go at her."

"Don't you get it," Rowdy continued, looking at Mick. "We don't have to sweet talk her. This ain't no date." Oh, yeah, he was laying the mountain accent on strong now.

Rowdy stood up and circled Becca, eyeing her up and down. Just his looking at her that way probably made Becca want a shower to get the effects off her skin.

Rowdy trailed a finger down her arm, and Mick could almost feel Becca trying not to slap him. But, she'd learned her lesson in the back of the SUV.

The guy was bigger and stronger than her, and well-armed as well. Southern gentlemanliness didn't apply here.

Stan and White's expression darkened. As if they didn't like it. What didn't they like about it? That Rowdy thought he'd be first?

Or were they just inherently against rape?

These guys had espoused high ideals, self-determination, etc. Though they hadn't used those exact words. If they were so set on changing the world, did they want rape to be the accepted norm?

Oh, hell, they were drug dealers. How moral would they be in other situations?

Mick slid his gaze around the room, looking for any unguarded guns or just anything he could use for a weapon.

An unoccupied straight-backed kitchen chair was his best

choice. He'd put that through Rowdy's brain before he let him rape Becca.

"You want a real man, missy?" Rowdy said in a low, disgusting voice. The insinuation behind his words, the mental image it was meant to evoke made Mick want to throw up.

Or kill Rowdy.

No woman should have to be subjected to that man's words or actions.

If he killed Rowdy, would the mission still be on? Would Stan and White be able to pull it off?

Hell, no. If he knew it, then the higher-ups orchestrating the bomb knew it too.

Would another cell move in, one Mick and the FBI knew nothing about? Was this group their only chance to stop this attack?

Rowdy continued circling Becca, getting so close to her she was almost forced to stand at attention in order to not actually touch him by accident. She seemed to sway away from Rowdy as he moved around her.

Mick's muscles contracted, every cell in his body raged against that man. Kill him, kill him now.

Rowdy puffed out his chest. "Lordy, I'd like to." He trailed two fingers down her forearm, then back up to her bicep, pushing the material of her shirt aside so that he was touching her from wrist to shoulder.

She shuddered, as if she couldn't stop the reaction, and Rowdy laughed.

Then, he stepped back, and blew out a sigh of frustration. "I would show the little lady some mountain pleasures. Give her the full real-man experience."

He cocked an eyebrow and moved away from her, plopping back down into his chair, kicking it back onto the two rear legs. "I would. But, I'm afeered my gal would cut off my man parts, if'n she heerd I was in bed with another woman."

The accent was in full force now, but more than that, his attention was caught by the message of his words.

48

Rowdy had a woman waiting for him? Mick didn't ask and hoped Rowdy wouldn't tell. Cause he sure as hell didn't want to know anymore than he'd already heard about the guy's "needs."

Stan and White stared at Rowdy, curious expressions on their faces, as if this was the first they'd heard about a woman waiting for Rowdy.

Rowdy's pompous smile turned to a glare under Stan and White's study. He snarled, "What about you boys? Either of you want her?"

Stan shook his head. "Nah."

Mick knew from Stan's constant talking about his ex that he was secretly hoping for a reunion. A man didn't talk constantly about a woman if he were through with her.

White studied Becca for a long moment, as if really considering it. He stood up and repeated Rowdy's circling behavior. Just not as close.

He looked her up and down.

Suddenly, Mick was more inclined to kill him, too. He might not be as dangerous as Rowdy, but any man who could treat a woman like that didn't need to be around.

The moment dragged on, and Becca's face got tighter and tighter until it looked like her skin would rip from her bones.

"Nope," White finally answered. "Never cottoned to rape. It ain't really fun less the lady wants it, too."

"How you know so much about rape?" Rowdy leered at White as if hoping for some lascivious tale. He really was an asshole.

That's what they should have nicknamed him. Asshole. Calling him the same thing to his face most people called him behind his back.

White's cheeks flushed when he seemed to get Rowdy's meaning. "No, it ain't like that. Had me a prostitute once when I was in the army. Really should have just jacked off rather than how dirty I felt afterwards."

He shuddered. "Ain't no fun less the lady wants it too."

Good words to live by, Mick figured.

He'd already known about White's dishonorable discharge from the army. The prostitute story hadn't been in the file.

Becca almost visibly relaxed but still she kept her eyes averted from the men, as if thinking at any moment they could change their minds.

"What a girl," Rowdy jeered. "Felt dirty."

"But, she is something," White said. "Almost makes a man rethink his rape policy."

Hell, the guy was gonna be bullied into rape?

Mick felt his hands tightening and tried to prevent them from forming fists. He wanted them in White's face. Or Rowdy's, didn't matter which.

"You gonna then?" Rowdy taunted.

White looked away. "Nah, never cottoned to rape, like I said."

Rowdy turned his ugly gaze to Mick who just looked back at Rowdy with a deadpan expression, not giving him anything. Trying not to reveal just how much he wanted to kill the guy.

"Yeah, all right, Mr. Charming, guess she's yours. Take her to the bathroom first. Don't want her defiling the bed when you defile her." He looked to his boys for their usual supporting chuckles and wasn't disappointed.

They laughed agreeably.

"Don't get too loud in there with her though, we might change our minds."

A shiver ran up Mick's back at the threat, a shiver that activated his need to kill impulses again.

"We're gonna start calling him George Clooney. Worrying all about her bathroom needs. Gots us a Mr. Debonair along for this mission."

How many more terms intended to be derogatory could Rowdy use for what was simply nice, decent, human, expected behavior? He'd simply backed up her request to use the bathroom, and Rowdy was decrying him as some special type of ladies' man.

The man didn't get better with age. The longer you were

around him, the more you wanted to kill him.

Stan and White grinned. Well, as long as they were all happy, Mick was fine with it.

Mick followed Becca down the hall.

"Hey," Rowdy yelled after him. "Listen at the door so she don't go out the window. Better yet, go in with her."

Becca whirled around, eyeing Rowdy indignantly.

Rowdy laughed derisively. The other two chuckled in unison.

Mick gave Becca a push to get her moving down the hall. She threw up her arm to knock his hand off her but he just kept pushing her.

His behavior looked in character for the jerks. The real reason he did it, to get her away from Rowdy and his gang.

But, damn, it killed him to manhandle her. He'd never touched her in anger. Not even as a hotheaded teenager.

After all he'd seen his father do, he would never touch a woman in anger. Yet, here he was treating her like shit.

Another reason to kill Rowdy. Rage boiled through him. It needed an outlet. Just keep it in check long enough to find the government target, and the men pulling the strings on these local yahoos.

Then, he'd kill Rowdy, given the justification. Say if he could provoke Rowdy to turn his gun on him.

Just hold the rage in check long enough. Two more days, he had two more days to unravel the tangled mess.

Two more days he needed to keep Becca alive. Unless he could get her out of there before then.

Barley followed along at his heels as if he would never leave him again, as if Mick had returned from the grave.

Becca walked into the bathroom, whirled and glared at him.

Sorry, he mouthed silently.

Her face was still furious but she gave him an acknowledging tilt of the head, then shot him a little point of the finger and motioned down the hall, as if to say, "Get away from this door." Then, she shut the door behind her.

51

A grin spread through him. Even under these circumstances, she could make him smile. He walked a few steps back down the hall to eavesdrop on the conversation in the other room.

"They're pushing it up now that we got her. It's perfect," Rowdy crowed.

"Sooner? Can we get ready?" White said.

"How soon?" Stan asked quietly.

"Two days," Rowdy answered, sounding proud of himself.

Two days? Hell, that was tomorrow.

"Wasn't they mad we got the girl?" Stan asked.

"Not after they thought about it for a minute, how it would make the point even more, getting a judge's kid. Whoo wee, they laughed. Didn't tell 'em it was our guy who helped us get the idea. He hates people who put away drug runners."

"But a female?" Stan stuttered. "Something 'bout it just ain't right."

"Hey, there will be collateral damage," Rowdy snarled. "That's how it works. If there weren't any women and children, it wouldn't be as dramatic. We're looking to inflict damage that will cut them to the quick."

He pulled the hunting knife from his waistband and stabbed the air, then, twisted and turned it several times. "Nothing says horror as much as little dead babies and bleeding women."

Mick's stomach curled at how easily Rowdy spoke of the blood of innocents.

Rowdy shook his head dismissively. "Can't be helped. They brought it on they selves. Government wants to take away the rights of the people, poking and peering into all our business, taking away near 'bout half our pay to fund their little governmental groups."

He puffed up now, strutting a few steps like a general addressing his troops. General Petraeus would have been proud. "They getting too strong, too powerful. We gots to push 'em back, start a revolution, put power back into the hands of the people. Power to the people, the little people."

Justifying murder in the name of some lofty goal.

Empowering the people, limited government. Sounded like a campaign speech, not what you used to justify bombing buildings with people inside.

This militia group was even worse than the people who'd flown planes into American buildings in the name of their cause.

Because these guys were willing to do it to their own countrymen.

And countrywomen and children.

Mick's jaw clenched, his hand curled with the need to choke Rowdy's throat, cut off his windpipe until he gurgled for air. Anyone who thought dead babies made a statement needed killing right now. He had to get out to the car and find the weapon that had been promised him. And the cell phone.

He sucked in a long breath, then blew it slowly out again.

He couldn't kill these Bozos straight out. If he didn't discover their target, how they planned to deliver the blow, and who led the group, there was no telling how much damage could be done.

Maybe even doubling their attack in retaliation. He only hoped the tracking device that had been put on the SUV had worked, that there was plenty of backup out there along the north Georgia roads just waiting to swoop in.

Hoped they'd taken down tag numbers and followed people to find the leaders of this group. Rowdy, White and Stan were just a small part of a larger group that would strike back harder if they weren't all dug out of their slimy holes.

"Jesus," Stan said, his face red, his jaw tight. Even from this distance, Mick could see the flush crawling up his cheeks.

"I didn't bargain for killing no babies. I thought we was just gonna take down a bridge or something, make a statement, not kill nobody."

"Oh, don't worry your little head, Stanley." Rowdy patted Stan's head. "We ain't really gonna be killing no babies. Maybe just kill a bunch of 'special agents'," he whined his voice up real high on the last two words. "Ever seen an un-special agent?" He giggled.

That madman's giggle said there was no reasoning with him, and scared Mick more than his words. It also made him sound stupid enough to be easily overcome. But, one thing prison had taught him was that smarts weren't necessarily needed to accomplish great evil in the world.

Mick had seen the mean intent that ran through Rowdy's brain more than once. Meanness could take you a long way, infuse a strength that ordinariness would never understand.

Also, he was beginning to wonder if the Feds even know who the real Rowdy was. The guy's accent and poor grammar seemed to fluctuate.

The guy was just playing a part for these people. How long had he been infiltrating this area, planning on using local people to attain his evil goals?

"We're just gonna kill FBI agents and their support people," Rowdy added.

"Still, a building full of people?" Stan stood up, sweat running down his face.

Rowdy stood up, too. From the dark hallway, Mick watched him physically menace the good ole boy who maybe hadn't realized just what he'd gotten into.

"You up to the job or not, Stan?"

Stan's gaze skirted away from the intensity, the insanity in Rowdy's eyes, and he sat back down. "Well, I guess if there ain't no children hurt. I mean," his voice rambled, going up and down in tone, as if searching for something to latch onto, to convince himself. "I been getting so tired of how this country is going. We ain't got nothing like the freedom we ought to be having. Nothing."

"That's right," White chimed in. "Every time you turn around, they usurping more and more of our rights. We got to do something. Got to turn this train around."

The way he said *usurping* sounded like it was an often used catch phrase of the group, like a kid repeating something his parents said.

"Got to turn this train around," Stan murmured. "Still, I don't want Mama and Daddy 'shamed o' me."

Rowdy looked at him, not saying anything. Couldn't question a man's not wanting to shame his parents.

"Maybe they'll understand what we is trying to do," White said. "Starting a revolution, taking back our country from those damned politicians up in Warshington and under that gold dome down in 'lanta. The original patriots didn't wait for the red coats to give them they's rights, they took 'em at the end of a musket barrel."

"I hear that," Rowdy said, and it seemed he was trying to imitate White's high-sounding tone.

But something rang false in his attempt. The man was just an angry guy looking for a fight and he'd found a cause he could get on board with, and bring others along in his quest for blood.

Did he even believe his own justification or was it just bits of grudges built on the shoulders of other grudges, slights and failed attempts in life that he blamed on the government?

A traffic ticket here, a lost job there. Somebody had to pay.

The only thing standing between innocent lives and this bastard might be him.

The toilet flushed, water in the sink ran for a moment, then the door opened, and Becca stepped out. She met his gaze, the connection sending a powerful kick to his stomach.

The reality hit him of what a complicating factor she was, the only woman he'd ever loved.

For most of his life.

A "fairy tale romance" some people had called them.

Before they'd gone down the hellish road that guys like Rowdy and his kind paved with their evilness.

She, at least, would come out alive. No matter what it cost him personally.

Rowdy's voice echoed from the den, emphasizing all Mick was up against in his fight to protect Becca, all the evil people backing up Rowdy.

Becca looked at him again with those sapphire blue eyes that always hit him in the gut. She would survive the next two days.

# CHAPTER SEVEN

Becca felt Mick so close behind her, escorting her to the back bedroom. His presence was a salve to the wound losing him had etched on her heart.

Barley trotted along behind them, looking up at Mick like he was a bag of treats, his eyes never leaving him.

A little pang of empathy flushed through her. Barley was afraid Mick might disappear at any moment. He'd grieved for Mick and Tess with a total lack of understanding, never really knowing why the two of them had deserted him.

On an emotional level, she hadn't understood Mick's absence any more than Barley, but at least she'd known the circumstances.

Barley had paced by the front door in the weeks after Tess' death, whining and looking out the side glass panels that lined the doorway from floor to ceiling.

Finally, he would curl up on two unwashed shirts, one Tess' and one Mick's. He'd found them in the laundry basket, pulled them out and claimed them as his own.

Becca had slept in one of Mick's shirts, wrapping it around her naked body, inhaling his scent, aching for his arms around her. But, finally the smell had vanished and she'd given up the shirt, the same way she'd given up hope of Mick ever coming back to her.

Apparently, Barley's nose had been keener than hers, detecting the faint scent she could no longer smell. Or just holding onto hope longer than her? The little dog had curled up on the shirts until the day he and Becca had been kidnapped.

She and the little dog had grieved together. Now, Mick was just feet away. If she turned quickly, she could wrap herself in his scent, inhaling him as if he'd never been away.

But, he wasn't back. Physically near her, he was still miles away emotionally, all his energy focused on another cop mission.

A kick of guilt hit her in the stomach at the selfishness of her concerns for herself, when many lives were at risk.

She opened the bedroom door to a small bed, a view more beautiful than the one off the back deck. The bed beckoned to her with a powerful draw, with the promise that she could climb in and sink into oblivion, forgetting everything that lay outside the bedroom door.

Inside the room, cozy comfort and a man she knew would never let anyone hurt her. If it was within his ability to control.

The only thing was, evil swirled outside of the room in a powerful vortex threatening to suck her and Mick down into its drowning depths.

The booming voices in the living room had carried through the thin bathroom door, painting a horrible picture. Buildings exploding? With people inside?

For just a brief moment, she understood what her twin, Tess, and Mick had fought against their entire adult lives. And her father as a judge had warred against.

Tess and Mick had volunteered for up-close and personal with evil. This stint with evil had been forced on her.

On a primal level, she wanted to reject the need to act, to involve herself and Mick, to jeopardize all the tomorrows they could share, all the tomorrows that Tess would never have.

She felt a duty to live, live for Tess.

But, once she knew what was at stake, babies bloodied, women and men screaming in pain and anguish, it was hard to walk away.

Even at the risk of her life?

At the risk of Mick's life?

Didn't they have a first duty to themselves, to keep their own lives safe? Didn't they owe it to Tess to live on, to remember her so that she lived on somehow?

That was the type of question Mick and Tess had confronted on a day-to-day basis. Were they willing to pay with their lives to save others?

This being her first time out, maybe it was understandable that all she really wanted to do was climb out that window and start running until she left evil behind.

Maybe her justification that she and Mick owed it to Tess to live was self-serving. But, the thought of losing Mick forever like she'd lost Tess seemed to justify any impulse to run, run away and take him with her.

Man, she hated this situation, these choices forced on her. But, Mick put himself into the situation.

His first impulse was to run toward the danger, heedless of his own safety, toward the possibility, high probability even, that he wouldn't come out alive.

Damn it to hell that she'd fallen in love with a boy who grew up to be a cop. Then, became an FBI agent, an uber-cop.

He wouldn't even think twice. But, what about her, what about the harm it would do to her if he died? He would say it was her choice to love him, but that he didn't have a choice to stop evil.

But, it hadn't been a "choice" to love him. She'd loved him for almost as long as she could remember until loving him had become embedded in her DNA.

Love didn't even begin to describe what they'd had. They'd been so entwined with each other that their future had seemed like one path.

Until the path had been dug up, and weeds had grown over what had once been a clear road. But, she ripped her mind away from all those thoughts, like Mick had seemingly done years before.

She needed to keep her mind in the present if she and Mick had a chance of surviving this situation.

Mick walked to the bed, pulled back the covers and scanned the sheets. "Looks pretty clean to me."

"Pretty clean?" She grimaced jokingly. "Don't know that's such a good advertisement."

He laughed, gravelly, deep in his throat, with a sound that pulled her toward him as surely as his scent. The sound of him, the smell of him, the look of him. Every damn thing about him.

"For a hotel, pretty clean may not be enough," he consented. "But for a hostage situation? Above average."

He smiled that killer smile that had always undone her. A curling hand of want stroked along her body, reminding her of the beds they'd shared together.

And the secret moments they'd shared, intimate, hot with connection. Moments that had held a lifetime's worth of passion.

That was why she'd not been with any man since him.

That and the brain numbing grief she'd dealt with so often the last two years.

Since she'd gotten the call.

The call that had changed everything and ended her and Mick's relationship with the finality of a gunshot.

Mick patted the bed. "Get some sleep," his voice coaxed, with the deep, sexy timbre that he'd used to convince her to do more sensual things than just take a nap.

Beds for them had had very little to do with sleep.

As if he read her thoughts, his eyes darkened with a hot passion she'd seen too many times to count.

He reached for her with one hand.

"Don't," she said, with a gasping, breathless voice, barely able to push out the protest. "Don't."

She couldn't handle this now, with everything that was already happening. Now was not the time to revisit the possibility of them.

He stood close enough that his scent wafted all around her, wrapping her in a blanket of want. She sucked in a deep breath, through her nose, luxuriating in the smell of him, like a dieter sniffing chocolate.

His hand stilled. He glanced away, the loss of the eye

contact as painful as when the final scent of him had vanished from his last shirt.

"Guess I'm as bad as that guy Rowdy, hitting on a woman under these circumstances," he said.

Guilt was a ready emotion for him, guilt for things he couldn't control, things no man could control.

A speeding bullet couldn't be controlled with honor and goodness.

Tess had been proof of that. Because she'd been the best person Becca had known her entire life.

Always, always, always, she'd done the right thing. And look what it had gotten her.

"Don't do this to yourself." She grabbed his hand as he started to let it fall to his side. "You are a world away from the type of man Rowdy is. Another species entirely."

Gratitude filled his face, then his eyes dropped to where she held his wrist. Hot need filled her, wanting him to touch her as he'd done in the old days.

Before he'd decided that looking at her face reminded him of just how badly he'd failed. His words, not hers.

She didn't know if she could ever allow herself to go back to that horrible place where she wanted him, needed him, but had no control. She thought that, as if she had a choice, since the want for him had poured through her fiercely when she'd first heard his voice in the car, as if no time had separated them.

It had been his decision to walk away.

When she'd needed him most, grieving for Tess, she'd also lost him.

A double killing blow at once, leaving an aching hole inside of her.

Now, no matter how much her body urged her to forget the past year and a half, her brain whispered that would never be possible.

Once you'd cut a hand off, you might imagine it back. But, you wouldn't extend the ghost limb again toward the pain that had severed it in the first place.

Survival instincts came in all sorts of forms.

No one would step into the path of a bullet.

Moving toward Mick was just that. Being shot once and standing up, asking for it again. She dropped her hand from his wrist.

Mick's eyes shuttered, telling her he'd read every emotion that had just flashed through her.

He pulled the bedcovers further back and patted the bed. "Get some sleep. You'll think clearer afterwards."

Would her brain ever really be clear where he was concerned? Would the sight of him ever stop the sudden flush of want? Would the smell of him be possible to resist, to steel herself against?

He looked different, leaner but more muscled, as if he'd strengthened himself to fight against the evil in the world.

His face had a new hard, almost jaded edge. Before, there'd been an openness about him, despite his hard childhood.

But, he smelled the same, inducing the urge to push up against him, inhale his scent, touch his bare skin.

More muscled, leaner and edgier, he was still Mick.

But, he wasn't her Mick any longer. He'd made that perfectly clear the last, long painful year and a half.

She nodded, kicked off her shoes and sat down on the bed fully dressed, then swung her feet onto the bed. Barley jumped up beside her, curling several times before settling next to her chest. She patted him comfortingly. Poor guy didn't understand what was happening today, or for the last two years for that matter.

Why Mick had gone away.

She knew the words for it, but her gut didn't really understand either.

She patted the little dog once again as he looked up at her then back over to Mick, hungrily studying his face.

Mick pulled the bedcovers over her, tucking them around her, gave Barley a pat, then started to pull away.

God help her, she grabbed his hand, unable to relinquish the comfort of his presence. After all this time without him, finding him like this was a gift.

Something flashed in his eyes. The same need for her that she felt for him?

Stop it, she warned herself. Stop the futile, useless hoping of the last two years.

That had gotten her nowhere. Though she'd been as relentless as Barley, refusing to give up hoping.

Mick's jaw tightened and he sat down on the bed, and began to rhythmically pat her shoulder, like you'd pat a child to sleep.

"It's going to be okay." Again, the words you said to a child, no matter the situation, just reassuring, offering the promise that things were normal.

Even if, like now, they were anything but.

She breathed in his essence, his goodness, letting it soothe her. A numb cloud of oblivion settled on her, and she felt sleep coming, sinking away into nothingness, even as she fought it because she was afraid when she woke, Mick would be gone.

As he'd been for the last two years, disappearing suddenly and completely. Leaving her wondering, like Barley, what had happened to the love they'd shared?

Had it been killed along with Tess?

She grasped his hand, willing him to be there when she awoke.

As tiredness clawed her down into sleep, she glanced up through leaden, nearly closed eyelids and glimpsed Mick, his eyes hungrily devouring her as if she were his last meal.

# Chapter Eight

Mick watched Becca sleep, her eyes shadowed with light purple against her porcelain skin.

Her complexion so pale and clear, with the beauty of a medieval painting he'd seen in a book, of a raven-haired woman leaning from a window.

Becca's beauty was of museum quality, the type of face that people would line up to stare at. He'd seen it in his dreams, in his fantasies, since that day when he'd had to walk away, when her face had become a constant reminder of how he'd failed the one person who should have been able to depend on him the most, his partner.

How could he have married Becca after that, knowing every time she looked at him, she'd remember all she'd lost? How he was responsible, and that when she needed him most, he might not come through for her, either.

Then there'd been the mission he'd undertaken, to destroy the drug network that channeled poison onto the streets of Atlanta and the surrounding metro area and outlying counties, to put away the men who'd killed his partner.

He'd had to keep away from Becca, knowing a connection to him would only bring danger to her.

That was the irony of their present circumstances; togetherness had been thrust on them because of the very mission he'd undertaken to avenge her sister's death. Chasing through the underworld of drug trafficking in order to find the person, or people, directly responsible for Tess' death.

That had thrown him and Becca back together. But, just as he'd believed, proximity to him brought danger to her.

God, he wanted to climb in that bed with her and claim her for his own once again. Wanted to fuse his body to hers, into one gigantic explosive device as it had been in the past, creating such heat and fire, such passion that they'd almost felt their climaxes shook the world.

It had shaken his world the first time they'd made love, so that he'd known there would never be another woman for him.

And there hadn't.

Even in the last two years, he hadn't been with any other woman.

He'd wanted, needed, the release that a woman's body could bring. But, he couldn't.

The only woman he'd ever really wanted was Becca, the one woman he'd no longer been able to face, or to endanger. It was so complicated.

Her breathing deepened. She was safely away in the land of dreams, hopefully where the last two years hadn't happened, with the death of his partner, Becca's twin sister.

He pulled his hand loose. He had to go attend to his mission. Barley leaped off the bed, trotting behind him.

"No, you stay here and watch our girl, Barley."

The little dog jumped up on Mick's leg, his two front feet hitting just below the knee. Barley looked at him with more love than Mick had experienced in the last two years. Gently, Mick caressed his face.

A hitch caught in his throat at the pure love flowing out of the animal. "I missed you too, Barley." His eyes felt hot.

"Damn idiot, crying over a dog," he muttered to himself. But, he continued to cradle the pup's head between his hands, lapping up the loving gaze the dog enveloped him with.

Then, he picked up the pup and set him on the bed with one last pat. Pointing at the dog to stay, he moved to the door.

Barley curled up next to Becca, his eyes fixed on Mick as if it might be the last time he would ever see him. So much emotion in one little dog's gaze.

"I'm coming back, boy." He met Barley's eyes which never left him as he opened the door then shut it behind him.

He took a moment to collect himself on the other side of the door. That moment with Barley had been like the homecoming he'd dreamt about for the last two years but never felt he'd deserved. Or could risk.

"A damn dog," he muttered under his breath then walked down the hall. Rowdy's ugly tone reached him before he even made it to the den.

A curling disgust clenched his stomach at all the hate inside that man, just looking for a place to land.

"We're gonna use her to get my cousin back from Tennessee. The Feds got him in the penitentiary up there. She's our bargaining chip. If they don't want to play, then." He pulled his pistol out of his waistband. "Pow!" A coyote grin spread across his face, dirty teeth exposed.

The urge to rip Rowdy's flesh from his body surged inside Mick. He compressed the desire to make the jerk scream in pain, pushing the need back into a box where he kept his animal urges.

At least he knew their plan. If Rowdy's cousin was in a federal prison, it was highly unlikely they'd be freeing him. Federal prison was a whole lot different than the state prison they'd been allowed to escape.

The federal penitentiaries took their escape statistics very seriously, not wanting to give prisoners the sense that any escape was possible.

Rowdy looked up as he entered the room. "You got Sleeping Beauty to sleep?"

Mick nodded.

"That was pretty quick back there." Rowdy looked at his boys for the expected laugh and they didn't disappoint him, chuckling along with him.

"Guess it didn't take long after being locked up like you were." Again with the ugly, teeth-exposed smile.

Mick wanted to knock those teeth down his throat. Maybe then he'd go to a dentist.

"So, what's the plan?" he said, ignoring the sex talk.

Rowdy's eyes crinkled with derision. "It's on a need-to-know basis. All you need know is, shut up and do what you're told. The real reason we popped you out of that prison is cause you was Stan's cellmate and would notice right away if he was gone."

Precisely why the Feds had stuck him in with Stan.

Mick shrugged like he could care less. "I meant what's the plan for food? I'm starving."

Rowdy stared at him for a long moment, apparently not anxious to give up his recent justification for annoyance. Finally, he shrugged and looked toward Stan. "Stan's the cook of the group. What's for dinner, Stan?"

Stan struggled up off the Naugahyde couch, the old sofa having softened around his shape so that it was like he was trying to get out of his own skin. The butt shaped indentation remained, the material slowly rising to a not quite flatness again.

Stan sauntered to the fridge in the kitchen that sat off from the den and poked around for a bit. "I could fix us up a meatloaf and some smashed potatoes."

"Emm, emm, emm," White sounded off. "Just like Mama used to make."

Suddenly, Mick could see White and Stan in their normal lives, good old boys that weren't really looking for a fight, but had traditional ideas that were offended by some of the changes of modern life, and were perfect picks for someone like Rowdy and his terrorism buddies to enlist in his hatefulness.

But, they'd run drugs too.

Justifying it in the name of the bigger cause.

Becca's daddy, "The Judge" as Mick couldn't help thinking of him, had e-mailed Mick about the arrest of these guys.

Some of the details of the drugs they'd been transporting and other particulars of the group had made him and the judge think these guys were part of the network that had led to Tess' death. The ones he and the judge were driven to bring down.

How much of all the collaboration between Mick and the judge did Becca know about? Had she figured out that it had become her father's life mission, as much as it had become Mick's, to bring the guys to justice who were directly responsible for his daughter's death?

"Are your families around here?" Mick looked at White, digging for any kind of information. Who knew where a conversation might lead, what nugget of information might be revealed about their connections in the drug world?

White looked at his feet. "Got none. My wife died of the cancer and my boy got killed in Afghanistan."

He'd never mentioned in prison that his son had died fighting for his country, making the ultimate sacrifice. It hadn't been included in the file on White either.

A sliver of sympathy for the guy slipped through the wall Mick had built up against any attachment for the people he was determined to put away for life.

With White's wife and son dead, he was the perfect conscript for Rowdy, no one left at home. Nothing left to lose?

Kinda like himself, a quick little voice inside Mick taunted.

Stan didn't meet his eyes, didn't need to say anything. He'd talked incessantly about his wife in jail, but more just as if sounding off in anger.

Though Mick had sensed his pain, the loss of his marriage and children on a day-to-day basis. A lot of guys like him disguised their pain with a covering coat of anger.

"So, where's your family, Atlanta?" Rowdy narrowed his eyes, focusing intently on Mick.

"Don't got none," he mirrored White's words, in a monotone, as if he'd said it a hundred times before.

"Don't got none?" Rowdy said sarcastically. "Everybody starts out with some, two at least." He cut his eyes at his boys

68

and they obligingly guffawed.

"What happened to 'em?" Rowdy persisted, determined to dig out the dirt on their newest conscript. A weakness would be an asset to be exploited. That's the only reason Rowdy ever showed an interest in anybody.

"Mom died of a drug overdose when I was eight, and Dad died drunk driving two years later."

That was all kind of true about him having no family, since he'd lost the last real semblance of a family when Tess had died.

"Grandma raised me. But, she don't have no truck with me no more. Since." He waved back toward the south. "Well, since all that."

The three of them stared at him. If he wasn't mistaken, he saw a glimmer of sympathy in White and Stan's eyes.

"Damn, that's rough," White said softly. "I thought I had it rough when my wife 'n kid died. But, I was an adult."

Rowdy looked around the room as if he knew he was losing the upper hand. "Enough trips down memory lane," he snarled. "We all gots a past. Now's all that matters, and the future. The future that damned government wants to snatch away from us and everyone else out here in the real world, 'cepting those folks in the capital towns of 'lanta and Wershington, DC. Cause those folks are privileged, special." His southern, mountain accent had become intense, as if trying to accentuate his likeness to White and Stan.

He stood up and paced a few steps, expanding his chest, breathing hard. "We're doing this for the children to come."

"Yeah," Stan said viciously. "My ex-wife's got my kids in a government school. Probably indoctrinating them into the government's way of thinking. I tole't her we need to home school 'em so they don't just accept everything the government tells 'em." Stan frowned like his ex-wife was just across the room, jabbing a finger accusingly. "That's what happens in them government schools."

"You mean public school?" Mick asked.

"Public schools is run by the government and them teacher's unions, teaching all they's communist ideas." Stan had never looked so mean, not even when he'd talked about his ex-wife leaving him. Usually, he was a pretty easy to get along with kind of guy.

Never once even talked back to the guards. But, get him fired up and Mick saw the type of guy he could be if really crossed.

Red cheeks, jutting jaw and curling lips made him look the equivalent of Rowdy.

Turns out the guy had his own triggers.

Mick scowled and nodded like he was on their side. Thing was some of the things they said made sense, with so much government and taxes.

Mick knew about layers of management from all the guys upstairs at FBI and before with the Atlanta Police.

He might have kind of liked these guys, except for the blowing things up and hurting people, and running drugs.

"So, what're we going to do about it?" he growled, in an imitation of Stan's indignation.

Rowdy's eyes narrowed. "You talk the talk 'bout bringing down the federal government. But, will you walk the walk of a patriot? Do you got the guts when it comes right down to it?"

Mick stared back into Rowdy's eyes for a moment. Then, he said, "I been knowing how to walk for a long time now. What I say and what I do, they're the same thing." He made a slashing motion with his hand.

Rowdy looked at Stan and White for a second, before all three of them gave a slow nod at each other.

"Well, your part," Rowdy said, for the first time not talking down to Mick, "is going to be driving the girlie up to Tennessee to drop her off to the Feds in exchange for my cousin when they release him from the Tennessee pen."

"Stan here will go along to help y'all." He nodded at Stan. "And White'll position the truck, so just after my cousin is released and you drop the girl off, it will explode." He gestured widely with his hands, lifting them into the air, illustrating a gigantic bomb. "And those fellas will realize they've been had."

He laughed, loud and long, a barking sound like a wild dog. "They'll think we was just after my cousin, then they'll see our real motive. To bring down the U.S. government and start a new kind of revolution, where the people have control again."

Stan and White nodded in unison. They might be a milder form of Rowdy. But, add a bomb and they were every bit as dangerous.

Damn, he sure hoped that tracking device, cell phone and the promised gun were attached to the SUV. He needed to get out and check that.

If they weren't there, he and Becca were really screwed. Or, as the bosses behind the safety of desks would put it, on their own.

# CHAPTER NINE

"So, Stan'll take the first shift," Rowdy ordered. Always ordered, never just stated.

"Gonna fix my meatloaf and taters while y'all get some shuteye. I'll sleep after lunch. Sides," he said. "Ain't enough beds for all of us to sleep at the same time."

Mick nodded. Everyone would be asleep except for Stan. How could he use that to his best advantage? Go out to the car and retrieve the phone, slip away and make a call, contacting his boss at the FBI?

"I'll share with the girl," Rowdy said, grinning at Mick. The guy liked to get under people's skin.

And it worked, distracting Mick from his initial line of thought. Ignore that comment and it was the equivalent of a male dog coming over and lifting his leg on another dog's lawn.

He couldn't let it pass and keep his guy certification.

In prison, people who took guff from anyone became an instant target. You couldn't be a pussy and not expect to become somebody's bitch. So, Mick had stood his ground in prison, against guys with shivs. Now, he'd have to stand his ground against guys with guns.

So, he turned, eyed Rowdy and swaggered just a bit, just a bit more than Rowdy's macho bravado.

He grinned at the supposed prison yard boss. "She's mine, we already discussed this. Bout your gal cutting off your man parts? So, let's not go over old ground." He met Rowdy's gaze, and held it, refusing to look away.

Rowdy held his gaze for a long moment, then something flickered way back behind his eyes as if he recognized another dangerous man. He finally looked away and guffawed, "Pussy hound." He laughed to his boys. "Knowed he was a lady's man all along. That's all right. She'll be jerking him around by the testicles."

Mick turned and meandered back toward Becca's bedroom in case Rowdy got any ideas about showing Mick who was boss.

Rowdy and White both followed down the hall and opened up separate bedroom doors.

"My own bedroom, that's the ticket," White said behind him. "Don't have to listen to Rowdy's snoring. This is living."

Rowdy just snorted.

Mick opened the door to Becca's bedroom quietly, shut it behind him, then pushed the button locking the door. It was only a privacy lock but it was something. He leaned a straight chair up underneath the doorknob.

Rowdy might like to eliminate him as a complication with a bullet to the brain while he slept. For good measure, he placed a small metal trashcan on top of the chair's seat. Then, grabbed a book and set it on top of the trashcan.

His own early warning system if someone tried to come through that door. He looked around for a weapon. A doorstop sat in a corner, a heavy metal antique iron. Mick picked it up and set it on the bedside table.

He needed just a bit of shuteye to clear his brain. Let everyone settle into a deep sleep before he tried going outside.

Padding across the carpeted floor, he peered at Becca. Asleep. An idiotic regret shot through him that she wasn't awake, ready to spoon back into him when he lay down behind her.

Barley moved to the foot of the bed, vacating Mick's usual place beside Becca. As Mick slowly slid onto the bed, her scent surrounded him, and a punch of nostalgia flooded him. For what had been, what could have been.

For what would never be.

He'd found home, family, and belonging in Becca, her sister, and their dad when the judge had decided to spare him juvie for punching his dad.

The judge could have sent him away so easily as Mick's dad had requested, and never given it a second thought.

The judge later told him he'd seen potential in Mick, from the way he'd addressed all the adults in the courtroom as *sir* or *ma'am*, and had spoken politely. Said Mick had looked him in the eye with an honesty the judge rarely saw in people dragged in front of his bench.

The judge had found Mick a place to stay where the fourteen-year-old didn't get punched in the jaw just cause he didn't get the right type of beer for his dad.

"Thirty two ounces, I said," his dad had bellowed the last time he'd hit him. "Don't be wasting my money buying six packs when it's cheaper to get the big boys."

Mick's mom had gotten in between him and his dad's powerful fists. The horror of seeing his mom beat hurt worse than any bruises his dad could inflict on him.

So, Mick had gotten a baseball bat.

"Son of a bitch," Mick muttered under his breath, his fists clenching, to this day aching for a few minutes alone in some dark prison yard with his father now that Mick was a man.

For what had happened later to his mom.

Life held lots of opportunities for regrets. Like the regrets the judge probably felt over bringing Mick into his daughters' lives?

Probably never would have taken such a personal interest in Mick if he'd known of all that would follow.

Mick and Becca falling in love.

Mick and Tess bonding in their shared mission to become cops, to make a difference.

Tess. An instantaneous knife of grief sliced through him.

He'd never see her face again, except in a photograph or his memory.

A horrible flashing image of the last night he'd seen her alive seared his brain and he grimaced, pain grinding through him, gripping his stomach, the scene playing out like a movie clip.

He closed his eyes, willing the memory away. But, that memory would never die. It was planted in his head for life.

Tess with her feminine brand of macho had been strikingly tough, with a sense of immortality they'd shared.

Nothing could hurt them. Death happened to other cops, careless cops, not cops as determined and tough as him and Tess.

He stopped, willing his mind away from the guilt, the sorrow, the self-recrimination, everything that had convinced him that Becca and her father were better off without his constant reminding presence. They'd both been too decent to voice the blame they must have felt was his.

In the privacy of their own grieving moments, they'd had to have thought it.

Cause he did.

When the judge's e-mail had started showing up in Mick's FBI inbox, he'd relished the contact, even if it was at a distance.

But, he'd never expected to see either of them again. Not the judge, not Becca.

Especially not Becca after he'd begun devoting himself to pursuing the drug ring he was convinced was responsible for Tess' death.

It was just too dangerous for Becca to be around him. Bad things happened to people he loved and he couldn't be responsible for anything happening to her.

But, here she was, like the angel she'd always been since the first time he'd met her.

He quietly levered himself closer to her, sliding until he was mere inches from her, where the scent that was pure her, sweet, clean, rolled over him. That estrogen-loaded essence of her punched him in the face, inundating his nostrils, then rolling down into his chest, filling every cell of his body with her.

And the desire to take her.

To take her underneath him and push into her center, feeling her surround him with all her goodness.

That goodness that he would never deserve again.

Not after what he'd put her and her dad through.

A soft purring sound emanated from Becca. She murmured, rolling slightly until she leaned into his chest, curling around him in her sleep. As if the last two years hadn't happened.

As if he weren't the person who'd cost her the highest price anyone should ever have to pay, the loss of her other half, her twin, the woman she'd slept beside in the womb, then shared beds with until they were teenagers.

She snuggled closer.

Then, God help him, he couldn't have moved away from her if his life had depended on it. If hers had depended on it?

That punch of guilt, of needing to protect her kicked in. He pulled back, fighting against the need that ached in his groin.

But, she curled into him again, soft, vulnerable in sleep.

As unsuspecting as the hundreds of people who'd get up and go to work one day soon and find their lives shattered, their bodies ripped with pain.

If the bastards involved with the Homegrown Militia weren't stopped.

This situation was impossible. He wanted to put a bullet into Rowdy's head, tie up Stan and White, and drive away in the SUV with Becca, punching a hole into the militia's plan.

But, most of all, saving Becca.

But, it'd be only a small hole in the militia's plan, easily filled, easily plugged. That wouldn't stop Homegrown's plan, only delay it.

Besides, he was firmly convinced that though Stan said they'd only driven the truck full of pot and cocaine as a one-time deal, a small operation, in order to finance their militia work, that in reality, the trio was connected to a larger drug

76

network.

Maybe even the one that had gotten Tess killed and himself laid up in a hospital with bullet wounds.

How could he save Becca yet continue on with his mission to root out the entire militia group? And maybe find the people responsible for Tess' death.

Becca pushed against him, murmuring in her sleep, and the physical pain of needing her once again hardened into a knife that twisted in his gut.

But, his tiredness overwhelmed him like a wave, pushing him down, rolling over him, until he slid under.

Into dreams of him and Becca making love, while danger threatened them like a dark force sweeping over the mountains.

# CHAPTER TEN

Damn. Just damn.

He ran his hand along the underside of the car, searching for the equipment he'd been promised.

His heart rate accelerated, pulsing blood through his veins, pushing panic throughout his body.

No. No. No.

The only word his mind could form was a simple negative response to the situation.

His breath came in quick panting spurts, the oxygen never managing to reach his brain.

An alternate plan. He needed an alternate plan.

Had the Feds managed to tail them anywhere near the area? Did they know where they were, unable to communicate that to him?

A thousand questions but no answers.

He could only hope backup was out there somewhere.

Until then, he had to come up with some way to reach them, to communicate the militia group's plans when the time came.

He had to get his hands on that cell phone Rowdy had in his pants pocket. How was that gonna happen when he hadn't even allowed Becca to touch it when she'd spoken to her father?

He glanced back toward the cabin and stubbed out the cigarette that had been his ready excuse to get outside if anyone questioned him on his return to the cabin. Never smoked, never would, even though he'd gotten pretty good at faking it.

Cause people got loose-lipped and chatty whenever they started smoking together. Gave 'em a bond.

Having cigarettes on you at all times in prison gave you an excuse to talk to people. They'd ask you for one, or you'd give 'em one just cause you knew they were jonesing for the nicotine.

As he walked toward the cabin's back door, the question of Becca chewed his insides like a rat on meth.

Should he take her and get the hell out of Dodge? Make sure Victim One was safe, since he might not be able to get communication out about the militia's plans.

Was a victim in the hand worth countless possible victims in unnamed government buildings? If it was Becca, yeah.

Even if many other people had to die?

Hopefully not. But, yeah.

Because, a world without Becca was unlivable, a planet without oxygen. You could walk on it, but you couldn't live on it.

Even when he'd planned to never see her again, just knowing she was out there had made life bearable.

If she were gone forever, how could he continue breathing?

Maybe he could kill two birds with one stone, get Becca the hell away from these guys, and also use the opportunity to communicate with the outside world.

He had to enlist her help, tell her the situation, make a plan. He walked quietly into the living room. Stan lay sleeping on the couch. That was a piece of luck. He must have fallen asleep after taking the meatloaf out of the oven cause a pan on the table emitted waves of aroma that called to his stomach.

Then, a glint of metal caught his eye. Stan's gun lay on the coffee table beside him. Mick padded closer, monitoring Stan's snoring for signs he was awakening.

Silently, Mick lifted the gun, turned it and slid the clip out. Holding his breath, he glanced back down the hall for signs of the other two men while listening to Stan's snoring.

Quickly, he removed four bullets from the clip, slid the clip back into place, then set the gun back on the coffee table.

Slipping the bullets into his pants pocket, he headed for the hall, passing the rooms of Rowdy and White, listening to their snoring echo through the doors. Quietly, he turned the knob to Becca's room and stepped in.

A silent swish of air alerted him as Becca swung something toward his head. He jumped back and grabbed her wrist.

Instinctively, he twisted the arm, pulling it down as Becca's big-eyed, half asleep expression said she'd just woken up.

He stopped moving for a second, taking control of his emotions, and letting her get a grip on hers.

Silently, she waited, breathing heavily herself. A small grin etched across her face and he felt an answering one welling within himself.

He reached back to quietly close the door behind him, took the heavy doorstop from her hand and set it on the bedside table. Then, he used his hold on her arm to pull her in further.

Her eyes widened. This time with a different feeling behind them. Awareness? Nervousness?

He slipped an arm around her back, leaning in close to her ear. "Morning," he whispered.

A slight chuckle breathed from her lips. "Sorry," she whispered close to his ear. "I was dreaming they'd killed you and were coming for me. Then, I heard someone in the hallway. I wasn't going down without a fight."

"You're a fighter," he whispered back.

So close to him, her scent whirled around him. An entirely inappropriate response spiked through him.

He'd learned with Tess' death that tomorrow wasn't promised, that in an instant you could be dead, so he savored the moment, for the briefest blink of an eye.

Savored her in his arms, safe, and close.

Then, he pushed back every male impulse he had and remembered where they were and what needed doing.

He released her. "Sorry if I scared you," he whispered.

"Right back at you." She smiled slightly. "I was so hoping to bash one of those guys in the head."

"I know you were." Their eyes met in a silent laugh, hers crinkling around the edges. He realized just how much he'd missed their shared sense of humor, laughing silently at each other across the room in high school classes, communicating without words when they'd each found something funny.

Which they'd done often. She and Tess had the best senses of humor he'd ever known, finding fun in so many little moments.

Damn, he'd missed them both.

He wrapped a hand around Becca's neck and pulled her to him, snaking his other arm around her back. The slightest resistance from her eased after a second. She hadn't tried to escape his grasp, just hadn't moved into his arms the way she did during all the years they'd been together.

Then, he felt her release and lean into him, wrapping her arms around him, holding him, letting him hold her. It felt so damn good.

So good, that for a moment, he wanted to forget everything outside that room and just think of nothing but her.

But, he couldn't.

Everyone was asleep and this might be their only chance.

"We have to get out of here while they're asleep," he whispered, his voice barely above a breath.

She jerked back and nodded vehemently, then sat on the bed and began putting on her shoes.

He pulled his gun out and loaded the four bullets, one for Stan, one for White, and two for Rowdy. Evil took some extra killing.

"We have to make it look like you're escaping," he whispered. "So even if everyone's asleep, you have to take off running and then I'll come after you just a moment later, as if I'm chasing you and only just realized you'd escaped."

Her eyes narrowed. "Why do you care if they know we escape together?"

Damn it. Might as well just say the truth. She could always tell when he was lying. He looked straight at her.

"I need to find a phone and let the Feds know where these guys are." And then he'd be coming back in, he didn't add.

She finished tying her shoes then picked up Barley as if she were going to carry him while they escaped. "You're not telling me the whole truth."

"Damn it, Becca," he hissed quietly. "Just do as I say. Your being here is making my mission much harder, trying to save you and still concentrate on what I need to do. It will be much safer for me if you're gone."

The tightening in her jaw said she wasn't having any of it. "Let's just concentrate on getting out of here and we can argue later," she whispered tersely.

"Okay then, how 'bout this reason. If they know we're in cahoots, they might put a bullet in my head."

She touched his arm, her eyes big. Instant impulses flashed through him. To take her into his arms and reassure her, comfort her.

Damn it, this was why he had to get her out of here. They'd already wasted so much precious time talking.

Looking away from her and everything that she inspired in him, he searched around the room for anything that could be of use to them in their escape. But there was really nothing that wouldn't immediately reveal their intent if they were caught.

He took Barley from her arms and set him on the floor. "You can run faster if you're not carrying him. And believe me, Barley can keep up with you no matter how fast you run."

Barley had accompanied Becca, Mick and Tess many times on runs. She nodded.

He took her by the shoulder and looked into her eyes. "Follow my lead and don't do anything if they're awake," he whispered.

The intensity in her responding gaze reassured him she understood this might be their only chance.

He tilted his head toward the door, dropping his hands from her, though it was like a falling man releasing his grasp on the last handhold before dropping to his death.

He sucked in a deep breath and willed away all thoughts except his mission and keeping Becca safe.

He opened the door. Not a sound echoed through the hallway except steady, even, male snores and an occasional snort.

Luck might be on their side. He gestured with his hand for Becca to follow and stepped out into the hallway, moving slowly, keeping his footsteps light.

Becca followed close behind him, Barley close behind her. They entered the den. And the sofa was empty.

Damn.

Turning toward Becca, he gave the slightest of head shakes. Her expression dropped.

Just the way Tess had done so many times when she was primed for action, then had to abort the plan. Just like Tess, Becca seemed to adjust quickly.

She could have been every bit as good a cop as Tess.

A toilet flushed and the bathroom door near the front entry way opened. "Hey," Stan said, eying them both. "You guys up?"

They nodded in unison. "You want to catch some shuteye now?" Mick asked, nonchalantly.

Stan shook his head, his cheeks reddening. Probably wondering if anyone knew he'd already done so by accident.

But, hell, no one could stay awake as long as they had and be expected not to succumb to the animal need for sleep.

"Lunch's ready." Stan cleared his throat and pointed toward the stove.

Should they try something now and make it look like Becca was escaping when there was only Stan? As he thought it, he could almost sense it going through her mind as well.

No. Too risky.

Mick took a step toward the stove, and Becca pushed him

from behind, sending him toward Stan. Apparently, she hadn't read his last thought.

But, Becca had already alerted Stan to her impulse to escape. It might be the last chance she got, so Mick barreled toward Stan with much more force than her push had inspired. Together he and the big man tangled up and fell on the floor.

"Hey!" Stan yelled. "Hey!"

Mick took his time getting off him, slipping and sliding back on top of Stan several times. "What the hell?" Mick glared at Stan as if he'd done something, instead of the other way around. Then, he glanced over his shoulder.

Barley stood by the door, whirling back and forth, whining, looking outside, then back at Mick, torn between leaving Mick, who'd been gone so long, and following Becca.

Mick motioned away with his hand and Barley took off, reassured by Mick's order.

"Get off'n me!" Stan yelled. "Get off'n me!"

Mick pushed down on the big man again, as if using him for leverage to stand.

By the time Mick got up and looked around, Becca and Barley were gone.

"She's getting away!" Stan yelled, heading for the door.

"What?" Mick stepped in front of him, effectively blocking him from getting to the sliding glass door.

Mick looked out the door and saw Barley's little hindquarters disappearing at a fast clip into the woods.

Stan pushed against him, too late to see anything.

"Where is she? Where'd she go?" He shoved Mick the rest of the way out the door, his head swiveling like a toy dog's on the dashboard of a car, bouncing around in all directions. With as little purpose.

She was gone.

Mick pointed down the driveway. "I think she went down there."

"Get up, get up!" Stan yelled back into the house. "The girl's gone!"

A loud scrambling sound like bears awakening from hibernation came from the rooms. Seconds later, two large burly, disoriented men emerged as confused as a bear must feel in his first seconds of coming out of a winter's sleep.

"She's gone!" Stan yelled. "Knocked us down and ran."

"What?" White and Randy asked in unison, as if they were just learning English.

"The girl got loose," Stan enunciated carefully.

"What? Where?" Rowdy seemed to be coming out of his daze the quickest. "Which way did she go?"

"I think she went down the driveway," Mick offered, his hands in the air as if he weren't certain.

"Stan, you go ahead down that way." Rowdy pulled his keys out of his pocket. "I'll drive. You run ahead and look along the brushy area in case she's hiding. White, you stay here in case she doubles back. Atlanta, you go up there." He pointed toward the woods.

A good piece of luck.

Maybe this was going to work after all.

Mick took off toward the wood line, praying he and Becca could avoid the other men.

This was their only chance.

# CHAPTER ELEVEN

Becca pushed through the undergrowth, limbs slapping at her face, vines grabbing at her feet, the landscape conspiring to help its homegrown boys.

This was their territory.

Her lungs burned and her side stabbed at her with the need to stop and let oxygen work its way into her bloodstream.

But, she couldn't. This might be her only chance. Her only chance to get to a phone and call the police for help, to let her father know she was safe. He must be going crazy with worry.

Losing one daughter to criminals was bad enough, losing his last child could send him over the edge into a maddening grief.

From below, she heard shouts and knew the chase was on full force. Would they alert their buddies, so that no part of the county would be safe, countless eyes watching out for her? Countless anonymous eyes?

"Girlie, come on out, girlie," Rowdy's voice cut through the greenery like a machete, slicing at her hope of escaping. Her only immediate need was to get away from him.

"Don't make me come find you. If I have to come in there and find you, I'm gonna be real mad." His voice careened up high into crazy territory. "Don't know what I might be capable of if I get that mad."

Clawing nails raked along her nerve endings, spiking into her flesh, visualizing all that a man like Rowdy could do. Would relish doing.

"Get me that deer hunting knife, Stan. I might have me some skinning to do." He laughed like a hyena on the hunt. "Come on out, girlie. Don't make me come in there looking for yoouuu," he yodeled out the last word.

She froze, paralyzed for a second, his words inspiring the sort of terror that almost convinced her to give herself up rather than provoke his wrath further.

Then, a fiery spike of anger cut through that insane thought and like a deer flushed out by the dogs, she ran, ran for all she was worth, ran for her life. Or from worse.

Ran from what a depraved monster like Rowdy could dream up.

Spurting up the hill, rocks raining down the slope, she must be alerting everyone to her exact location. She couldn't worry about that, needed to put as much distance between herself and the cabin as possible.

She ran like a mad woman, like a fox with hounds after it, baying for her blood. Felt as crazed as the little creatures must feel. Ran for what seemed forever, through dense, malicious clawing greenery. Barley ran at her heels, his eyes frantic, unhappy, seeming instinctively to realize what was at stake.

Her breath came in ragged gasps, ripping, burning breaths racketing through her lungs. Finally, she had to stop, panting for oxygen. Half collapsing against a tree, she listened, trying to hear over the blood pounding in her ears.

Then, she heard it, a faint sound of footsteps, kicking loose gravel, bringing someone closer and closer up the mountain.

Nearly shrieking with terror, she sucked in the sound that would reveal her whereabouts, pivoted and ran in a half limp, half stumble, leaning to favor her right side, where the ribs threatened to rip through the skin.

If they caught her, even Mick might not be able to keep them from killing her, or merely torturing her to make her pay for her escape. If Mick tried to stop them, they both might end up dead.

And Mick would try to stop them.

The crazed blood fear that prey experienced pulsed through

her body. Her pursuers might be equally crazed with bloodlust that the chase excited. Who knew what would happen if they caught her?

She ran then, ignoring her side, only knowing she had to get away. Get away from the monsters.

\*\*\*\*

"Becca," Mick called quietly, hoping his voice wouldn't carry down the hill. He stood, silently, listening.

Nothing.

Again, he began running up the hill, following the faint trail, a hiking trail that climbed the mountain behind the house.

It was only natural she'd keep on the path. The path of least resistance that most humans would take. Put the greatest distance between yourself and the people chasing you.

But, he stopped and looked around for any sign she'd veered off it.

A faint shuffling sound ahead told him she was still on the path. So, he ran for all he was worth.

Which wasn't much. His heart pounded in his chest. Even the few months he'd been locked up had taken a toll.

Becca was running like a deer on speed. She'd always been fast but she must have upped her daily runs more than usual since Tess' death.

He knew instinctively she'd used her daily runs as her way to burn off the emotions from losing Tess, losing him, losing the future they'd planned together.

Damn it. He couldn't let his mind go there.

Now was about survival, catching up to her and getting her somewhere to safety.

"Becca," he wheezed. "Becca, stop."

A blur to his right, off the path, almost hidden in the greenery, caught his eye. She was running downhill, through the dense undergrowth.

Damn. He'd nearly missed her.

He took off running after her, slipping and sliding down the mountain, brush and vines trying to trip him at every step. "Becca," he called again. He was close behind her.

Loose, slippery leaves gave way beneath his feet and the ground came up to meet him like a giant fist, slamming into his body, sucking the wind from his lungs. Then, gravity flipped him over and over, tumbling him downhill.

Finally, he slammed full force into her, carrying her with him in his fall. Together, they rolled another fifteen feet then crashed into a tree.

He hit the tree first and the blow knocked out the little wind left in him. Unable to breathe, he sucked at the air, his compressed chest locked up, nothing getting in.

Though intellectually he knew it was only temporary, his animal instincts lurched with fear that he couldn't get oxygen into his body.

Before he could catch his breath, Becca began attacking like a cornered cougar, clawing at his face.

He grabbed her wrists. But, she kicked at him, her back arched. A crazed look altered her features into a wild animal fighting for its life.

In a long wrenching gulp, he sucked in air just as she bared her teeth and aimed for his neck. "Becca," his strangled lungs pushed out.

Inches from his jugular, she jerked to a halt, her eyes rabid, gasping breaths rasping from her mouth.

Her eyes met his, and slowly, as if she had to force herself, her jaw muscles eased. Slowly, she became Becca again.

She fell back onto the ground.

A jagged pain ran from his hip to his shoulder. God, he'd hit the tree hard. He felt along his side to see if he'd actually broken anything.

Becca sat up, watching his hand as it checked out his side. "You okay?" she huffed out, barely understandable in her breathless voice.

"You okay?" He raised an eyebrow.

She heaved air rather than answering his smartass remark. Barley nosed them both. "It's okay, boy," she reassured him, then her eyes fastened on Mick's face.

"Your face, I scratched you."

He swiped at his face, coming away with blood.

"Geez, I guess you did." He laughed darkly. "That's okay, will make my story look good that you fought to get away from me."

"Your story?" She leaned in. "What do you mean?"

Have the argument now or later? Might as well start the wearing down process now. She always took a lot of wearing down to convince her against an opinion she'd taken to so strongly.

"The story I'll have to tell as to how you got away." Too many words, too little breathe. He sucked in air.

She arched an eyebrow.

"When I go back," he added.

"You're not going back," she stated definitively, taking his shirt into her fist.

He looked down at that little hand, fisting into his shirt, so determined to control her world.

"Those men are monsters," she snarled. "We're going to find a phone, get some help in here to take these men into custody. There is no going back." She laughed dismissively.

He felt one of his eyebrows raise reflexively, as if it couldn't help itself. But, he said nothing, not fighting with her anymore now about what was a done deal. Just let the idea sit and fester, and work on her subconscious, help her come to the conclusion that he was right.

He had to find some way to get her safely off this mountain and then resume his mission.

She tilted her head, eyeing him with narrowed eyes. "I know that look. Mr. Big Shot Undercover Cop is going to bring them all down."

He averted his eyes, not meeting contact with hers.

"Bring them all down." She waved her hands dramatically

90

in the air, using her imitation of a big city accent.

"We don't have time for this." He struggled to his feet, a jagged pain shooting through his side. He refused to grimace or react, not wanting any more lectures about what he needed to do.

He held out a hand toward her.

She took it and he gave a tug, pulling her to her feet. Pain shot all through his left side, wrenching a groan from deep inside him that he couldn't hold back this time.

Damn, he did not need to make her argument for her.

"You're hurt," she said, touching his arm.

"I'm okay." He looked around, ignoring her and the pain. His side peppered him with lingering agony, but her hand distracted him, lacing the pain with shots of heat, awareness, want.

He didn't need that. He needed to get his bearings, to remember the little bit he'd seen as they'd traveled through the mountain darkness on their way to the cabin.

"I remember some smoke coming from the distance when we were out on the back patio. Figure it's a cabin," he said, ignoring the obvious concern still in her eyes.

She turned and looked around. "I ran up the mountain, then to the right and down. That means we're going toward the view we saw from the back."

He tilted his head at her. "Very good. Someone was listening when Tess and I talked about navigating towards landmarks."

She smiled slightly, then shrugged. "Not really. I was just running on the path, then took off down this hill by instinct when I thought whoever was chasing me was about to catch me."

"Yeah, but your instincts were right, since this was the way I would have chosen if I'd had time to plan a route," he said, meeting her eyes.

A hint of pride flashed in hers, then she looked back in the direction of the militia cabin, which was far away now since they'd been running for quite some time. They were virtually lost in the woods at this point, the heavy wooded mountain providing cover that no sound could penetrate unless someone were right up on them.

They were far enough away that their voices would never reach the road or the cabin. These mountains were a lot bigger once you started hiking them than they looked from a distance.

"Do you think they'll figure out where we're going?" Becca said in a tight voice.

"Maybe not," he said as much for her benefit as trying to reassure himself. "I told them I saw you heading down the road. Maybe, they'll just go back along the road, figuring you'll be heading toward civilization, thinking that's the quickest way to help. If we're lucky."

"Better to be lucky than good," she repeated the old saying.

"We're gonna have to be both," he said, then wished he hadn't because fear slipped from underneath the tough cover she'd carefully put in place, coming out into the open where he could see full force its effect on her.

And he didn't like it. Hated it.

Hated the men who'd inspired that look on her beautiful face.

He had to get her out of danger. If those men got their hands on her after this, he didn't even want to think about what their anger might drive them to do.

# CHAPTER TWELVE

Dusky night was falling. Through the blue, smoky haze covering the mountainside, a cabin materialized up ahead, through the trees.

"Finally," Becca gasped, relief suffusing the word.

He put a hand on her arm, one finger to his lips. Leaning close to her ear, he whispered, "We've got to make sure none of these guys or their buddies are up there."

She nodded, her eyes connecting with his. Damned if her nearness, looking up into his eyes like that and the feel of her under his hand didn't excite some primal urge.

Despite the situation.

All day, he'd watched her butt as she'd hiked up and down these mountains, watched the strength and determination in that small tight body. She was one hell of a woman.

And he'd walked away from all of that?

What the hell was wrong with a man who'd do that?

No matter the reason.

Memories burned through his mind. The two of them touching, unable to get close enough. His breathing became more shallow. All he wanted was to pull her up against his body.

A flicker in her eyes said she'd taken note of everything that had just run through his mind.

A hint of summer heat hazed behind her eyes, left over from a long ago mid-summer night. A night that had belonged to them when they were still lovers. When they had a future.

He jerked his mind back to the hard, cold now, in which they could never be together because he brought nothing but danger into her life.

He forced his hand to drop from her arm.

"I'll go first. I want you to stay here. If you hear anything, and I mean anything, that sounds off, I want you to start running and keep running away from here." He pointed a finger at her, hoping she'd take his direction for once.

She nodded.

"I mean it," he whispered. "I don't want you trying to come in there and save me."

She half smiled and he found his own lips turning up.

What the hell did he think talking to her like that, she was thinking. The mind reading went two ways. They'd known each other just so damn long.

When they'd lost each other, they'd each lost a huge part of their past.

A smoky mist floated across her eyes much like the mist that covered these mountains. More beautiful than these mountains even, those eyes held an ancient passion that they'd shared for most of their lives.

If this were the last time he'd ever see her . . .

To hell with everything else.

He'd make sure she remembered and felt just how much he'd always loved her, just how much he still loved her.

He pulled her to him. She didn't resist, leaned into him, as if she'd craved this as much as he had.

Her body melted into him, her arms slipping up around his neck. The instant explosive heat that erupted in his body threatened to blow him apart.

Like jet fuel, it burned through any resistance he could muster. With a sudden fiery need, he took her lips, his mouth molding to hers, feeling the same fire blowing back from her.

In a wild explosion, their mouths melded and they pulled each other closer and closer until their skin almost combusted into flames.

He needed her, wanted her, had to have her.

As he'd always wanted her.

Heat columned into the air, swirling around them, threatening to consume them both, making him forget the situation.

Almost.

Almost.

The need to protect her rose up underneath the desire that singed his skin. There wasn't much light left.

He needed to use it.

Pulling back from the kiss, he gasped for air, for the strength not to take her here on the forest floor, to make her his again.

If only for one last time.

Molten desire in her eyes called to him with a wailing siren call. Every cell in his body screamed for the release only her body could provide.

But there was a higher overarching need. He had to get her to safety and then figure out a way to save all those unaware, innocent victims these monsters intended to kill.

No matter the personal cost to himself.

Now was not the time to indulge himself, assuaging the long overdue need he'd felt for her.

Now was about protecting her and getting her to safety. Then, going back in and finding a way to stop those bastards and their buddies from hurting so many other innocent people.

He stepped back from her, the hardest thing he'd ever done.

But, the misty, passion-hazed want still swirled in her eyes. "God, you are so beautiful," he murmured, rubbing his thumb across her cheek.

Her eyes cleared and she looked directly at him, taking in everything about him, as if memorizing him for a lifetime. Because she knew just how easily you could lose someone you loved.

An instant with her was worth a lifetime with anyone else. They'd packed so much feeling into every second they'd shared together.

An understanding flowed back and forth between them, an understanding of just how much they'd missed each other and just how hard the separation had been on both of them.

He shook his head. "Stop it," he said.

"Stop what?"

"Stop being all that stuff that drives me crazy, beautiful, sexy, knowing, deep with passion."

She laughed softly. "You were paying attention in Mrs. Green's English class. So poetic."

He smiled, then leaned his head to meet her forehead, savoring her alive and warm and safe.

For the moment.

He pulled back and took the gun from his waistband, putting it into her hands. "I'm going in. And it will help me immensely, take a huge burden off me, if you promise that if anything happens, you'll run as far away from here as possible, and try to make your way into town to the police."

He looked into her eyes, willing her to understand just how much was at stake. Willing her to save herself, if he couldn't. "Do you promise me that?"

Her eyes half closed, then she opened then, meeting his gaze steadily. "I do."

They stared at each other, she, like him, probably remembering a time when they'd thought they'd say those words to each other in a different context. He'd set her up to expect those words. Then dropped her on her rear, walking away.

She half shook her head, as if pushing away the same thoughts that were racing through him.

To hell with this. He had a mission to concentrate on.

He stepped back, moving away from the dangerous attraction of her body with its gravitational pull. Steadily stepping backward, he whispered, "I'll whistle if it's safe to come out."

She nodded, then he turned from the sight of her, turning

toward what needed doing.

Becca watched him go, calling Barley to her so that he didn't follow Mick, then hunkered down to wait with the dog leaning against her. The heat from Mick's touch still burned on her skin.

At least, they'd had one last moment of "them". No matter what happened now, she knew they'd had their good-bye.

The good-bye that so many in the line of duty never got. Police officers, firefighters, soldiers, federal agents. So many left the house in the morning not knowing if they would come home in the evening.

They said a casual good-bye to their loved ones and never got a real good-bye, a final good-bye.

The good-bye that she'd never gotten with Tess.

Tears rose in her eyes. If anything threatened Mick, she wouldn't be able to run into the woods and save herself at the risk of losing him. She'd promised but knew it was a promise she wouldn't be able to keep.

She sucked in a long quivering breath that never seemed to reach her lungs.

If anything happened to him . . . Would living be possible?

Time elongated, losing all meaning until every heartbeat seemed an eternity, the eternity she might have to endure without Mick.

She listened, the forest sounds mixing with the heartbeats that pounded in her head, until she wasn't sure what she could hear and what she was imagining.

A crow squawked and she jumped, at first thinking it was Mick yelling. She stood, waiting.

Waiting, waiting, waiting.

The trees whipped back and forth in the wind like they were rubber bands, the wind howling through the trees, screaming of the danger to come. Dark clouds raced across the sky, bringing the storm. It would be a bad one.

An omen?

She tilted her head back, letting the wind lift her hair to

swirl in the breeze. If only the wind would carry away some of the anxiety that simmered along her skin.

Finally, through the trees, she heard a low whistle, the same whistle Mick had used to direct her to him when she'd sneaked out of her father's house in the night during those long, high school years.

When they'd been unable to keep their hands off each other, had lived only for the moments they could share in each other's arms.

Tess had laughed at them. "You guys are unbelievable. You see each other all day at school, after school, and still you can't make it through the night without a few kissy poos."

Those nights. The heat that had burned them, the nights that they'd barely been able to stop, when they'd almost consumed each other with the need to consummate their love.

It had always been Mick who'd pulled back. He'd finally revealed why one night. "I promised your dad that we wouldn't do it until we'd graduated high school."

"You what?" she'd shrieked, her voice rising so high that only dogs could hear it. Mick had sworn he'd heard dogs barking for miles around. "You talked to my dad about this stuff?"

He'd laughed and shrugged. "He talked. I listened."

She'd leaned back against the seat of his car. "Oh. My. God." Embarrassment had flushed through her to think of her father even imagining her this way. "Did you tell him anything?"

"Hell no. Like I said, I just sat there dumbfounded and listened. He laid it all out there. Said I owed him that much at least." His eyes had shone with serious intensity. "He was right. I owe him. The fact that he didn't kill me right off when I took up with you, for one thing."

Laughter had boiled out of her. He'd seemed to mean that.

"For another." His eyes turned dark. "I owe him for everything good that has ever come into my life." He met her gaze with an intensity that had rocked her. "I couldn't throw all that back in his face by disregarding this one thing so important to him."

He'd stroked one finger down her arm. "Even if it is the hardest thing anybody has ever asked of me."

"Hardest?" she'd said impishly, leaning in to run her finger down his chest, stopping just at his beltline, and then only because he grabbed her hand, heat flashing across his face.

"The hardest," he answered before taking her mouth with a passion that seared through her every cell, had made her ache to be his.

But, he'd pulled back. That had always been Mick, fighting with himself to do what was right.

She knew why it was so important to him, to be trustworthy, to respect the word he'd given.

Because he'd never wanted to turn out like his parents. Like the people her father had told her and Tess about, who'd turned their back on their little boy, only caring for the instant gratification of the bottle, leaving their little boy's interests behind every time liquor or drugs called to them.

She'd known she'd have to wait until graduation, and her father's implied consent, to make love to the man she'd loved for all her teenaged years.

Now, his whistle evoked the same excited draw it had in high school.

She headed toward it, wishing for just one more night with him. One more heat-filled night with memories that would last a lifetime.

# CHAPTER THIRTEEN

Dusky twilight allowed her to make out the cabin where Mick stood in the doorway. He waved her inside and Barley darted behind her.

"It's a group of rental cabins," Mick said quietly, still watching the driveway that curled up the hill.

"There's a phone," she said, excitement rising in her chest. "The sheriff should be able to get here pretty quickly. I don't think we're that far out of town."

He didn't meet her eyes.

"What?" She narrowed her eyes, knowing what that expression of his meant. "You're not going to call the sheriff. Damn you, Mick."

He shrugged. "You're going to call them."

"Me?"

"Yeah, you're going to call them to come get you and Barley. I'll wait in the woods to make sure they come and get you out of here safely."

Steel tension coiled in her gut, jamming into all of her vital organs, as surely as if she'd just heard the news that he was dead.

"No, I'm not leaving you to deal with those guys alone. You'll get yourself killed."

"Damn it, Becca." He shook his head. "It's what I do. I go in and get the bad guys and protect the innocent. It's what we all do, law agents."

"It's what I do," she mimicked, all of the fury that ate at her dousing the words with acid sharpness. "And what about me?"

"You'll be safe," he said with a surety that she'd do what he said.

But damn it, she wouldn't. She wouldn't go down that mountain in the safety of a sheriff's car, wondering if Mick would see the night out alive.

"I won't do it." She narrowed her eyes against the sharpness of his expression, refusing to allow his influence to gain grip on her, refusing to waiver in her determination.

"Becca," he said in that tone he used when he thought he was absolutely right and just had to convince her of that. "I will have a better chance of living this out if you're gone. I have got to stop these men and I can't do it worrying about you every step of the way."

"I'm going to call my father." She turned her back and picked up the phone.

But, his hand closed over hers, holding the handset in place.

"And tell him what?" His face was so close to hers, his expression so scary that if she hadn't known him since they were fourteen, she might have actually given in to his demands, based on fear alone.

But, she wasn't afraid of him. Never had been, never would be.

She flung her hand back, knocking his hand off hers, then picked up the phone.

"Becca."

His tone stopped her with its intensity more surely than physical strength could have.

"What?" She waited, not looking into his eyes, not letting the power of his expression sway her.

"You need to listen to me."

She didn't move, didn't look at him.

"Innocent people will die if these men get their way."

Still, she didn't look at him.

"Remember September 11th?"

The memory cut through her. They'd watched the images together on television, huddling against each other in horror. Tess and her father had sat together on the couch, likewise horrified.

When Becca had started to cry, her father had waved her over underneath the safety of his arm, and motioned for Mick to join them on the couch, extending a hand to grasp the teenaged boy's shoulder.

The four of them had survived the fear and dismay that had suffused the entire American population

They'd survived it by sticking together.

"I won't leave you up here alone," she said in almost a whisper, barely able to force the words out past the terror in her chest.

Terror that she could lose him.

"I couldn't take it if they killed you, Mick." She turned her face up to look into his eyes. Their gazes connected like a match to the side of a matchbox, sparks arcing through the air, threatening to catch fire.

But, he looked away, steadily refusing to meet her eyes.

"We'll talk about this later. First, we have to call the Feds and let them know our location." He sucked in a deep breath as though the oxygen wasn't quite getting to his lungs. "Then," he said with a weak shrug. "We'll call your father and tell him you're safe."

She nodded. "He must be going through hell worrying about me." Her heart began beating faster in sympathy for her father's worry.

Mick squeezed her elbow, a grim smile on his face. "You've been kidnapped by some really bad guys, are running for your life and you're worried about your dad worrying about you?"

"I just don't know how much more he can take . . ." Her voice fell silent when Mick looked away. "I'm sorry, Mick. I didn't mean to bring it up."

"It's okay. I understand." He didn't meet her eyes, just lifted the phone to his ear.

"Damn." He looked back at her, his eyes flashing darkly. "We've been arguing for nothing. It's dead. The wind must have knocked out the lines further down the mountain."

"Storm's coming," she said. Wind whipped around the cabin, howling like a wolf hunting a lover.

"Gonna be a big blow," Mick said.

A shiver rippled through her. The wind keened like doom descending on them.

Mick turned to the desk, opening drawers. "Looking for a cell phone," he explained.

She tried to ignore the wind beating against the cabin walls and joined Mick in the search for a cell phone, looking anywhere that someone might stash one.

After a few minutes, Mick shrugged. "Guess we're gonna have to hole up here tonight, ride the storm out and hope the phones get back up during the night"

He said it calmly, but she sensed the tenseness behind the façade he wore for her benefit.

Turning, he walked down a hall to a back room.

A dog bowl sat by the back door. "They've got a dog," she said loudly toward the hallway. She filled the bowl with fresh water and set it down. Barley began lapping at it, his little pink tongue hitting at the water like typewriter keys.

Mick returned with a shotgun and a small backpack. "They had this and two other guns and ammunition that will fit the gun I got from Rowdy."

He pulled a pistol out of the backpack, loaded it and stuck it in his waistband.

She walked to the little kitchen that took up half of the front room of the small cabin and began rummaging for dog food for Barley.

Mick joined her. Opening doors, he began to pull out food. "Soup, oatmeal. Cookies," he said with forced delight, turning them so that she could see the Double Stuffed Oreos that were her secret obsession. "Rolls."

He loaded the food into the backpack.

"Here's some dog food." She lifted a bag from underneath a cabinet and shook it then grabbed a plastic grocery bag from a drawer and dumped some in. Then, she replaced the original bag where she'd found it. "Don't want their dog going hungry if we take his last bit."

Mick grabbed a bag of coffee and stuffed it into the backpack. "That ought to do it. Unless you want to look and see if I missed anything else you want."

He flipped over the rentals pamphlet sitting on the front desk and studied the map of the resort layout. "They've got a new cabin, just added, the honeymoon cabin." He laughed but his voice caught on the end of the laugh as his eyes met hers.

His gaze darkened, then he looked away. He was thinking, same as her, that if it were their last night together, at least they'd have the honeymoon suite.

"It's new so maybe even if the guys know this place is up here, they won't know about the new cabin since they were in prison. We'll take the pamphlets so if they come looking up here, they won't notice the addition."

He shrugged. "It's something, might work." He was trying everything to reassure her.

A huge crack of lightning lit the sky, followed quickly by thunder that rattled the windows. "If this storm comes up bad, they might give up the search till morning," she said hopefully. "They don't seem like the type to want to struggle against all odds."

Mick laughed. "I think you have them pegged."

A few heavy drops of rain began to hit the cabin's tin roof.

Mick opened a small key box behind the desk and took out the key labeled *Honeymoon Suite*. He grabbed the rest of the pamphlets. "Let's go."

They walked down the path leading away from the office, Barley trotting happily along with them. At the first sign, they turned right, following the map. Luckily the signs hadn't been updated yet to include the honeymoon suite.

Two more paths diverged until they came to a fork with a

barely visible path, not apparently having been used by much of anyone except the construction crew. A hand painted, temporary sign marked the path, reading *Honeymoon Cabin*.

Mick handed her the pamphlets, then yanked upward on the sign with both hands, leveraging it back and forth several times until it came free.

He took it with him and continued on toward the cabin. They needed all the help they could get if Rowdy and his boys came looking for them. He didn't say it. He didn't need to. Because she got it just as clearly as he did.

A shiver ran through her, thinking how much they were depending on luck.

"Maybe we should hide in the woods," she said.

Mick looked back at her as if he were considering it when a giant lightning bolt streaked toward the earth, followed instantaneously by bone jarring thunder.

They both jumped and Barley yelped.

"Come on." Mick touched her elbow "It's coming in hard."

Like he needed to say that. Rain pounded on the trees in the distance, whipping them. It would be mere seconds until the main rain event reached them.

They ran, Barley right beside them, sliding around several turns.

Then, the rain began sluicing down, pelting her skin like BB pellets, as hard as hail. Instantly, she was soaked, her shirt plastered to her skin.

Running up onto the porch, she almost collided with Mick's back. He was shaking his hair out of his face like a wet dog. Barley skidded to a stop beside them and also began shaking himself.

Becca began laughing. "You guys are a team."

Mick looked back at the dog. "We're all shook up."

He met her gaze and grinned. The craziness of the past few seconds, running from the storm, had gotten both of their adrenalin going. They'd been attacked by the rain as if it didn't want to let them get away dry, unleashing a torrent of soaking water.

"Great hairdo, missy." He ran his fingers through her hair, pushing it back out of her eyes.

Then he stilled, just stood there, his hand falling to her shoulder, looking at her.

She met his gaze, felt the electricity. Knew that a storm was descending on the two of them, with more force and bone jarring power than the raging wind that screamed around the cabin, with the wild rain beating down on the cabin's tin roof.

# CHAPTER FOURTEEN

She met his gaze for a long moment, feeling the power behind it, remembering just what that look could mean. Not sure if she was really ready for all the emotions it could evoke.

But, could she let the opportunity to be in his arms one more night pass? To feel his passion, his strength of being.

No man had ever seemed as alive as him. No man had ever made her feel so alive.

Still, the pain of experiencing him again, then losing him once more...

She tore her gaze away from his and nodded toward the door. "Want to see if that key works."

He turned and moved woodenly to the door, fumbling with the key. Until finally, it turned and he pushed the door open.

He flipped a switch and the room illuminated. "Electricity works," he said.

"I wonder if there's hot water." She looked back at the rear of the cabin. "I could really use a shower. It's been two days now since I had one and a lot of running, sweating and getting kidnapped in between."

His eyes ran down her frame, hesitating where her shirt stuck to her chest, translucent. She pulled at her shirt, plucking it away from her skin.

Mick's gaze flickered away and he turned to shut the curtains.

She grabbed some paper towels from over the sink and

began to dry Barley who wiggled in enjoyment of the puppy massage. "Feels good, huh, boy?"

Mick turned and watched her and Barley for a second then began rummaging through the cabinets.

"Wonder if this honeymoon place has any candles. A honeymoon cabin ought to have some candles. Don't want to light up this joint like a beacon for those guys if they come looking for us."

"We better start making a list of the stuff we've scavenged off these people so we can pay them back," she said, hating the idea of the owners feeling victimized.

"Already ahead of you." Mick nodded. "Was planning to have the Feds cut them a little check when this is all over for the trouble we'll have caused them."

"Broken window at the first cabin." She glanced at him.

He was staring at her as she still leaned over drying Barley and she realized her shirt was gapping open in the front over her breasts, probably providing a pretty good view down her shirt. A quick flash of heat threatened to sizzle the remaining moisture from her skin.

She stood up and he turned back to his search for candles.

She retreated to the back of the cabin, looking for the bathroom, Barley right behind her. "It's okay, Barley." He'd never really liked lightning but thankfully the lightning had faded after the first few flashes. Now, only steady rain pounded on the roof.

She opened a door and flipped a light switch. A bathtub sat in the middle of the floor, the largest claw footed tub she'd ever seen. A real couple's retreat. "A brownie troop could get in there," she said to Barley who trotted around the room, taking its measure by sniffing at everything.

"Here," Mick said.

She jumped. He'd walked up behind her, quietly.

In one hand he had a dish of dog food, which he set on the sink. In the other hand, he balanced two vanilla-scented candles, the vanilla wafting around smelling like normalcy, back when life was about getting home from work, walking the dog, then sinking into a warm, scented tub of bubbles. The candles threw off a soft, honey colored glow that softened the edges of Mick's face.

She reached up to caress the face that looked more like the Mick she'd known, a sweet young man who'd been yanked around by life but still believed in the power of good. And believed in love.

When she touched him, wariness dodged around his expression, followed by a hint of want. Then, he looked away, leaning away from her to set a candle on the sink, then stepped further from her to place another next to the tub.

"Any hot water?" He leaned over and turned the tub's tap. The water ran for a second before he put his hand under it. "Oh yeah. All the comforts of home. Can't tell you how long it's been since I had a bath."

"Why don't you get in?" she asked, moving closer to him, running her hand along his back. He started, as if she'd stuck a shiv in him.

Leaning over, she put the plug into the tub and together they watched the water fill, enticing, promising.

"No baths in prison and always watching over my back for some guy sneaking up behind me in the showers," he said as if trying to joke, but it fell short, darkness hinting at the truths he'd seen in the big house.

"Didn't the Feds have anyone in there to watch out for you?" she asked, suddenly fearing that perhaps he'd been victimized.

He laughed and turned to her. "Yeah, there was that. I had my own specially-placed guards in the joint to make sure I didn't get any unwanted male suitors. Kept an eye on me."

But, he'd seen stuff, of that she was sure.

"Still. I'm sure you'd appreciate a shower or bath without a bunch of guys eyeing your cute behind."

He laughed, more tiredly this time. "Let's not keep talking about it, Becca. I shouldn't have brought it up. I just want to forget that whole stinking hole and so many of the people in it."

She nodded. He seemed to be great at not thinking about things that bothered him. The way he'd walked away from her and her father's pain. Forgot everything about them and just moved on with his life.

When Tess had died, it was as if everything she and Mick had shared had died with it. But, maybe they had a second chance now. Or at least tonight.

She turned toward a hook that held two robes. "One for you," she said teasingly, trying to pretend it wasn't something she wanted desperately, needed even, to connect with him, to be as physically close as two people could be.

He looked at the extended robe, his eyes hooded, unreadable.

What was he thinking? What was he feeling?

He reached behind him and dimmed the lights.

Her heart accelerated, anticipating what she'd dreamt about night after night when he'd left her, the reality before her now so much more powerful than her imagination.

The thought of making love to him heightened every sense. Raw need filled her body.

Mick turned his back on her, hiding any reaction he might have had. "Why don't you take a long soak?" he suggested. "There'll be soup and Double Stuffed Oreos waiting when you get out."

He reached for the saucer of dog food and set it down on the floor. Barley attacked it, wolfing down bites.

"Good boy," Mick said, then left without looking back at her.

Becca watched him retreat, tears threatening to erupt in her eyes. But, she pushed them back.

"Been a long time since you had anything to eat, huh boy?" She leaned down to rub the back of Barley's neck. He looked up at her, but continued crunching the dry food.

She sucked in a deep breath, the pain of Mick's rejection prickling her heart. Unbuttoning her wet shirt she peeled it off, then unzipped her pants, dragging them away from her skin. They were stuck as tight as if Elmer's glue had been dripped down her legs.

Mick rattled around in the other room. She shimmied out of her underpants and bra. Then, she heard footsteps in the hallway. Mick walked halfway down the hall but stopped, before he could see into the bathroom, just stood there silently in the hall.

Waiting. Wondering should he go in? Wondering if she was going to renew her implied invitation to join her in the bath?

The cool air prickled her naked skin.

She sucked in a deep breath, measuring the possible fresh pain of losing him so soon after they'd made love, if that's what tonight held. The memories, the need, the want for him refreshed full force.

Life could be over in an instant. You had to grab what you wanted while you still could.

She slid into the water, making a splash as she did so. "Ahh," she moaned, not for his benefit but because she couldn't help herself. Her muscles embraced the warmth, her skin feeling as if it were her first bath ever.

She was naked, with him just on the other side of that half closed door.

"Mick," she forced past the constriction in her throat. "This feels great. Aren't you worried there might not be enough hot water for two baths? Maybe you should join me in here."

She held her breath, listening for any sound from him.

He inhaled deeply. She could hear the breath as clearly as if it came from her own lips, as if he dragged in and out of his lungs all the conflict he felt, the same as she did. The conflict over eventual pain versus immediate need.

The silence dragged on for a long moment. What would he do?

"Let me look around out here, secure the place."

His footsteps down the hall, taking him away from her, were like the sound of her deflating expectations. Was it just an excuse? Or would he return to join her in the bath?

Barley whirled and followed Mick. Animal magnetism, the guy had animal magnetism.

The small shelf next to the tub held scented bubble bath. "Might as well add that to the list." Sprinkling it generously under the running water, she watched it foam. A vanilla scent floated into the air, enveloping her with a feeling of safety. "How ridiculous," she muttered. "We're anything but safe."

She was determined to enjoy the bath. "Small comforts," she whispered her motto of the last year and a half. She couldn't bring back Tess, those jerk militants were still out there somewhere, and she and Mick had been unable to contact help.

But, she could enjoy soaking in the foamy, hot water. Tess would want her to, had used the same coping technique many a night after a bad day as a cop on the streets of Atlanta.

The warmth enveloped her, the bubbles slicking over her skin, the heat soothing the muscles that had never experienced a workout like they'd been put through today.

Slowly, she slipped down into the ever-rising water until her chin was just above the waterline. Then, she leaned back, letting the water wet her hair, until finally all that remained above the water was just her face.

Slowly, she waved her head from side to side, removed from the world above, sensory deprivation almost allowing her to believe that none of the last twenty-four hours' events had happened. Her hair flowed around her head like a mermaid's.

She savored the comfort, the simple basic things that she'd taken for granted, a clean body, a warm soothing bath.

And tried not to let her mind stray to other things.

Like the man she'd missed so much her nerves had screamed in agony with the physical pain of his loss. Only recently had the pain numbed into a stunned disbelief that he was gone.

She sat up, listening for him. Would he join her in a few moments? Barley trotted into the room, looked up at her, the quizzical look in his eyes reflecting her feelings.

She smiled at him. At least the little dog should be reassured. "It's okay, Barley. We're safe now."

If only she really believed that.

\*\*\*\*

Mick stood on the front porch, listening to the heavy downbeat of the rain on the tin roof. There was nothing like a tin roof in a rainstorm.

He savored the moment, the wildness of the rain, the trees whipping in the wind, fresh pine-scented air blowing on his face. The lightning had stopped, or he never would have let Becca get into the tub.

Becca.

Becca naked in the tub, just in the other room. All he had to do was open the front door, walk down the hall and get into that tub with her.

What would follow was without doubt.

The way they'd almost exploded into a fireball when they'd kissed earlier would be nothing compared to naked skin against naked skin.

Wet naked skin against wet naked skin. Yowza. He shook his head, willing the image away. But, it was impossible to get it out of his brain because it was emblazoned there as if with a fiery brand, part of his consciousness now.

The sight of her dressed drove him insane with want, with the lust for her that no other woman had ever inspired.

But, could he do it?

Could he touch her like that and not feel all the guilt return, the pain, the heartbreak, the self-loathing?

Stop being such a girl, every male cell in his body screamed. Don't over think it, don't over analyze it. And for God's sake, don't wonder about how you'll feel later.

Just go in there and take what she was offering so willingly, what they both wanted. Take her. And to hell with the consequences of tomorrow.

A noise in the bushes to his right jerked his attention back to the moment. He stepped behind a porch column and turned sideways to shield as much of himself as possible. The gun in his waistband was readily accessible.

He leaned for the shotgun that sat beside the front door of the cabin.

Being well armed felt good.

Silently, he waited.

A tree rustled and a deer nosed out of the trees, looked him straight in the eye, took his measure for a long moment, then bolted.

What was that buck doing out in this storm? He ought to be laying up underneath some bush, scrunched down into the leaves, sheltering from the storm.

But, almost like a warning, he'd appeared to remind Mick just how easily someone much more dangerous could slip through that tree line and take him and Becca out.

He looked out into the storm riddled woods, peered for anyone sneaking up on the cabin and listened for any sound that would give away their stealthy approach.

People thought an FBI operation was a planned precision event. But it was really just people plopped down into an unpredictable situation, where anything could and did go wrong without notice.

Like these guys having a grudge against the judge who'd sentenced them and going after his daughter. He'd known he was just asking for trouble going undercover into the county where he'd grown up. But he'd expected different trouble, like running into a prisoner he knew, maybe from high school.

Or even his own father. Since he'd long ago lost track of that man, didn't even care to know what sorry hole he was imprisoned in these days. If he was still alive. He might be since he hadn't gotten the death penalty.

But, his father wasn't in the prison where Mick had ended up. The Feds had run a detailed list of every prisoner and guard in the facility. He'd studied it for days, referring to Facebook accounts and old yearbooks the Feds had secured for him, comparing them to mug shots from prison.

They'd arranged for transfers for any guard or prisoner who seemed to have any connection to Mick. Had been overzealous in making sure no one would recognize him.

No one had thought to check the sentencing judge.

There was always some unpredicted complication like that.

So, the one person who shouldn't be here more than any other person in the world was here.

What a disaster if he let himself be jumped while they were making love. That complication could be avoided. He would never forgive himself for such a failing.

If he made love to her tonight, afterwards his mind would be so messed up with thinking about her, with the lust and emotions it would excite. He wouldn't be able to concentrate on his mission.

Yeah, there was no way he could go in there and do what every cell in his body wanted.

Because of the mission.

Nothing to do with emotion.

Or the desire his body felt, the desire that could only be quenched by her.

Yeah, that wasn't happening.

He stepped out into the wild rain, letting it run down his face and body, praying it would cool his body's thirst for Becca.

## CHAPTER FIFTEEN

Becca lay in the tub, lukewarm water lapping at her skin.

She leaned up to run more hot water, but stopped at a rustling in the bushes outside the window. Her hand stilled on the faucet. What was that?

"M . . .," she stopped herself just short of calling out his real name. "Atlanta? Is that you?" she stage whispered, in case one of Rowdy's crew had sneaked up on them.

A louder crashing in the woods outside shot panic threw her. She leaned up and blew out one candle, then jerked around to extinguish the other one.

The wind blew outside, crashing the limbs in the trees against each other in what almost sounded like a gunshot. But, it wasn't, she told herself. That wasn't the sound of gunfire.

The front door opened and she grabbed a towel, as silently as possible. If she stood up now, the water could alert intruders of her presence. So, she held her breath, waiting, ready to leap out of the water if someone came through that door that wasn't Mick.

"Why are your candles out?" Mick called from the front room. She let out a huge whoosh of air, as if a balloon had just been released from someone's grasp. The huge hand that had gripped her lungs.

"I heard some noises," she called back, hoping her voice didn't sound as pathetic and weak to him as it felt.

"Yeah." He laughed roughly. "That was a buck. Took off out of here pretty fast."

"Oh, okay." She dried her hands on the towel, then relit the candles. She'd be damned if she was gonna let this bath be ruined for her.

She ran some more hot water, slid down until her entire body was covered in the comforting liquid. Then, she just waited. Deny it all she wanted, that was what she was doing. Waiting for Mick.

Damn him.

She moved her foot up to flip the hot water spigot off. After a few more minutes, she finally gave up the ghost. Mick wasn't going to join her.

"Just accept it," she muttered to herself. She got out, toweled off and wrapped one of the honeymooner robes around herself.

"Honeymoon, my eye. Why don't you just pour salt on it?"

Humiliation at Mick's rejection rubbed at the good mood the warm bath had brought. But she pushed back at the feeling and just tried to accept it as a reality.

How many times would she put herself out there like that and be slapped in the face before she accepted that there just might never be another "them"?

Their time had come and gone.

Like a death, she could mourn it, rage against it, deny it. But the final stage had to be acceptance. She'd probably been through every stage in the last two years. So why was she going backward? She'd already processed it.

One minute they'd had a future, everything was laid out beautifully.

The next, it was gone as surely as Tess.

She'd never be able to speak to her twin and she'd lost the Mick that had been.

The Mick who'd loved her and accepted her advances happily.

Hell, she'd never had to make advances because Mick had always been coming on to her.

But that Mick was gone.

There was only this new Mick, the man who pushed her

away.

Sure there was the sexual tension, the fire waiting to explode between them.

But, this new, thinking Mick, this guy who put up all sorts of barriers between them...

He was a man she'd never known before.

The Mick she'd been in love with would have been in the tub before his clothes even hit the floor, given the invitation she'd extended.

But, not this Mick. This Mick was harder, more controlled, the edginess of his face apparently extended all the way through to his heart.

Her heart spasmed with grief, and a tear threatened to escape. But, she narrowed her eyes.

She just had to accept it. Accept it, like so many other hard things in life that were impossible to come to terms with.

That day had changed everything, the very essence of Mick altered.

God, she wanted back the old Mick.

She leaned over to pull the bathtub stopper to let out the water, but stopped. Maybe he'd like to jump in real quick and get clean.

"Soup's on," Mick's voice rumbled from the other room, the timbre sounding just like the old Mick. But, he wasn't.

Well, she'd changed too, had learned to deal with reality and go on.

A spicy scent drifted in and her stomach overruled any objections, pulled her out of the bathroom and into the main room.

Mick set a bowl on the table and two rolls on a napkin beside it.

Then, he took his bowl and rolls, ripped a huge bite of bread off with his mouth and walked out onto the front porch. Barley followed on his heels, slipping through the door just before Mick closed it.

A searing sadness punched into her stomach, seeming to

leave no room for food. But, she looked at the soup and her stomach roiled with emptiness and her mouth salivated with desire. She'd eaten nothing for twenty-four hours, and the food drew her to it.

She spooned up a bite. Like heaven in a bowl. She closed her eyes, savoring it. Canned soup had never tasted so good.

Deprivation could do a whole lot to make you appreciate simple things like a bath, soup, heated rolls. She downed the bowl of soup as fast as Barley had wolfed down his food, hardly taking time to breath. Then, she pulled apart a roll.

At the first bite of one of the yeasty, warm rolls, she made animal sounds of appreciation.

Mick opened the door and caught her moaning. "Good, huh?"

She laughed, only the slightest bit embarrassed. "Oh, man, caught me."

"Hiking all day will do that to your appetite." His eyes crinkled in the old way. He could seem like the old Mick.

And then change so quickly.

His expression went grim and he reached for another roll, turned his back on her, saying over his shoulder, "Why don't you get some rest."

"Why don't you?" she replied. "This rain will keep them away and you haven't had much sleep at all."

He looked back, the steel edged muscles of his jaw tight. "I can't count on the rain keeping them away."

"That's the Mick I know and love."

At the word *love*, his eyes glinted darkly, and his mouth twisted with some undetermined emotion.

He held her gaze for a long moment, the connection heated, promising. She wanted to wrap her arms around his neck, draw him to her.

That would probably just bring the humiliation of being pushed back, of being told he needed to watch out for the bad guys.

"Don't you ever relax, Mick?"

A fierce play of emotions ran across his face before he pushed them back, the stern exterior cementing in place.

"Not while I'm on assignment. I'm all business then. You've just never seen that side of me."

"I've heard about it."

He met her gaze, darkness swirling in his eyes because he knew who had told her.

She and Tess had laughed in his face at times about the toughness he displayed on the streets of Atlanta with truly bad guys.

"It's like he's another person entirely," Tess had guffawed later to her in private. Then, her face had softened. "But, when he deals with the victims, you just want to eat him up, he's so sweet and tender."

Tess had looked her in the eye. "I can see why you fell in love with him when he's dealing with a victim, an old person or a child, even a cat or dog."

She'd flashed Becca one of their secret twin smiles that said she was going to divulge something because they were sisters first of all, even before she was Mick's partner.

"You know he carries dog and cat food in the car in case we run into a hungry stray."

"Yeah?"

Tess nodded. "He stocks up and he also buys stuffed animals and coats in the winter for kids we meet. I don't know how you guys are gonna pay your bills when y'all get married with all the stuff he gives out."

Becca had tilted her head, something coming into a new focus. "That time we saw him out at the discount mall and his face flushed all red when he saw us. He was pricing stuffed animals?"

Tess had met her eyes, nodding, confirming it.

"He also buys shampoo, bubble bath and shower gel, gives it to women victims, women who get dropped off at battered women's shelters with a suitcase if they're lucky. 'At least they'll have a nice bath or shower to soothe them,' he'd say."

She and Tess had teared up a little.

Becca sucked in a deep breath. That was then. This was now. She glanced up, meeting Mick's eyes.

He looked away, reaching for the package of Oreos, ripping them open, snagging a handful. "I'll be outside." He leaned down to give Barley the last half of his roll.

The dog grabbed it in his mouth and followed him, eyeing the Oreos.

"No Oreos for Barley!" she yelled at the closing door. She finished her last bite of roll, then looked at the Oreos. They'd been invented just for her.

Sugar between two cookie wafers. Life didn't get much better than that.

"Heck, I've been hiking half the day." She took four and looked into the fridge for milk. No luck there. "Oh well, how bad can Oreos without milk be?"

Then, she looked toward the front door.

Another evil little voice urged to go out there, said to indulge, said Mick was like Oreos, something to be enjoyed when available. It had been so long since she'd been able to spend any time with him.

Now, he was just ten steps away.

She walked the short distance and opened the door.

His gaze took in her presence then swung back to the outside perimeter of the cabin's surroundings. But just that quick glance had filled her entire body with awareness.

And memories of the two of them. Hot, passion-filled memories of nights spent sating their desire for each other. Want vibrated through her, followed by a quick pulse of frustration.

She stepped up to lean against the front porch column just feet from the column he was leaning on.

Above them, the wind swirled clouds through the dark sky.

"Gonna be chilly tomorrow," he murmured, his voice husky and low in his chest. "That front's bringing in colder weather."

She shook her hair, reveling in the coolness, the freshness, the mountain feel to the night.

Then, she looked over at him. "Why don't you take a bath and let me keep an eye out here?"

He hesitated.

"You've got to be filthy. I left the water in the tub so you can just jump in and out real quick."

He looked back toward the door, then nodded. "Stand inside the front door, and keep the gun ready. Watch out here cause if they come, this is the only way in."

He opened the door, positioned the shotgun inside the door, then shut it behind her. Walking toward the hallway, he looked back. Making sure she was on the alert.

She smiled. "Get er' done," she said lightly.

He grinned at her blue collar motto impression.

Almost as soon as he disappeared, she heard a splash of water, telling her he was naked in the other room. Hot curling impulses swept through her, working on her self-control.

But, she shook her head, pulled aside the curtains an inch and peered out into the dark. If she failed to detect Rowdy approaching, Mick wouldn't blame her. He'd blame himself.

She wasn't about to heap another helping of guilt on the man's shoulders.

Faster than she would have thought anyone could even get undressed, then dressed again, he was back, already pulling his pants over his hips and buttoning them.

He zipped them closed, closing the door on the possibility of her accosting him unaware while he was nude. A little gulp of disappointment accompanied the shucking on of his shirt. He shoved his feet into his boots, without even stopping walking hardly, then grabbed the shotgun and went back outside.

Well, that was probably one relaxing bath. She shook her head and followed him out onto the porch.

He sat in a rocking chair and laced up his boots, then stood again, and took off from the porch, circling the cabin, before returning.

"Everything okay out there?"

He nodded and leaned up against the front porch column, as if the speed bath had taken his breath away.

"Did you notice the Jacuzzi function on the tub?" she said with a grin.

He arched an eyebrow, with half a grin. "I didn't take time for a massage either."

His shirt was only half buttoned and what was buttoned clung to his damp body like a second skin. A clean Mick, warm from the bath. She could live with that.

"I could still take care of the massage if you're up for it."

A heat began in his gaze that shot straight to her self-control, easing back any doubts she could muster.

She looked into his eyes and sensed he was as close to the edge as she was.

Then, the sheer draw of him was too much for her.

She stepped closer, angling herself under his arm. The sharp, immediate scent of him shot through her, reaching into her core with the desire to get closer and closer to that smell.

At first, he kept his arm stiffly away from her, then with a deep inhalation, he lowered it, wrapping it around her, bringing her in against his body.

She nosed into his neck, drawing his essence inside her, reveling in the comfort and sense of home it brought.

His other hand tangled into her hair, bringing her closer. He leaned in, nosing into her mop of damp hair.

"Damn it," he sighed.

"Exactly," she murmured. "Just damn."

He laughed slightly, pulled back to look into her eyes with a soul searching gaze as if it might be the last time he ever saw her, as if memorizing her features for a lifetime.

"It doesn't have to end tonight, Mick," she read his thoughts out loud.

His gaze skirted away, not willing to admit she'd gotten him right.

"It doesn't have to end, Mick. It never had to end."

He glanced back at her, meeting her eyes.

"Talk to me, Mick."

"What do you want to hear?"

She tapped his chest with one finger. "I want to hear you say we have a chance. That maybe we can get back what we once had."

He laughed roughly, dismissively. "I don't think that's possible."

"Why not?" She angled her head, making eye contact with him, no matter how difficult it seemed for him to meet her gaze. "Why not, Mick? Don't you know how hard it was for me, losing you and Tess at the same time. I needed you then, Mick, more than ever."

His eyes met hers directly, with an intensity that burned into her soul, gave her hope.

"I needed you," she whispered. "And at the time I needed you most, you disappeared on me."

He lifted a shoulder in acknowledgment that she was saying the truth, pain filling his eyes, then he looked away.

For a long moment, he stared into the darkness before saying in a husky voice, "I'm sorry I let you down."

He stopped, sucking in a deep breath then choked out, "I'm sorry I let Tess down." His voice broke on the name Tess, barely getting it out.

His pain stabbed into her, harsh, aching, as if coming from inside herself. She'd give anything to release him from its grip.

"You didn't let Tess down, Mick." She leaned forward, trying to make him look at her, to no avail.

His eyes glimmered with unshed tears. He coughed roughly, straightened, pulling his body away from hers almost indiscernibly.

But, she felt it.

She'd become an expert at noticing him pulling away from her.

"I don't blame you for turning away from me," she said quietly. "I know just looking at my face reminds you of losing

124

Tess. I know every time you look at me, you feel that sharp loss."

She ran her hand across his chest, patting, comforting. "But, that's when you need your family the most, when you're hurting. That's when you needed us the most."

He laughed, a ragged, hoarse sound that had nothing to do with humor. Then, he stopped and drew in a deep breath, pausing, fortifying himself as if what he planned to say would take enormous effort.

He looked directly into her face. "I didn't only remember losing Tess every time I looked at you or the judge, I remembered how I'd failed her." He sucked in another desperate breath. "How much I'd cost you and the judge. I couldn't face you every day, on an ongoing basis. It was too painful facing my failure."

He shrugged, looking away. "I justified staying away from you, thinking it was probably easier for you, not having to see me. A constant reminder of all I'd cost you. Of just how much you'd lost."

"Oh Jesus, you're dense." She'd needed him so much and it had hurt her father so badly when Mick had stopped coming around.

"My dad never said anything about you vanishing, Mick. I think because he might have cried in front of me if he had. But, I know he felt he'd lost a son as well as a daughter that night."

He tilted his head, as if he hadn't realized just how much losing him had meant to them. And for just an instant, she could see the hurt, undervalued little boy whose parents had placed no priority on him at all.

He hadn't mattered enough to his parents to stop the drinking, the fighting, and the going to jail over drugs.

Every time they'd left him home alone to go out drinking and partying, he'd learned a bit more about how little he mattered.

And how to do without love.

"You matter, Mick," she stated emphatically, trying to

reach to the core of him, willing him to accept what his parents had taught him wasn't true. And hoping he would believe what the loss of him had meant to her and her father.

Then, she broached the even harder subject.

"And neither my dad nor I ever, ever," she lowered her voice. "Ever thought of losing Tess as your fault. You know why, Mick?"

She waited for his response. But, he simply looked at her as if words were beyond him at the moment.

"Because it wasn't your fault."

He glanced away, dismissing her comments, rearranging the facts in his mind to fit into his worldview.

"It was not your fault, Mick. It wasn't. You and Tess just met a couple of bad guys that night who got in a lucky shot."

His eyes narrowed and he struggled to drag in air, a ragged breath sawing across his lips. He was seeing the entire event happen again in his mind, the shooting of his partner, Tess dying in his arms.

"Quit it," she said harshly. "Quit thinking of that night. Just accept that it happened and move on."

"Move on?" he barked. Barley jumped, the whites of his eyes showing as he looked up at Mick. "Move on? I failed my partner that night. I can't move on. I cannot stop reliving it in my mind, imagining reacting just a second sooner."

A muscle in his jaw worked, a vein in his neck strained. "She and I split up that night, separated. I should never have let that happen." His voice cracked on the last word.

Becca knew the story as well as he did, had gotten the police report to read the parts Mick wouldn't tell her, finagled the entire report from Reggie, a cop who'd been sweet on Tess.

Mick fell silent, a thousand-mile stare in his eyes, telling her he'd gone back to that night.

"You didn't know there was another guy out there."

"I should have known." His hands fisted and he glared at nothing. "Should have realized that guy wouldn't be alone."

She tried to meet his eyes. "It's called survivor's guilt." A harsh laugh erupted from her gut, hurting her lungs as it spilled out. "People call it survivor's guilt as if the person is sorry they lived and the other person died."

"But, it's not that simple. It's the guilt of thinking over and over again about how if they'd been just a little bit quicker on the draw, had just realized earlier, had done something, anything just a bit different that they could have changed the whole course of events."

She reached to tap his forehead with one finger. "The movie plays over and over in your mind."

His shocked expression said she'd gotten it right.

She grasped his forearm, shaking it to emphasize each word as she spoke. "Stuff happens, Mick. Just accept it. Stuff happens in life that we don't have complete control over. As long as there are people, there will be moments when people wish they'd reacted just a little bit different."

She shook her head, meeting his gaze directly. "Only good people do that, Mick. Only good people take on the blame for the actions of such terrible people like the ones who shot Tess." She laughed darkly. "Do you think the buddy of that guy who got shot after he shot Tess is feeling guilty? Hell no. He's just mad you guys busted up a drug deal."

She raised an eyebrow. "Marcos didn't feel the need to quit the force after that day."

"Marcos just happened along." Mick blew out a burst of air, as if he could force out all the guilt he felt with it. "He wasn't the one who saw his partner split off to go around the other side and catch the perp, yet kept running after him, not knowing what she'd encounter when she got to the other side."

"Still," she shrugged. "Marcos was there before you, and I don't get the sense he's racked with guilt over his failure."

Marcos had come out a hero, since he'd shot the guy who'd shot Tess and Mick. He'd actually risen in the ranks since the incident.

"It eats at me," she said. He glanced up, meeting her gaze. "I know it must eat at you." She needed to get him to talk about it.

"My dad can't let it go. All he does to investigate drug rings and drug movements through Georgia, hoping to get as many of these guys as possible."

Mick nodded. "I know. He e-mails me all the time with info."

"But, you'll never know if you get the right guy," she said.

Mick laughed dryly. "I guess it'll be a lifelong crusade against drug traffickers." He met her gaze. "For me and the judge."

"When will it be enough, Mick?" She knew the answer to that already. Never.

"None of us are perfect, Mick. Nobody's infallible."

She could see the impact her words had on him, how grateful that she'd put into words that she and her father didn't blame him.

Even if he couldn't stop blaming himself.

"What would it take for you to forgive yourself, Mick?"

He looked at her sharply, as if he'd never thought anything could make up for his failure the night Tess died.

"How much penance are you required to do before you forgive yourself?" she stated matter-of-factly, as if she were a trial judge asking for community work service. "How many times do you have to risk your life before you feel you've done enough good?"

He stared off into the distance, his eyes blacker than any lightning riddled storm clouds on the darkest of nights.

"Exactly," she concluded. "Nothing will ever be enough."

He met her gaze with a dark laugh. "Not unless it brings Tess back."

"Nothing will bring her back. That ain't happening, Mick." She laughed, her voice twisting with all the pain she'd felt since that horrible day. "I know more than anyone that she's never coming back."

Tears pushed against her eyes, threatening her composure. But, this wasn't about her loss. It was about his and the enormous guilt burying him.

Burying him?

The idea hit her hard, taking her breath away so that she had to wait a moment, then suck in a deep breath before continuing.

"Is that what it's going to take, Mick?"

He looked at her, her riddle of a question unclear.

"Is it going to take you dying to make up for Tess' murder?"

His shocked eyes told her she'd guessed it. Nothing would ever be enough. He'd keep chasing absolution to his grave.

An early grave?

"I won't let you kill yourself because of Tess, Mick. I won't," she ground out fiercely, her voice sawing on every word.

He looked into her eyes for a long moment, his eyes giving nothing, as if he might walk off the porch and into the storm without warning, leaving her the way he had two years ago, alone, wondering about him and if she'd ever see him again.

"Damn it," he cursed sharply, then pulled her into his arms, her body slamming into his steel hard chest, his arms wrapping around her, his face pushing into her hair.

Suddenly, another wave of rain swept across the mountain, descending on the cabin with a mighty roar, slashing trees almost sideways. Hail began pounding down and green lightning lit the sky.

Barley whined and scratched against the front door, begging to be let in, to escape the storm.

Mick pulled back to look into the storm's threatening face. They both knew when hail began the storm was at its worst, that the possibility of tornadoes was greatest. A lifetime of living in the tornado-ravaged South had taught them the warning signs.

"Come on." Mick grabbed her hand and turned, pulling her with him into whatever safety the cabin could provide.

## CHAPTER SIXTEEN

The storm turned into a raging monster, ripping at the cabin as if it would toss it into the air and over the mountains into a thousand pieces.

Mick knew it could do it. He'd seen the aftermath of such storms many times, helped the victims recover the bodies of loved ones, seen the treasures of a lifetime thrown into the winds, wedding photos sailing into the next county.

He grabbed the mattress off the bed and dragged it into the hallway. Becca brought the pillows and bedcovers, tossing them all onto the makeshift storm shelter in the hallway.

"If it gets really bad, we'll go into the tub or closet," he thought out loud.

The storm rampaged against the roof and walls of the cabin, with a deafening roar.

"This will be close enough that we can jump right into the closet," Becca added, wincing when a branch slammed against the tin roof. Barley shivered against Mick's leg, whining and looking up at him, the whites of his eyes showing.

Mick grasped the dog around the back, reassuringly, comfortingly. "It's okay, Barley," he lied. Anything could happen.

He then walked to the front door, jamming a chair under the knob. Barley followed him, circling nervously at his heels. "It's okay, Barley," he repeated gently to the little pup.

"He loves you." Becca smiled lovingly at Barley, then her

gaze directed at the chair. "No one will come out in this storm, Mick."

She was probably right.

The animal instinct in any human being would have them cowering before this raging force of nature.

"Come here." Becca motioned with her hand. She lay down on the mattress, as if he'd intended it for a bed, instead of to cover themselves with. She pulled the bedcovers over herself as if they were going to bed down in the hallway for the night. As if this were just any other night.

Suddenly, all thoughts of survival boiled down to surviving the next hour in her arms. The thought of burying himself inside of her became a storm raging inside of him, as powerful as the one outside the cabin, an animal reaction that was so primitive it threatened to drive out every human, thinking part of his brain.

If the storm worsened, if he heard the roar of a train coming up the mountain, that often-described train sound of a tornado, then they could get into the closet, he told himself.

If he could hear it over the roar of blood in his head, the roar of blood flooding out of his brain to other parts of his body, making it hard to think, easy to feel.

Easy to do what his body demanded of him.

"Here Barley, get in the closet. We'll join you if a tornado comes." Barley willingly scooted into the closet. Mick threw a towel onto the floor of the small space and Barley circled it several times then lay down on the makeshift bed, his eyes meeting Mick's with love and connection. "Good to see you too, boy."

Then, he looked back at Becca, lying on that mattress as if the last two years had never happened, warm, inviting, with the same lack of recrimination as he saw in Barley's eyes. Just affection, and something else, something much more dangerous. A passion he knew he shouldn't act upon.

Still, she reached up to him with one hand, beckoning him down. Offering what he wanted more than anything in the entire world.

With an inner sigh, he lay down and pulled her underneath his arm. As if that were all that was going to happen. That he was just going to reassure her, comfort her, provide the strength of a body beside hers during the storm.

A jagged flash of light lit up the entire cabin and she leaned back to look at him. In that moment, he read her eyes clearly.

She wanted him inside of her as much as he wanted it.

She curled her body toward him, wrapping one leg over his, sliding her hand up underneath his shirt.

Skin against skin. His body erupted with a force as great as the storm outside.

He turned toward her, meeting her hips with his, skimming his hands inside her robe, pushing it back, leaving her naked to his gaze.

A deep, shuddering gasp ripped from him, a painful breath that savaged his lungs. She was so beautiful. He'd never forgotten how she looked beneath him, how she felt when she wrapped her legs around him, opening for him, making herself completely vulnerable.

He wasn't going to make love to her. He wasn't.

Just hold her, touch her, kiss her.

It would be enough after all this time.

It had to be because he didn't have any protection. Didn't know if she was using any.

They couldn't make love. He wouldn't die, leaving her carrying his child without being around to take care of her, of the baby.

She ground her hips into his, lifting them in an undeniable invitation. Her hand slid down his body, to his pants button, fumbling to undo it.

"Don't." He took her hand. "I'm not that strong."

She half laughed. "What do you mean?"

"We can't make love tonight. If that hand gets where it's going, I can't be responsible," he finished with a ragged laugh he meant to sound like a joke, but failing.

"Then don't be responsible," she murmured, her lips

against his neck, a hot brand sliding down his skin, heating him, melting his resistance, hardening his body for her.

He relaxed into it for a moment, her softness against his hardness primal, enticing, right. Damn. He was losing all control, acting, not thinking.

He jerked to attention. This couldn't happen. Pulling back, he met her eyes, those blue eyes heated to a sapphire sharpness, cutting into him like tools. He almost relented, doing what was natural, what he wanted to do.

Then, he broke away from the power of her gaze.

"I can't do this." He sat up, leaving her lying there below him, like she'd lain in beds beside him so many other times. Times that had ended so much better.

Naked and unashamed, not attempting to cover herself, her hair flowing down over her porcelain shoulders, partially covering one round, soft breast. She was everything he'd ever wanted.

Here in the flesh, what he'd dreamt about so many nights. But, this wasn't a dream. All he had to do was relent, give in, quit fighting it.

"I can't," he repeated. "Knowing that we could make a baby and I might leave you and the baby without a father, without someone to help take care of the two of you."

She pulled back to look into his eyes. "Because you might get killed on this operation, you might not come back."

Hard as it was to look into those eyes, he did, then nodded, acknowledging what they'd both known all along.

"If it means me dying to save those people, to stop those men from a terrorist act, and to hold them accountable for that and all the drugs they've helped bring into this state, that's what has to happen."

"I step into the gap, do what needs to be done, like so many other lawmen and women before me, and like so many that will come after me. It's what has to be done to protect innocents."

He shook his head. "I may die. If I do, I won't leave a woman behind, pregnant with my child."

Her eyes glazed with a passion that misted out across her body as she sat up and curled closer to him, wrapping herself around him. Naked, warm, mind-altering.

"If you were to die on this mission, if I were to lose you forever," she said close to his ear, her breath brushing across his neck, warm, enticing. "I would want to have your baby growing inside of me, to have a small part of you left to treasure for the rest of my life, to give my life meaning. To know that you hadn't really died, because I held a small part of you in my arms."

She ended on a whisper he almost couldn't distinguish.

She looked him directly in the eye, with those powerful eyes, those convincing eyes that had always made it impossible for him to say no.

With her voice full and strong, so that he couldn't miss her words, she said, "I want you, Mick Hampton. I want you tonight. If you don't come back, I want a little piece of you growing inside of me."

The animal need she felt to carry his child flashed in her eyes and an animal need of his own answered it.

Overriding it all, the intensely human love for her he'd known for the greater part of his life pulsed through him.

An accompanying desire surged through him, to take her, to make her his once more, merging their bodies into one.

He was responsible for so much loss in her life, and if leaving her with a part of him inside of her if he died, with someone to love, to focus on, to live for was what she wanted then he would give her that.

Becca knew when he relented, felt it as surely as a wave washing upon the shore, sweeping across the sand, carrying with it back into the ocean all resistance.

He moved his body to fit hers, to fit into her arms as he'd done so many times when they'd made love in the past, all hesitancy gone, molding to her, meeting her body's need with a powerful hunger of his own.

Pulling her closer, he mouthed the sensitive skin of her neck just below her jaw. She shuddered, flashes of heat

134

running through her. He trailed down to her collarbone and she gasped, anticipating the next touch, knowing what he was about to do.

She dropped her head back, awaiting the feel of his mouth on her breast.

But, he stopped, his hand behind her head, tilting her head upward, and took her mouth in a soul searching plundering that wasn't about sex but about connection, about them, about all the years they'd known and loved each other.

With a passion that spoke of loss, of the time they'd been separated, and the consummation of finally finding each other again after all this time, all the nights of tears and loneliness and wanting, he took her mouth.

He was hers. If only for a little while.

It was enough. It had to be enough.

As he kissed her, his hands wandered down her body, trailing fire across her skin, sliding along her waist to her hips, pulling her into and under him.

A deep shuddering want thundered through her.

He broke the kiss, pulled back, kicking his shoes off, undoing his pants, sliding them off in one movement. She unbuttoned his shirt at the same time so that when he moved back to cover her, he was as naked as she was inside the robe.

He didn't push the robe off her shoulders, instead left it around her, forming an intimate capsule that he moved inside of, so that they were insulated even further from the storm outside.

He stopped for a second, pushed the closet door closed with Barley inside.

She laughed slightly. He met her eyes with a smile. "Just seems wrong, making him watch," he said what he always said.

Then, he tilted his head, and listened. "Tell me if you hear any trains coming up that hill." He gave a rough laugh. "I don't know if I can hear above this blood rushing in my ears."

Outside, the storm raged with a power that said no one would be venturing out to find them tonight.

She pulled him in, with her hand curled around his neck, brought his mouth to hers with a visceral connection that made him hers.

If only for this night.

One last night?

# CHAPTER SEVENTEEN

The storm had passed, leaving the morning light sharp and clear, its rays reaching the hall where Mick and Becca had spent the night.

Mick stood and picked up his shirt and his gun. He'd replaced his jeans and his shoes when Becca had fallen asleep. Didn't want to be caught naked if the militia boys had suddenly changed personalities and come out in the middle of the storm.

He opened the closet door to let Barley out.

The dog wagged his tail, wiggled and smiled at Mick. Mick gestured with his head toward the front door and Barley trotted to it, waiting for Mick.

Mick looked out the front window, scanning the trees carefully before pulling back the chair and opening the front door.

Barley trotted happily away to do his business, as if nothing momentous had happened during the night, as if nothing had changed.

But, everything had changed.

They might have made a baby. Part of him couldn't help but hope they had, despite the circumstances, despite everything that had happened and that still could happen.

If anything, it made him more determined to take down these guys. And come out alive. He couldn't leave his child and its mother alone in the world.

If there was a baby.

If there was, he had to swallow his guilt over failing Becca's twin, suck it up and be there for them. The decisions made in the night had to be lived up to in the day.

First though, he had to stop these guys from killing innocent civilians, and FBI agents, people who worked to better their country in the best way they knew how.

He also needed to find out who these guys were connected with in the drug ring. Did they even know who was at the top of the organization?

But, most importantly, he needed to get Becca to safety.

If the phone in the rental office was out, he'd have to get her out another way, without giving up his cover. Maybe hike toward town, hiding in the woods, until they could find help, or maybe another cabin, hopefully inhabited, or with a phone so she could summon help.

When she was safe, he would return to the escapees' cabin, hoping they would believe his story about getting lost in the woods.

The extra bullets and weapon he'd taken from the office last night would help. Those guys thought he didn't have a loaded weapon, and that might give him a jump on them if they tried to harm him.

He walked onto the front porch, sat in a rocking chair, and retied his shoes, then put on his shirt, covering the pistol he'd stuck in the back of his pants.

He stuck the second pistol in the side, ready to grab. Then, he headed up the path toward the office.

As he hiked up to the main cabin, he checked for signs that anyone had come up the hill during the night.

The same as last night, the area was deserted, no recent tire tracks showing someone had driven through there after the storm.

He went inside and checked the phone. No luck there either. So, he headed back to the honeymoon cabin.

As he approached it, the front door opened and Becca stepped out, carrying two, steaming mugs, the scent of coffee rising above the clean smell of pine given off by the woods around them.

Dressed now, she looked great.

Fresh from sleep, no makeup, her hair loose around her shoulders, un-styled, she was the most beautiful woman he'd ever seen.

Always would be.

She sat down in a rocking chair and extended one of the mugs to him. He took it and sat down in the other rocking chair, then saw a flash of them at seventy-five, rocking in chairs on their own front porch, kids and grandkids scattered around them, gathered for a family reunion.

He wanted that, wanted it badly.

A steel determination rose up in him that he would have it, would take it, wrench it back from these bastards that threatened his and Becca's future together.

A future he hadn't even hoped for until last night.

"So, what are we doing today?" Becca looked at him over the top of her coffee mug, then took a long sip.

Her blue eyes reflected back the clear, new sky.

A little surge of love for her billowed up inside him. How could he have been away from her so long? Willingly given this up?

"It's almost normal, huh?" He smiled at her, enjoying the smile she gave back to him, looking like her old self. "Like we're a couple on a getaway up here in the mountains."

She grinned. "In the honeymoon cabin."

For several seconds, they rocked and drank coffee, just enjoying the morning and the fact that for the moment, they weren't in danger.

Barley bounded down the trail, a baseball cap in his mouth, proud of his prize.

"Where'd you get that, Barley?" Becca reached for it. Halfway to Barley's mouth, her hand faltered and stopped.

The cap was covered in something dark reddish. "That looks an awful lot like blood." Her voice caught in her throat and cracked on the last word.

Mick stood up and took the cap, turning it from side to side. "That is blood." Her voice rose sharply. "That has to be blood."

Mick didn't meet her eyes but walked back inside for the shotgun and the daypack, stowing the leftover food inside. He returned to the porch and handed the pack to Becca.

"Where'd you get this, Barley? Show me." He motioned with his hand in the direction the dog had appeared from.

Barley just stood looking at him.

Becca stood, her face pale, her hand shaking as she set her coffee mug on the porch railing. "Where'd you get it, Barley?"

She started a playful motion with her body, back and forth on the balls of her feet as if she were going to run and get whatever he'd found. The little mutt darted toward the woods, then back toward Becca.

Mick's stomach dropped. What was in those woods?

Together, they followed Barley, Becca playing the game that encouraged him to show them.

Finally, they reached an area behind the office cabin, off the path, deeper in the woods than the average person would walk on a normal day.

But, this wasn't a normal day. There was something lying behind a tree, crumpled on the ground.

Adrenalin shot through Mick's body, pumping blood through him, until he was ready for a fight, ready for whatever Barley had discovered. His gut knew what it was, a sick feeling rolling through him.

"Maybe you should hold back, Becca." He took her by the back of her pants, tugging her to a stop.

She didn't resist, just stood there, her face wan and ghostlike, peering toward the tree.

And what lay behind it.

"Here." He pulled the pistol from the back of his pants and handed it to her. "It's ready to go. Just point and pull the trigger."

She'd trained with him and Tess at the gun range. Her

competitive drive to beat them at target practice might stand her in good stead.

"Stand behind this tree," he said. "It'll give you some protection."

She just stood, staring toward the figure, so he gently moved her to a position where the tree would block her from anyone who might be lurking in front of them.

She was in shock. He patted her arm once more. "It's gonna be okay. You're gonna be okay."

She met his eyes then, with a look that conveyed it was a lie that there was anything okay about this situation. She gave a little head nod that she was ready.

For whatever lay behind that tree. He set the shotgun on the ground beside Becca, just in case, then turned, pulled his second gun and edged forward. A shotgun would be a better bet if Becca really needed to take someone out.

But, right now, with her in that dazed state of mind, he didn't want her accidentally pulling the trigger and blasting him and Barley with a load of buckshot.

"Hey," he called toward the mass of clothing lying on the forest floor. What he wouldn't give to hear a moan or a groan right now, telling him it wasn't a dead body.

But, the awkward angle of the collapsed figure didn't give him much hope.

Slowly, he walked closer, looking around as he did for anyone who might be hiding in the dense undergrowth.

He stepped around the tree so that he got a full view of what was now clearly a person. A man lay crumpled over, his face visible, with eyes staring into the dense woods around him.

Mick's heart rate spiked as he stepped forward to check for a pulse. None. Looking the man over, he felt sure he'd been dead for a while, maybe yesterday, maybe earlier.

He looked back toward the cabin, where the driveway was empty. "No car," he said. "Don't know when this happened."

Becca gasped, as if she too had been hoping the person was

somehow still alive, that they could help him.

There was no helping this guy. They just had to make sure they didn't end up like him.

"Come on." He took Becca by the hand, pulling her toward the office. "Let's see if by chance that phone is working now."

She went with him, letting him pull her limply behind him, compliant, almost without a will of her own, as if she'd been shocked so greatly that she'd left her body.

Scoping out the area for anyone still lurking around, he took his time walking toward the back deck, the shotgun in one hand, his other holding onto Becca.

She gripped his hand like it was a rope thrown to her when she was drowning, holding onto it like it could pull her back to reality, out of this nightmare.

He turned, looking her in the eye, forcing her to meet his gaze. "It's going to be okay, Becca. I'm not going to let anything happen to you."

"It had to be Rowdy and White, right? Who else? They killed him," she said, disbelief glowing in her eyes. "He was alive, then he wasn't. How could they do that?"

She looked at him as if for answers, but he had none. He'd seen a lot of bad that couldn't be comprehended.

He shook his head. "When we can understand them, then we're in trouble, Becca. I don't ever want to be able to understand people who can do stuff like that. You and I aren't like them. We can only take care to not let that type of person hurt us."

She nodded. But, he could tell she wasn't listening, was lost in her own head.

He turned, walking toward the cabin, pulling her limply behind. Then, he stopped.

It couldn't be.

Barley sniffed around a dark mass that lay still on the ground.

Mick turned Becca away, praying she'd stay in that position.

Then, he turned back. A closer look revealed it was two figures, one underneath the other. He leaned over, touching his hand to one throat, then the other. Both dead.

Becca gasped, and he realized she'd turned to look.

Quickly, he swiveled, trying to push her away.

But, she gasped with a sound that swirled up into a shriek, screaming, with her hands to her mouth as if trying to hold back the horror, screaming with a high-pitched, freakish, metallic screech.

He set down the shotgun and grabbed her, pulling her to his chest, hiding her eyes with one hand, holding her against him with the other. "Don't look, Becca. Don't think about it."

Long, convulsive sobs shuddered out of her, as she leaned against him, holding onto him as if she were a child, wanting only to think what she'd just seen hadn't been true.

"It's too much," she wrenched out in a voice that sounded like a stranger. "A little girl? And her dog? They didn't have to kill them. A dog? Why kill a dog? It's not like he could testify against them? And a little girl? They're so precious."

She tried to pull away as if to go to the child but Mick wouldn't let her, knowing she'd already seen too much.

She sobbed against his chest, and he just held her because he could think of nothing that would make it better.

The dog had probably tried to attack whoever had hurt his master or mistress. And the natural reaction had been to shoot.

But that little girl? That would haunt him into the next world. The little pink shirt. She and the dog were curled together, as if the dog had used its last few breaths to comfort his young mistress.

Tears rose to Mick's eyes, imagining the scene.

The person or people who'd killed the little girl were going to hell. And they wouldn't have a chance in any courtroom in the country.

Or any prison for that matter.

They'd virtually signed their own death warrants. No one on earth could tolerate that, not even the worse criminal.

Killing a child put you in a whole other category of evil.

Barley stood quietly by Becca's heels, staring up at her, his eyes nervous, concerned. Barley would have done the same as that dead dog. He'd protect his mistress.

"She's okay, Barley. Everything's okay, Barley," Mick soothed in a calm voice, lying to the little dog, who whined in response.

Becca looked down at Barley, then leaned and pulled him up, holding him, cuddling him, pushing her face into his fur. "I'm okay, Barley," she quavered in a voice that said she was anything but.

Barley let himself be held, quietly soaking up her tears.

Dogs knew death. Barley also seemed to understand his mistress' reaction.

The dog let her hold him as she cried, a mirror image of the child clinging to her dog.

Becca's sobs finally quieted, and Mick picked up the shotgun, then turned Becca toward the cabin and walked her so that she wouldn't see the little girl and the dog again.

Opening the back door he'd left unlocked the night before, he didn't even bother at a pretense of calling to see if anyone was home.

He sat Becca down in a chair, leaned the shotgun against the wall, then walked to the phone and lifted the receiver. A dial tone. "Thank God," he murmured.

Quickly, before the lines could go out again, he dialed a number. Hernandez answered immediately.

"Hey, it's me," Mick said.

Becca had to focus even to hear Mick's words. A fog seemed to float like gray Jell-O between them, with Mick a great distance away.

She needed to focus. Her life, Mick's life and Barley's life could depend on her staying present, putting the horror she'd just witnessed behind her, waiting until a later time to process it. Waiting until later to grieve for that little girl, with her little pink shirt, her arms wrapped around her dog.

But, the image kept playing in her mind. The Golden Retriever's head had been tucked under the girl's neck, as if he'd nuzzled her into the afterlife.

A sob shuddered through her, but she pushed away the image, and steeled her mind.

All grieving for that trio in the woods had to wait, so that she, Mick and her dog could survive, and not end up like them.

She stood up and walked closer to Mick. He reached for her, pulling her underneath his arm. She leaned into his warm, living body, a sense of comfort and security flowing from his body into hers.

They were alive. For now.

All she wanted was to get out of there, take Mick with her and get out of this whole damned north Georgia area and go back home.

To hell with everyone else. She wanted to keep Mick alive. To keep Barley alive. And yes, to keep herself alive.

She wanted time with Mick. Wanted to have his baby. The future beckoned her away from this horror that the present had become.

But, a noisy torrent of words rumbled from the phone, cementing her firmly in the present. Mick began talking again, and she savored the reassuring timbre of his deep, masculine voice.

"I know. Couldn't be helped."

He nodded, listening to the other person.

"Yeah, the gun wasn't there, the phone wasn't there, the locator wasn't there. Figured you guys had no idea where we were."

Another second of listening.

"We're up in the mountains, Georgia still. We're at a vacation rental right now. Dogwood Resort. You need to tell the cops that there's two bodies out back."

He hesitated for a second, listening. "Don't know," he replied to a question Becca couldn't hear.

He read off the address from the pamphlet he'd stuffed into his pocket yesterday. He turned the pamphlet, looking at the small map on the back. "We're off Johnson's Mountain Road, the closest town is Hawk's Peak. We're northwest of there."

He seemed to calculate for a minute. "That means their hideout cabin where we were is on up that same road, heading away from town.

He murmured agreement to something the other guy said.

"Yeah, she's with me. Says she's not coming with you guys, won't leave me alone with the bad guys, says I need her help."

He laughed, along with the harsh laughter that filtered from the phone. "I know."

He listened for several minutes to a long diatribe from the other end.

"Emm, yeah, but she says she's not going. Says she's going to tell the sheriff everything and have them go pick up the guys who kidnapped her. That'll blow any chances we have of getting the rest of their group." He listened as another few seconds of angry ranting came from the phone.

"Agreed. But, she's worried about me," he said, not meeting her eyes. He listened for a minute, before answering, "Okay, it's a plan."

"Tell them to come up the hill without sirens but with blue lights on so we'll know it's them," he said, then hung up, and began to outline the plan as if she'd never protested against leaving him.

"He's going to call the sheriff, say he got a call from a family member, have them come pick you up."

A firestorm of protest welled up inside of her. He couldn't end up like that man and his little girl lying out back.

It was probably too late to stop the sheriff from coming. Mick's Fed contact had probably already made the call.

She had to come up with her own plan.

Mick dropped his arm from around her shoulders and moved away.

She felt the distance harshly, as if she'd just been put adrift on an iceberg, flowing with the ocean away from him, wondering would she ever see him again.

He was all business, walking through the cabin, opening drawers, rummaging through them.

"Ahhh," he said, pulling out a map, unfolding it slowly. "The guy was a hiker, obviously." He smiled with true pleasure. "A topographic map as well as a map of the hiking trails that ribbon this mountain."

A scream was forming in her gut, racing toward her mouth, armed with marching orders for him that didn't involve any maps. All he had to do was get in the car when the sheriff's people came to pick her up.

"Maybe once the sheriff picks you up, I can find an easier way back to the militia cabin." Satisfaction laced his words as if he'd just gotten an award at the annual police banquet. Or whatever the FBI equivalent was.

"Do you even hear yourself?" Her voice ripped the air, harsher than she'd meant to, ice from the cold ocean she'd been set afloat on seeping into her tone.

Along with desperation and fear. Fear for Mick.

His eyes turned compassionate. "Let's not fight, Becca." His voice softened. "This is how it has to happen. Let's not take it out on each other."

Tears formed behind her eyes but tears meant she was giving in. She wouldn't give in. She had to fight. Fight for Mick, fight for them.

When he'd left her alone the first time after Tess' death, she'd given in so easily. Not this time. This time, his life was on the line.

She'd gotten him back, a second chance with him. If he didn't die.

She would not be sweet and obedient, waving him off to his death, so he could end up lifeless and cold like those bodies in the woods, all essence of Mick gone.

A gravelly, crackling came from the road, a vehicle coming toward the cabin. There was no time to gather just the right argument. "Mick, you can't go back to that cabin," she lurched out the words.

Mick glanced at her then walked to the window, peering out intently, his body stiff. In a flash, he whipped around, grabbed the shotgun and reached for her hand, and dragged her toward the back door.

"We have to get out of here. That's not the sheriff's people. Barley," he yelped. The dog leaped to attention, bolting in front of them toward the back door, as if Mick's tone of voice had told him all he needed to know.

Panic roared through her body, as they ran after Barley, knowing as instinctively as the canine that all their lives depended on it.

If it wasn't the sheriff's people, then it couldn't be good. The three of them had to stay alive until the local authorities got there.

# CHAPTER EIGHTEEN

Mick's arm propelled her along faster than she thought she could ever run, his momentum pulling her through branches that ripped at her, clawed as if to stop her long enough for whoever was in that car to catch them. Everything blurred past in a green curtain.

Blood pounded in her head like a locomotive, and her lungs ached with the need for oxygen. But the memory of that little girl's body, lifeless yet still clutching at her dog, kept Becca moving longer than seemed humanly possible.

She would stay alive, if for no other reason than to make sure those murderous jerks paid for what they'd done.

They ran until the air wheezed from Becca's lungs, burning through her windpipe, as if acid were spilling out her mouth.

They had to have run miles from the vacation rental cabins, going up and down steep grades, pushing through heavy undergrowth at times, before Mick stopped, looking back in the direction they'd come. She leaned over, gasping for air, leaving him to worry about who was behind them because all she could do was try to suck breath in through ravaged lungs, oxygen never quite filling her body's need, as if she were sucking in deep ocean water, looking toward the surface, desperately wishing for air.

Mick also gasped, but still he kept his gun in hand, pointed up toward the general direction of the rental cabins. After a moment, he whispered, "Don't breathe."

She stopped breathing, going against everything that her

body screamed it needed. Mick looked intently through the greenery. She did the same. In the silence left by their suspended breathing, she heard nothing.

No men's running footsteps, no rustling in the brush, no one coming to kill them.

"Breathe," Mick said on the released breath that pushed from his lungs. He sucked in another long gulping breath, then leaned over onto one knee.

She pulled in air. Barley watched her as if they'd only just gone for a little park run, as if he could keep going all day. His little tongue hung out though, curling into an upside down, pink comma. The little tongue quivered in the air. Barley wanted water more than she wanted air.

Had the water bottle she'd stuck into the small day backpack survived the mad run through the woods?

She struggled with the zipper, her exhaustion making it difficult to maneuver. Mick reached over and opened the pack.

She pulled out the water bottle, her breathing starting to resemble something normal, like she'd only done a half marathon. Leaning down, she poured a bit of water into the little Tupperware top she'd originally packed for Barley.

Barley lapped up the water, his gaze on her face, making eye contract continuously.

"It's okay, Barley," she whispered.

"Oh yeah, lie to the little guy," Mick said with a grim laugh.

"Everything is okay right now," she answered. "Right now, this minute, everything is okay. We don't need to worry him about things that might happen." She patted Barley who'd quit drinking and leaned against her leg.

Patting him was as good for her as it was for him, the feel of his warm body comforting under her hand.

"He's lucky to have you," Mick said.

She met his eyes, smiling with her gaze at him.

"You're going to make a great mom," he whispered.

A quick pulse of hope shot through her, hope that they

might have a baby and they might live to raise it together.

Mick's eyes glimmered with unspoken thoughts. That she'd be the kind of mom he'd never had, the kind of mom he'd deserved, the kind of mother her mom would have been to her and Tess.

If she hadn't died too early.

Then, his face went serious, as if he'd pushed back superfluous thoughts.

They didn't have any extra emotion to expend on that line of thought.

Now was about survival. And keeping Mick alive.

"What now?" she said, already knowing what he would say.

Mick looked away from her eyes, those eyes that always saw right through him. The words he chose right now were perhaps the most important conversation he'd ever had with her.

He had to convince her to cooperate with his plan. He glanced back at her.

"What are we going to do?" Becca repeated, her eyes large in her pale face, dirt smeared on her cheek. The knees of her pants were ripped and dirty, with leaves tangled in her hair.

Wiping away the dirt from her face, he pulled a stray leaf from her hair, then another. Dropping them on the ground, he waited while she ran her hands through her hair and shook it back.

"You look good enough to go to town," he said, waiting for the explosion.

She brushed at the dirt on her pants then straightened, looking at him, her eyebrows raised. Bracing for a fight?

He reached for her, pulling her into him, wrapping his arms around her. For just a brief second, she let him hold her, then resisted his embrace, stiffening herself.

"The plan?" she said tightly.

"Well, we're going to use this hiking map to find a way into town, and you're going to the sheriff's and say you had a fight with your boyfriend and he dumped you on the side of the road, you spent the night at the rental cabin, then found the family out back this morning."

"Make sure you talk to the sheriff. His name is Grant Campbell. I know him. You can trust him," he continued.

She stared at him. "And you're going to be where?"

He tilted his head. "You know where I'm going to be."

"Nooo," she dragged the word out, her body language mirroring her negative response.

"Becca, have you ever known me to beg?"

He looked into her eyes, psychically willing her to go along with his plan.

"Nope, can't say I've ever witnessed that indignity."

He laughed. Despite the circumstances, again she was making him laugh. Gallows humor?

Laughing because of the tension jagging through his nervous system.

"Can we just assume I'm begging?" He arched an eyebrow, seductively, he hoped. She was much more vulnerable to manipulation when she was sexually aroused and wanting him.

"Without all the groveling and knee bending?" she returned, smiling coldly, telegraphing she knew exactly what he was trying to pull on her.

"Exactly." He sucked in a deep breath, summoning up the reserves of strength he needed to convince her. "I don't have time to take you into town myself."

"Why?" she snarked slyly. "Won't those three still be stupid and dangerous tomorrow?"

Exactly. Tomorrow. Who knew what the world landscape would look like tomorrow. They didn't have until tomorrow, the plan had been moved up to today.

"Accept that I don't have the time," he said, striving to keep his voice level and not set off her innate desire to dig in her heels.

Cooperation, he needed cooperation.

"No." She shook her head, took a handful of his shirt in her fist and pulled him toward her, as if she could manhandle him into town with her. "I am not leaving you out here with these people. I'm not."

"Becca, I have a mission. You've seen what these maniacs are capable of. They want to kill a lot of people. I have to stop them."

"Even if you're one of the people they want to kill?" She leaned closer until her face was inches from his, that beautiful face that he would remember into the next world or wherever he ended up after his time on this planet was done.

His time with her was some of the most precious he'd ever experienced. What had he ever done to deserve this woman's love?

"Becca." He looked into her eyes, willing her to understand. "As long as I know you're safe, that if you're carrying our child that the child is safe, then I can do whatever I need to."

She closed her eyes, shaking her head slowly side to side. "That's what you don't understand." She opened her eyes, the blue around the irises pulsing with intensity, darkening then lightening, as if in time to her heartbeat. "If you're not safe, then I'll never be okay again. If anything happens to you, then I will never be happy, content, okay as you put it, again."

He opened his mouth to speak but she put one finger to his lips, stopping him.

"I'm not leaving. Accept it." She smiled darkly. "And let's plan what you're going to do with that information."

His mind threatened to explode. Everything told him to fight this, to convince her no matter what it took.

But, the thing was, he'd known her too long not to realize she meant it. And there was no changing her mind when she got like that.

Besides, since the militia's attack had been pushed up till today, he was jeopardizing his ability to stop the attack just by arguing with her. How many lives would be lost if he continued his futile attempt to convince Becca?

He needed to get back to Rowdy's cabin.

No matter how much danger it involved for him. But, Becca? He needed a plan that would keep her safe while stopping them.

He had to make a plan that included her.

"Okay," he said. Pivoting to pace, he began to formulate a new plan. "You'll come with me, but you'll stay up in the woods, out of sight. You'll keep the shotgun. And when we leave to go down to Atlanta to execute their plan, you'll come out, hitchhike into town to the sheriff or find a phone somewhere."

"Look in their cabin," he continued. "If I find a cell phone, I'll try to hide it in the bathroom, under the sink, or in the bedroom we were in, under the mattress. You'll call the Feds at the number I'll program into the phone and tell them where you are. I'll leave a note as to what I know about their plan and you'll tell the Feds."

She looked away, as if measuring the plan.

"I'm hoping the phone call I made from the office gives them time to get up here to tail us."

Damn, he hoped that. "But, if not. Then, maybe they'll be able to catch up to us with the information you give them." He looked at her, to see if she was agreeing.

She just continued to look at him, expressionless.

He laughed harshly. "If none of that works out, then I'm on my own."

She met his eyes, with an intensity he'd never seen before. "Leave me a note no matter if you get a cell phone. I'll make sure help gets to you."

He nodded.

A plan. They had a plan.

But, plans often had a way of going bad.

All that had happened the last couple of days was the perfect example.

# CHAPTER NINETEEN

Mick sucked in a deep breath of pine-scented air. Jesus, he hoped this worked, and hoped Becca stayed hidden in the trees if things went bad. Hoped that, for once, she listened to him and did what he asked.

Didn't try going up against guys who would wipe her off the face of the planet like a buzzing gnat.

His heart began beating in his chest, every human survival instinct telling him to run. These men were planning to kill hundreds, even thousands. What would stop them from killing just one more?

A sweaty sheen covered his skin, turning to ice as the cold air hit it through the thin material of his shirt. He shivered, seeking heat in the anger at these men and what they were planning-murder and mayhem.

They wanted to inflict death, injuries and grief on innocent people. And to cripple all Americans with fear.

He sucked in one last, fortifying gulp of mountain air, brought the image into his mind of all he wanted to prevent, then walked into the open, heading down the path to the back deck of the cabin.

As he neared the deck, Rowdy stepped through the sliding glass door from the living room.

"Well, lookie here," Rowdy crowed. "The prodigal son done returned."

Stan and White pushed through the blowing curtain behind

155

the sliding door. The trio moved toward him, like a pack of hunting wolves, stalking closer, their eyes wary, darting back toward the trees behind him.

"You didn't find her?" Stan asked.

Mick shook his head. "You?"

Both Stan and White shook their heads. Rowdy just stared at him, his gaze hard.

"Where you been?" Rowdy said, flatly.

That man always looked like he meant something entirely different from what he said. As if he already knew the answer to his question.

"Frikin' got lost in the woods. Got all turned around in the storm."

"Man, that was something, wern't it?" Stan shook his head. "We quit looking when it seemed like a tornado was 'bout to hit."

"Did one hit anywhere up here?" Mick kept the conversation diverted from what he'd been doing.

"I think one might have hit over the east part of the county. The radio was saying they got tore up over there." Stan's eyes rounded. "Glad it weren't over here."

"We didn't find the girl," Rowdy turned the conversation. "Wonder where she got to?"

Mick looked back down the driveway. "Maybe someone picked her up."

"We've been thinking the same thing," Stan said. "Been thinking we ought to hightail it out of here."

Mick nodded. Let's go with that.

Rowdy stepped forward and shoved Mick, hard. He nearly went down but caught himself at the last minute, keeping his footing. Which was important when you were in a fight with an animal like Rowdy.

Rowdy pushed forward again, jamming his hand into Mick's chest with a blow that threatened to stop his heart.

Mick gulped in a breath, willing the blackness away from in front of his eyes, trying to focus on Rowdy. Before he could get his equilibrium, Rowdy swung on him, catching him on the side of the head, knocking him down.

Mick should have taken Rowdy out when he'd first gone physical on him, should have knocked him cold. But, he hadn't wanted to turn it into a fight to the death, which it would have been if he'd hit Rowdy the way he'd wanted to.

If he hadn't completely knocked him unconscious, the guy would have gone off like a rabid coyote, totally aborting any chance Mick had to find where they were planning the bomb and when.

And, on a secondary note, ruined any chances he'd had to find out who they were selling drugs for.

He hadn't wanted to get on Rowdy's bad side. He'd forgotten that all Rowdy had was a bad side.

Before Mick could get up, he heard barking.

No.

No. No. No.

He struggled to his feet as Barley charged out of the woods, heading straight for Rowdy, biting at his legs.

Rowdy laughed and kicked the little dog, hitting him squarely in the chest with a solid sound that hurt to hear, knocking the pup several feet away.

Barley yelped, then jumped up and came back like nothing had happened, charging Rowdy's ankle again. Rowdy leaned over and grabbed the little dog by the scruff of the neck, swinging him up, holding him in the air.

Rowdy looked toward the woods. "Where are you, little girl? I know you're up there. Come on out. I got your dog."

He swung the pup by the skin of his neck, and walked toward a tree. "I'm gonna bash his brains out on this here tree if you don't come out."

Stan and White both sucked in air. They knew just how mean Rowdy was, knew he'd do it.

Slowly, Mick began to walk toward Rowdy. Could he stop him before he had time to swing Barley? Before the pup's head had time to connect with the trunk of the tree in the crushing noise of a skull being bashed in?

Then, an even more terrifying sound cut through Mick's thoughts, the clear racking of a shotgun pumping a shell into the chamber, ready to make mince meat of a man.

Rowdy growled like the animal he was and pulled his pistol out of the side of his pants and held it to the dog's head.

Mick stopped.

"You shoot at me and this pup don't stand a chance." Rowdy's mouth twisted in an ugly grimace. "You love this dog. I saw how much you loved it. If you don't drop that shotgun and come out now, I'll blow this pup's head off."

"I'm counting to ten then the dog gets it." Barley yelped and swung, his feet kicking the air. Rowdy laughed loudly. "Dog knows I'll do it."

"Ten," he started slowly. "Nine."

He poked Barley with the pistol and the dog howled. "Eight, seven, six, five, four," Rowdy sped up.

"Three." Then, he stopped and smiled with an ugly snarl toward the wood line.

Becca appeared on the path leading out of the woods, the shotgun aimed at Rowdy.

"There she is, our little dog lover. Can't believe you'd risk your life over a stinking dog." He shook his head and gave a dismissive, harsh laugh. The guy probably couldn't imagine risking his life over anything or anybody.

Becca walked slowly, closing the distance between Rowdy and her shotgun. "Put your hands up, White and Stan." She motioned with the gun toward them and instantly both men's hands shot up.

Rowdy snarled, "Think I'll shoot the little mongrel, just to teach you a lesson, girlie."

Stan swiveled his head toward him. "Don't," Stan said.

Rowdy's snarl intensified. "Don't tell me what to do," he said, in a low, ugly voice that sounded like he'd spent years practicing to achieve maximum meanness.

"If'n you shoot the dog, she's still got the shotgun and we got no leverage," White reasoned.

As White talked, Mick pulled his gun and stepped behind Rowdy, placing it to his head before the guy even realized he was moving.

Rowdy growled then gave him a knowing look. "That gun don't have no bullets."

"Really?" Mick moved the gun, slightly, and fired a bullet into a beer can that had been left on the back picnic table.

The can skipped off into the dirt.

Stan and White's faces paled. Rowdy's snarl lessened.

"How many bullets you got in that thing? It was empty when I give it to you."

"At least one more," Mick said, his mouth close to Rowdy's ear, his gun poking into Rowdy's skull. "Set down the dog and put down the gun."

Rowdy sucked in a few breaths before he tossed Barley down. The little dog skittered on his side in the dirt before getting to his feet again and heading straight for Rowdy's ankle.

Rowdy kicked Barley away.

Mick shoved the gun against Rowdy's head. "If you kick that dog one more time, I'll blow your brains out. Now, drop your gun," he said, as Barley continued to savage Rowdy's pant leg.

White slid his hand toward his waistband.

"Don't," Mick warned.

"Like he said." Becca pointed the shotgun at White, closing the distance. "I've never really seen what a shotgun can do to flesh. But, it tears up a target real bad. At this distance, you probably would never even survive long enough for an ambulance to get here."

Malevolence tarnished her face, a look he'd never seen on her, never thought she was capable of.

"That is if we even call an ambulance." Her expression said she meant it.

Damn, he was glad she was on his side.

Suddenly, he knew where he'd seen that look before. On Tess's face. She'd given that same face to a man who'd beaten his two young kids.

Becca could be every bit as tough as Tess. He'd known she could be tough in an argument with him, but he'd never seen her go pure hateful, ready to inflict pain.

"Drop your gun, Rowdy." Mick nodded toward the two. "You guys, too. Or I don't know what she might do."

Becca's face backed up his threat and with a final snarl, Rowdy let his gun drop beside his feet.

"Kick it away," Mick directed.

Becca was getting too close, and Stan and White still had their guns. Anything could happen. His breath clawed raggedly out of his chest, painfully.

"I'll blow his brains out if you try anything," he said, directing a fierce glare at the two.

"Do like he says!" Rowdy yelled.

Apparently, violence only bothered him if he was going to be the victim.

Stan and White leaned over, setting their guns on the ground. Becca continued advancing. He shook his head at her but she approached anyway.

As she got closer, he shoved Rowdy away, then leaned over and grabbed his gun off the ground, then moved over to get Stan and White's guns.

When he stood up, he saw in their eyes that they knew the whole game had changed.

But, damn, he wished Becca had started running, and kept running. Now, he had to make sure Rowdy didn't kill her out of pure anger if things went bad.

And everything had changed as far as his plan to convince them to give him information.

What was the plan now? Beside blown all to hell?

Becca joined him, standing with the gun pointed toward the trio. Suddenly, without planning to, he grabbed the shotgun from her hands.

Her wide, pale eyes said that was the last thing she'd expected.

Rowdy raised an eyebrow. It was the last thing he'd expected, too.

\*\*\*\*

Half an hour later, Rowdy, White and Stan were securely duct taped to chairs.

The mission was sure as hell blown. What now?

He sucked in a deep breath, cursing inside himself, hoping not to put any guilt onto Becca. Things went to hell on operations. You just had to roll with it.

First things first.

Mick tilted his head at Becca to follow him out the patio door, which he shut behind them.

Walking away from the building, he lowered his voice in case the guys could possibly overhear.

"You have got to get out of here," he whispered tersely, hoping she'd listen to him and just obey his orders. Although that had never been the case before.

"Yeah, and then what happens?"

"I'm going to try and flush out the other militia members. Find the head of the snake. I may try to act like I did what I did just now because I didn't want them to kill you or Barley."

She rolled her eyes, saying more with that physical expression than any words could convey. But, she added the words for good measure. "Yeah, like they'll buy that" she whispered vehemently. "Give it up, Mick. Give it up. You are risking your life."

He narrowed his eyes. "You risked your life for a dog."

"I didn't do it for 'a dog.'" Her eyes fastened on him, fire flashing. "I did it for Barley."

He almost laughed at the vehemence in her voice.

"I couldn't let him kill Barley, let him put a bullet in him."

He nodded. He reached for her to pull her in for a hug but she resisted, rolling her shoulder to shuck off his hand. "I get it," he said. "I know you couldn't let them hurt Barley."

"Just like you couldn't," she said, knowingly.

He met her eyes for a second, reading the demand for an acknowledgement, and nodded. They had to find some common

161

ground in order to move on. Maybe it would remind her that they were on the same page.

Besides, it was the truth. "I couldn't have let them hurt Barley."

Hurting dogs, or any animal for that matter, was right up there with hurting kids. It would have driven him crazy. It wouldn't have happened on his watch.

Even at the cost of saving human lives?

No. He'd have stopped them from hurting Barley and then found another way to stop them from hurting people.

"I couldn't let them hurt Barley," he said. "Like I can't let these jerks go after innocent people up in Tennessee."

"You didn't know for sure you'd die if you came out of the woods in order to save Barley, just like I don't know for sure I'll die trying to save the people the militia wants to kill."

Her mouth narrowed into a thin line that she began to work with her teeth, twisting and chewing on the inside of her lip.

He tilted his head. "It's the same. You're the same as me. You put your life on the line for another living creature, put yourself into danger."

She nodded. "You're right. When I thought he was going to kill Barley, I felt a superhuman strength come over me, like no one could hurt me, that I just had to go and save him."

She met his eyes straight on, with an understanding that seemed somehow new.

"That's what you and Tess felt all those times you put your life on the line as police officers, trying to save victims, get the bad guys." She half smiled. "I get it. I know exactly how you felt then, how you feel now. If you knew you were going to die, of course you wouldn't do it. But, there's that adrenalin surge that says you can make a difference."

Something released inside of him, to hear her describe exactly how he felt all those times, how he felt now.

Could they pull this off, could they bring these guys down?

# CHAPTER TWENTY

"This is what we're going to do." Mick looked Rowdy, Stan and White in the eye. All three were still duct taped to the chairs. Stan and White eyed him with interest, Rowdy with undisguised vitriol.

"I believe in what you guys are trying to do, with your mission to bring down the federal government. State's rights and the individual's rights have to be reasserted. This has been a long time coming. It's gonna take something big to start the revolution back to putting power into local hands."

Even Rowdy looked more interested. The ball was rolling back his way.

"I just don't think this girl has to get hurt in the process." He tilted his head and saw agreement in Stan and White's eyes.

But Rowdy looked away.

He was just dangerous all the way through. He couldn't be part of the plan. He had to be controlled.

"Look, Rowdy, I can drive up to Tennessee and exchange her for your cousin. Two birds with one stone. And you said something was gonna blow up?"

Rowdy looked him in the eye, with a sly look that said his evil brain was simmering with devious plans.

"I can do that," Mick offered. "Show you guys I'm with you."

Becca gasped, believably, as if she was just hearing this for the first time. "What?"

"Shut up." He motioned toward her with his gun, but was careful to keep the barrel pointed away from her.

"Untie us then," Rowdy said, leaning forward, his foul breath blowing on Mick.

Mick looked him up and down. "Emm, no. Can't say as I trust you. But, I want to show these guys and your other buddies, that I mean business, that I want to be part of the movement. Then, I'll have standing. You'll see I'm with you."

He shook his head at Rowdy. "Right now, you got your anger up, might make you do anything." That, at least, wasn't a lie.

Rowdy glared at him. The guy was calculating payback, all right. He didn't like being put into the down position, told what to do.

"So, what's the plan, boss?" Rowdy snarled, his words compliant, but everything else saying trouble.

"We're going to call your buddies, tell them I'll be taking the girl up to Tennessee to meet the Feds, that Stan will go with me for the handoff."

"Stan, huh?" Rowdy swiveled his ugly gaze toward his buddy who flinched under the pressure of the distrust shooting out of Rowdy's eyes.

"I don't have nnnnothing to do with this," Stan stuttered out. "Nnnothing."

"Yeah, uh huh." Rowdy turned back to glaring at Mick. "So, girlie here goes free and so does my cousin?"

"Yeah, you said you had people working it out, didn't you?"

"Yeah, yeah, that's right." He glanced at the cell phone on the coffee table. "Go ahead, make the call."

Mick's stomach turned at how willingly Rowdy agreed. Becca's eyes got big, and she played with Barley's collar, rubbing his rabies tag between her fingers. She was gonna rub out the tag number if she kept it up.

"Can I call my father and let him know I'm okay?" She looked at Mick, not at Rowdy.

The request caught him off guard. He was so into getting in touch with the militia's contacts that he'd forgotten completely about the judge. A sliver of guilt cut through him that he could lack such consideration for the man who'd half raised him.

Becca's gaze tore at him, how she'd been dragged into this mess.

"Sure," he said.

"Ladies' man," Rowdy said with derision. "That tells you clearer than anything that he got some last night."

"Well, why shouldn't she put her dad's mind at ease?" Mick looked at Rowdy, not really expecting an answer. But, what he saw in White and Stan's eyes spoke volumes about the type of people they were.

They understood, almost nodding at him.

"Here." He picked up the phone. "You dialed the number before, Rowdy. Which one is it?" He scrolled past the judge's number, checking out the last few numbers on the call list. Those would be important information for the Feds. Maybe they could use them to trace others in the network.

Rowdy looked at him with a smirk, like he was in the driver's seat again.

To hell with that.

He turned the phone toward Becca, as if he didn't know the number by heart. "Do you see your dad's number here?"

"Hey, don't let her see them numbers," Rowdy growled. "She might 'member them and tell the Feds."

Mick wanted to laugh in the guy's face. He was so easy to play.

"Here, then." He turned the phone toward the bound criminal. "Which one is it?"

"The fifth from the top." Rowdy was really pissed now. He wanted to get up and beat Mick to death with the chair he was bound to.

Mick kept his face empty, not showing the fun he was having with the guy.

He hit the number, getting ready to dial, and looked at

Becca. In a tough guy tone, he said, "No funny business if you want to see your pappy again."

"Pappy?" She laughed in his face.

Stan and White both grinned along with her. "Getting a little mountain, ain't you, boy?" White said.

Mick smiled at him. "Just trying to fit in."

"I ain't heered pappy since." White's face fell. "Well, since my daddy said it about his daddy. He always called him Pappy."

He looked away. "Said it was an inside joke with him and his daddy. Something about his daddy's daddy. Never really got the straight story on that."

Becca looked at him, empathy on her face. "Is your father still alive?"

Here we go again, with the life story of these guys.

"What's it matter?" Mick said tersely to Becca.

She shot him a hurt look. Getting ready to get out of character, respond to him as Mick.

"No," White said quickly, looking Becca in the eye, with a soft smile, as if he'd been touched by her question. "My daddy's dead."

"I'm so sorry." Becca leaned forward to put her hand on White's shoulder.

She was actually feeling sorry for the guy who'd kidnapped her? The girl was a walking bleeding heart.

He had to get back in control of the situation.

"Hey, you want to talk to your father or not?" he bit off the words, glaring at Becca like the hardened character he was supposed to be.

"Ooh, the ladies' man gets tough," Rowdy cackled.

"I'm sorry, sweetie," Mick changed his tone to a soft one meant to get a girl to give up her panties.

She slashed her eyes sideways at him, and Rowdy laughed under his breath.

Then, he toughened his tone again. "I'm gonna let you make this call. But, not one word about where you are, hear me?"

"Got it," she said, in a cutting tone. She started to stand, but he narrowed his eyes, and moved closer, towering over her. She sank back into the chair and nodded. "Got it."

He gave her a quick, assessing glance, hoping she didn't give away anything to these guys. "Look, tell your father you're okay, don't mention any of this, don't mention militia, just say you were kidnapped, but that a nice couple took you in and you're going to call the sheriff, but they're afraid the phones will go down cause of the storm so if he doesn't hear from you before tomorrow, don't worry."

"Say the roads are blocked too, cause of downed trees," he added.

He held the phone next to her ear, and with a stern look repeated, "Don't mention any of us, nothing about a cabin in the north Georgia mountains, don't mention the militia. Don't mention anything but that you're safe."

Then, he punched the connect button and held the phone to her ear.

She nodded, her face pale, her hands shaking. This was a lot harder on her than she wanted to reveal.

He knew how badly she wanted to reassure her father. The girl was all about other people's feelings.

"It keeps ringing," she said. "Voice mail." Tears began to well up in her eyes as she listened to her father's voice.

"Daddy. This is Becca. I'm okay. I was kidnapped but I got away. I'll call you tomorrow. Don't worry if you don't hear from me cause a storm's been making the phones go in and out."

Mick hit the disconnect button.

He wanted to take her in his arms and comfort her.

But, if he did, she might break down completely.

If she lost it, he didn't know how he'd react. Call this whole thing off? Call the Feds to come and get the ones they'd already caught and make them get the info out of them?

He needed her to be strong, to keep it together.

For her. For him.

For all those people that might be victimized by these guys' buddies, if he didn't stop them.

# CHAPTER TWENTY-ONE

Becca saw the doubt in Mick's eyes. He was worried about her.

He'd never been able to stand seeing her cry. If she'd been that type of girl, it would have been simple to get her way. Turn on the tears and watch him fold.

She'd never used it against him. The pain in his eyes hurt much more than any fight was ever worth. She'd always caved rather than see his pain.

"I'm going to take Barley out," she said, tilting her head toward the little dog.

"Nice try," Mick spit out. "I'll come with you."

"Ladies' man," Rowdy sing-songed.

That image was working out. The guys thought whatever he did concerning Becca was because she was a female. Just any old female.

That was okay. Let them think that.

"Hey, I got me a question," Rowdy said slyly.

Mick deadpanned a look at him.

"If you don't trust her now, how come she had that shotgun up there?" Rowdy's eyes narrowed.

"Cause I didn't trust you guys. Besides." He shot a look a Becca. "You didn't think it was loaded did you? I'm not that stupid. Just the sound of that shotgun racking is enough to stop any man in his tracks."

Rowdy snarled an indiscernible sound. Stan and White tried

to hold back grins. It was never good to laugh at Rowdy's expense. He'd pay you back twice.

Mick tilted his head at Becca to go ahead and he walked out behind her, followed by Barley before Mick slid the glass door closed. They walked to the front of the house, next to the SUV.

"I wonder where my phone is, forgot about that." Becca went to the back of the SUV and began looking for it.

"I'm gonna call my contact agent at the FBI." He dialed the number by heart as Barley sniffed around the bushes.

Quickly, he outlined what had happened and the change of plans. As soon as he knew where the event was to happen, he would call with as many details as possible.

Then, he paused before continuing, wanting his question to come out right, not accusing, not finger pointing. Even though the screw up could have ended with him and Becca dead.

"The sheriff never got up here, we ended up having to run like nuts through the woods. Becca is still here with us. She's a loose cannon, almost ruined the whole thing."

Hernandez blew out a disgusted breath. "Those yokels, I told them to get in there as quickly as possible. I think there's a mole in the sheriff's department, someone sympathetic to their anti-federal government beliefs."

"Yeah," Mick agreed. "I'd been worrying about that too."

Hernandez snorted angrily. "These homeboys have the home court advantage."

"Yep. Okay. I'll be in touch."

"Hey," Hernandez said quietly. "Be careful."

That was as close to a person as his boss had ever been. Usually a by-the-book supervisor, all business.

"Will do. Just get me the backup when I need it."

"Will do." The phone went dead. Hernandez was already probably regretting the emotion that had played in his voice.

Becca walked around the SUV, holding up her cell phone. "Found it in a side pocket."

Mick looked at Becca. "You've been great in there."

An evil darkness filled her eyes. "I kinda like pulling one

over on Rowdy after all he's put me through."

"Payback's a bitch," he agreed.

"Just call me payback from now on." The grim intensity on her face made her look more like Tess than ever before. Always she'd been the light one, Tess the destroyer, the avenger.

Lines crinkled between her eyebrows, and she leaned in, looking him in the eye. "So, how's this gonna go down? The devil's in the details they say."

As if she were going to be involved.

The hell she was. When they got into Tennessee, he was gonna set her out on the side of the road, near a convenience store, and let her call her dad for a ride home.

She wasn't going to be anywhere nearby when all hell could break loose.

Becca noted that expression Mick got when he wasn't telling her the whole truth. If he knew that his right eyebrow went up when he was lying to her, she'd be screwed. He didn't do that with anyone else but her. Cause she'd watched him enough to know.

So now, she knew. He was planning to pull this whole thing off by himself.

"The hell you are," she said, not worrying about the non sequitur. "I am not going to let you drive off by yourself to be killed." She stepped closer, leaning in. "You are seriously outgunned in this operation."

She met his eyes, though his gave nothing away. "Somehow you got the gun with no bullets. The tracking device and cell phone you were supposed to get weren't there. Whoever is helping you back at the FBI is doing a hell of a bad job."

A dark fury burned in his eyes, then he reached for her, pulling her up against his chest.

She wrapped her arms around him, feeling him safe and warm. And alive.

She had to keep him alive.

He might think he could win this alone, but he'd find she

wasn't going anywhere. She was going to make sure he came through this alive.

He'd have backup he could count on. Her.

\*\*\*\*

Nearly three hours later, the location of the bomb had changed three times. First, they'd gotten a text the location had been changed from Tennessee to the federal courthouse in Gainesville, Georgia, so they'd headed south. Then, it was changed to Macon.

The last text had come when they were approaching the downtown Atlanta area, said the location had been changed to the federal courthouse in Atlanta, which Mick suspected was their target all along.

They'd just changed it, minute by minute, in case someone in their group was a mole.

Now, noise and chaos that was the highway system of metro Atlanta surrounded their SUV. Smog, congestion and horn-blowing. A guy behind him rode his SUV's bumper.

That guy should watch it. You just never knew whose car you were bumper surfing. A car full of militia guys, who were more than ready to blow a few Atlantan's heads off, had little sympathy for anyone living inside the perimeter.

Yeah, blow your horn at that.

The bumper-riding guy swerved around Mick and gave him the finger.

What would Rowdy do?

Mick did just the opposite and clenched his fingers onto the steering wheel. Then, the road-raging guy purposefully slammed on the brakes in front of him.

Mick and Becca's bodies both jerked forward into the shoulder harness of their seatbelts as Mick hit his brakes to avoid hitting the jerk.

Barley woofed and tried to scrabble up over the dashboard to get at the car. Becca pulled him back, clasping her arms tightly around him.

Muffled yells came from the back of the SUV as Stan and White were thrown about by the sudden braking. Tied up as they were, it was probably hard to brace against the lunging of the vehicle. Life was tough once the tables turned on you.

Mick accelerated slowly as the jerk sped up and disappeared into the traffic ahead, zipping between lanes just to gain one extra car length.

Becca leaned over, placing her hand on his arm, and patted him as if he were Barley or one of her school kids. "Maybe some cop will ticket him up ahead."

A bit condescending, but still. It wasn't all bad having her on an assignment.

They'd left Rowdy tied up and in a closet with a chair and a broom locking him in. The guy was just too volatile, and Mick knew something would go wrong if he was along for the ride. So, he'd taken the chance of leaving him bound up, hoping the Feds got there before Rowdy had a chance to get loose.

He'd needed at least one of the three guys to talk to the contact in the militia group, hopefully keeping them unaware of any disruption of their group's identity until it was too late.

He'd brought both of them, figuring there was less chance of Rowdy escaping if he didn't have someone to help him, perhaps to untie his hands.

It wasn't a perfect plan but he was kind of making it up as he went along.

Hernandez had promised the Feds would get there quick to take Rowdy into custody.

They exited the freeway and began to weave toward the final location Stan had been given when they'd held the phone to his ear half an hour ago. Mick had texted the information to Hernandez, allowing the bomb squad to get in place, to evacuate buildings before Mick and his crew showed up.

Suddenly, blue lights filled his rear view mirror. Hernandez had made the call in time.

Sirens prompted Mick to pull over as a frenzy of police cars zipped by him. Woosh, woosh, woosh. Car after car blazed down the street.

There was nothing more impressive than a gang of police driving like they meant business, cutting the corners on turns, flying to intercept the danger.

Everything Mick had endured in the past few months, the jail time with the bad food and lousy company, and the danger, would be worth it.

Thank God, it was all coming together in the end. Despite the obvious screw-ups along the way.

A team would follow the guys who left the bomb back to their hideout and hopefully catch more suspects as they weaved in like roaches to a roach bait station.

Once they'd caught some guys in the act of trying to blow up a federal building they'd be willing to give names to save themselves, to get out of prison in time to have some final years with their families before they died.

But, if the Feds had been on top of this thing, following him, Rowdy and his boys up to the cabin, they could have gotten tag numbers, maybe figured out who was making the bomb before it had gotten this far. Had enough evidence to break up the network.

Nothing had gone as hoped on this mission so far.

But, now, now things were leveling out. Nothing more reassuring than a stream of blue lights.

He inhaled slowly, then eased off the brakes and continued toward the bomb site. His car would be stopped. Then, he, White and Stan would all be taken into custody, keeping the appearance of Mick's cover intact.

But, as they approached the address, his heart began to pulse like a police light, beaming out the message that something else had gone horribly wrong.

In an area close to the Gulch, as it was called, a nearly vacant area between the CNN building, the Georgia Dome and the Federal building, they spotted the expected box truck parked along the curb, innocent-looking but loaded with death.

But, what the hell?

All of those blue lights had gone somewhere else?

Where did those cops all go and why? Why? Hell, it was clear. Clear that this whole operation was a total SNAFU, or in other words System Normal, All Fucked Up.

# Chapter Twenty-Two

Becca's eyes were as wide as searchlights, looking around and behind them for all of those cops who'd blazed past them so reassuringly just moments ago.

But, nothing had gone as hoped on this mission. Why should this be any different?

Slowly, he pulled the SUV to the curb. Federal agents, SWAT and bomb technicians should be swarming this area by now, evacuating the buildings close by, preparing to disarm the explosives.

He'd texted the exact location to Hernandez. There was no excuse for this. "Damn it," he muttered under his breath.

Becca looked over at him, those telltale lines between her eyebrows scrunched together like a couple of dogs in a doghouse on a freezing night.

"No agents, no backup," she whispered.

"Just that damned deadly truck, parked way too close to the buildings around it. If that thing goes up now, people will die."

He looked out into the Gulch, with its vacant area between the triangle of federal buildings, the CNN building and the Dome.

"We need to get that truck further out into that area," he whispered to Becca and pointed. "The collateral damage to people will be much less if that thing goes up out there."

Her breathing accelerated. Damn, he didn't want to upset her but she was part of the team now. Every bit as much as Tess

176

had ever been.

Becca wouldn't end up like Tess, no matter what it took.

He threw the SUV into reverse, backing up at a breakneck speed, putting distance between Becca and that deathtrap of a truck. No telling if it had been set on a timer. Stan had gotten very little information from his phone contact.

Mick scanned the buildings around them, searching for watchful eyes, anything that looked out of place. Someone could have their finger on a trigger device right now.

The keys to the box truck were supposed to be underneath the front seat. One of them was to drive the truck underneath the federal courthouse, leave it there, and then run like hell.

All of the federal marshals running outside toward the illegally parked truck would increase the casualties.

Meanwhile, Rowdy's cousin would be released from the Tennessee penitentiary in exchange for Becca. A car was supposed to be waiting to meet her at the nearby Federal Administration building.

After the release of Rowdy's cousin was assured, the militia members would have driven away just in time to escape the mayhem that the bomb's explosion would cause.

"Damn it, where are they?" he muttered. Where was his support team, the agents, the bomb squad?

Becca's eyes got bigger and her breath came in quick, short pants. "Something's wrong," she whispered so White and Stan wouldn't hear.

"The truck's parked right where they'd said it would be," he replied.

"But no agents," she said.

"They should be all over this place." His gut wrenched with the need to punch whoever wasn't getting them help.

"It's another Oklahoma bombing if we don't do something." He looked at Becca. What had he gotten her into? A terrorist plan set into motion without any disruption.

"Damn it. We need to get that truck further out into the Gulch." He wheeled the SUV around, facing away from the

Gulch, ready to drive like hell. "Call 911, tell them what's happening, to get people away from the windows in those buildings. Then, turn off the phone."

"My battery's about dead," she said.

He tossed her Rowdy's phone, then threw open his car door, stalked around and yanked White out of the back of the SUV. He pulled off White's blindfold and ripped off the duct tape from his mouth.

"Oww," White protested.

Mick shoved him around toward the Gulch. "See that truck," he pointed.

White squinted from the sudden exposure to sunlight. Mick jerked him by the shirt. "See that truck?"

"Yeah, I see it. Right where it's supposed to be. What's the problem? You knew this was the plan," White said indignantly, self-righteously, as if killing people was accepted, something in the course of normal human events.

It was part of this group's constitution. They had a political justification for all the blood they were prepared to spill.

Mick yanked him hard, spinning him around to meet his eyes. White flinched, tried to step back but Mick pulled him in close, pulling his gun from his waistband and sticking it to White's head.

"Drive that thing out into the middle of that area over there."

White looked at the parked box truck, then began shaking his head fervently, repeatedly. "Nnnoo," he stuttered. "You're supposed to."

"Me? Why is that, White?" Mick hit him with the butt of the gun, scuffing it against the side of his head, scraping skin so that blood spilled out, running down White's face.

Mick leaned in, glaring into White's face. "You have two choices. Either I shoot you now, or you move that truck out into that open area."

White looked into Mick's eyes, calculating Mick's level of craziness. Mick pushed the gun's barrel up under White's chin, communicating exactly what he was prepared to do.

White nodded.

"They said the keys would be underneath the front seat. Just drive it out into that middle area, then what you do after that is up to you."

"Untie me, then." Sweat began popping out on White's face like popcorn, turning to melting butter running down his cheeks, mixing with the blood dribbling down his face.

"I wasn't born yesterday, White. Just do the best you can with your hands and feet tied. It's not far out to that spot."

He'd tied their feet loosely with about a foot of rope between them so they couldn't run.

Mick looked at White's hands, and figured he probably did need to untie them. Quickly, he undid the rope, then pointed his gun at White.

"You try running anywhere but toward that truck, and you get a bullet in the back. Got it?"

White nodded but didn't look at Mick. Instead, he scanned the surrounding area, frantically, his breathing accelerating like a sputtering old pickup truck, looking up toward the buildings, as if he too knew there might be a trigger-happy finger waiting to push the button for the bomb to explode.

With a last gulp of air, White swerved unsteadily toward the truck, tilting like a drunkard.

He reached the truck, glancing back one more time toward Mick, who pointed his gun menacingly at him, then White struggled into the truck and began driving.

In the distance, Mick could see marshals from the Federal Courthouse emerging, running toward the truck. They were still far enough away that even if the bomb went off soon, they would live. Hopefully.

Mick waved his arms, signaling for them to stop, to get back. Yeah, right. Like that was about to happen. These were men programmed to run toward danger, to stop it.

Even if it meant their lives.

He'd done all he could do right now.

"Part one," Mick said, then ran to the SUV, jerked it into gear and accelerated away from the area, pushing the vehicle as fast as it would go.

"Put Barley in the floorboard," he said insistently.

She glanced at him, did what he said, then turned backward, looking toward the truck.

"Get your head down!" he yelled. At any moment, the bomb could blow.

She continued to stare, seemingly fixated on what was happening with White.

He shook his head, grabbed the phone, and began to dial 911, to make sure the operator understood just how dire the situation was.

Before he could even dial the three digits, a huge explosion behind them rocked the air. Debris flew from the Gulch, raining down around the SUV, pelting the back windows.

Becca screamed and Barley yelped out a startled bark. A loud, secondary explosion ignited with a powerful boom.

Mick grabbed Becca's head, jamming it downward just before a large rock blasted through the back window.

Stan yelped through the duct tape over his mouth. Barley began barking like there were several cats and a squirrel running through the car.

Mick kept driving. Another explosion could be set to go off nearby. Sometimes these guys set multiple bombs to catch the first responders.

Anything could happen now.

Becca leaned forward and pulled Barley into her lap. She tried to sit up, but Mick kept his hand on her head. "Stay down."

She knocked his hand away, forcing her way up, and looked backward. She screamed, a loud screeching expulsion of noise. Then, she covered her mouth with her hand, smothering the sound, pushing it back, though she still screamed with her eyes, wide and terror stricken.

Barley whimpered and looked up at her with white showing

in his eyes. "It's okay, boy," she soothed, her voice strained, like she'd damaged her vocal chords. She stroked his head, pulling him into her body.

"White never even got out," she said weakly, as if she'd used up all the air in her body screaming.

They'd both known already. She just needed to say it to push out some of the horror and disbelief.

Stan yelled with a muffled sound from the back of the SUV.

Mick jammed down the accelerator, pushing the vehicle further and further from danger.

Had the truck exploded on a timer or had someone seen White driving the truck into the open space, known their operation wasn't going off as planned and decided to detonate it before it got too far from any buildings? Had they knowingly sacrificed one of their own?

Mick drove like a deer being chased by dogs. Any minute now, the police would swarm the area and they'd be caught up in the sweep. He couldn't hesitate. They had to get away.

"This went real bad wrong," he said.

"Ya think?" Becca's eyes were a wide blue in her pale face. "What was that back there?" She looked through the back window, as if expecting an explanation to appear, to see something different than floating dust and smoke.

She held onto Barley as if the little dog could erase the horror of this new reality.

Where were the agents who should have stopped that truck before it got that close to the federal complex?

Why hadn't Hernandez directed support to the area?

It was almost as if he'd purposefully left him hanging in the wind.

Set him up to die?

# Chapter Twenty-three

Mick screeched around another corner and Becca grabbed the door grip. Still, she was thrown from side to side, only the seatbelt and her fingernails holding her onto the seat.

"Like a banshee out of hell," she muttered. Did he want to finish getting them killed? They'd escaped the bomb but would they die from his driving?

"Slow down," she said insistently. He hadn't listened the numerous times she'd already said that.

"We gotta get away," he said through tight lips, his eyes intent on the road, breaking away every few seconds to look in his rearview mirrors, furors deep between his eyebrows. Who was he watching for?

The same people she was watching for. Anyone coming for them. Because now she didn't know who that might be.

"Why weren't the cops and FBI agents and Homeland Security and . . ." She struggled to come up with more names for types of police. "Why wasn't anyone there?" she finally blurted out. No one had been there. No one.

"Are we on our own?" That's how it felt, like she and Mick were in a hurricane whipped ocean, flailing in the water, sharks possibly just underneath the surface.

Unseen danger below, help invisible beyond the lurching horizon of the ocean.

Mick reached over and grabbed her hand, taking his eyes off the road for a brief second. She met his gaze then took his hand off hers and put it back on the wheel. "Both eyes on the road and both hands on the wheel if you're going to keep driving like a crazy man."

His eyes crinkled a bit.

"I take that as a yes, you're going to keep driving like a banshee out of hell," she said, putting her hand on his thigh, needing the contact.

And like a banshee out of hell, fleeing demons, he drove until they left the city behind, drove on two-lane black top roads, until they reached a green, tree-lined rural area.

Finally, he turned off into a roadside picnic area, blowing dust all the way to the back of the lot, hiding the vehicle behind some bushes so it couldn't be seen from the road. Or at least that's what she assumed he was doing.

He looked intently back at the road.

"I've gotta go to the bathroom." Becca staggered out of the car, her legs numb, deadened limbs that didn't quite connect her to the earth. She staggered toward the little restroom building.

Her legs might be asleep but her mind was wide awake, racing over every second of the last two days as she tried to get her left leg to respond to her mind's commands.

This was a nightmare that only kept getting worse. She looked behind her just as the door closed, her gaze fastening onto Mick, the only reason she felt they still had a chance. As long as she was with Mick, nothing really bad could happen to her.

She held onto that belief. Because it was all she had right now.

Mick shoved open the car door and lifted Barley out onto the ground. And tried to wrap his mind around all that had happened.

"Do your business, boy," he said to reassure the little guy. Getting out himself, he stood, looking around at all the greenery, dragging in deep breaths that held no bomb blast residue. If you just looked at the immediate surroundings, you could believe all was right in the world.

Barley circled the area looking for the best place to go. Everything was just fine in his world. "It's a dog's life," people would say as if that were a bad thing.

Looked pretty good right now.

A few moments later, Becca pushed open the bathroom door, and walked toward him. As beautiful as ever. With no makeup, she looked like the fourteen-year-old girl he'd fallen in love with so long ago.

A deep pulse of relief flowed through him. Just seeing her made everything seem all right in his world. She was all he needed to feel good.

But, he wasn't the man for her.

She deserved a guy who would go to work in the morning and come home every night like clockwork.

Not some guy who could end up in a body bag by the end of his shift.

She deserved better.

Like now, for example. He couldn't believe that this would have happened to her if not for him.

Sure, her dad had been the guy who'd sentenced these guys to prison.

But, something told Mick that if he hadn't been part of the plot things would have been different.

A niggling feeling told him he was missing something vital.

As Becca neared, he sucked in the sight of her. So beautiful. And she wanted him.

Well for now, they were both alive. And like a dog, that had to be enough for him, to live in the moment, in the present, not worrying about the future.

She walked to stand in front of him, inches away, and he pulled her close, wrapping his arms around her living, breathing form, inhaling the smell of her, vanilla soap and fruit scented shampoo and that other smell that was her. Pure her.

"Ah, Becca," he exhaled into her hair.

She leaned back to look into his eyes. "We're okay for now, Hampton," she said, deep in her throat in that voice that seemed

TARGETED TO KILL

designed to drive him crazy. To make him want to do bad things with her that felt so good.

She pressed her hips into his, as if needing to connect with him on a primal, sexual level. God, he wanted to take her right here, right now, in the grass, under the blue sky.

"Later, sweets," he promised her, promised what they both wanted.

"Will there be a later?" she murmured, inches from his lips.

He nodded, as he stared down at those lips. "I promise." Then, softly, he touched his lips to hers. That was all he trusted himself to do.

Because if the kiss went further, there might be no stopping himself.

But, there wasn't time for that.

Later, he promised himself. "Later," he promised her.

A loud banging against the inside of the SUV's back area punctuated the end to the moment.

He released Becca and went around to the back, opening the SUV's back door, pulling the blindfold from Stan's eyes, yanking him to his feet, then jerking the duct tape from his mouth.

"What the hell is going on?" Stan yelled as soon as his mouth was free. He squinted from the light and looked around.

"I'm taking you out to use the toilet is what's going on. Unless of course, you don't need to go." He grabbed him by the shoulder as if he were going to put him back into the SUV.

"Hell yeah, I need to go. I almost pissed my pants when that explosion went off." Stan looked wildly about. "Did White really die in that explosion?"

He'd had to have heard them talking but with the noise of the moving vehicle and not being able to see or hear anything that had happened outside the car with his interaction with White, he obviously wasn't certain.

Or just hoping for the best for his buddy?

"Use the bathroom," Mick said, tilting his head toward the small primitive building.

185

"Oh, God." Stan started to hyperventilate, leaning forward, panting for breath.

"Calm down. You're gonna make yourself pass out."

"But, he's dead? I can't believe he's dead."

A raging anger filled Mick that this guy could so callously plan to blow up women, children, men, anybody, but now whimper over his own friend. He shoved Stan hard, the rope tied between his feet causing Stan to fall.

"Oh yeah, you're so worried about your buddy," he growled out the disgust he felt for this guy and all those just like him. "But, you didn't give a damn about all those innocent people who were gonna die in that explosion."

Stan struggled to his feet, still panting, his eyes wide. "I never thought they'd do it. Never thought they'd really blow people up. I always thought we was all just talking big inside the pen, passing time with evil thoughts of revenge until we could get out."

"Then when you got out?" Mick ground out.

Stan looked around, wildly. "Then, when we got out and back to the cabin, everyone started coming round. I didn't know how to get out of it."

"Yeah, save it for the jury," Mick spit out. "All I know is a bomb went off today, down near the federal building. And if I hadn't made White drive that truck away from the buildings, instead of toward them like your buddies wanted us to do, lots of people would have died."

He swallowed hard. "People may have died anyway."

News reports had been nonstop on the radio as they'd driven out of town but had been unclear as to how many people had been injured or if anyone had died.

He shoved Stan toward the john. "I don't want to hear any more of your bull."

"I'd be dead if I'd been driving that truck," Mick said to Stan. And Becca would have been all alone in this new nightmare landscape where he didn't know who to trust.

God, he had to figure things out. Had to make sure Becca was safe. But, he didn't know who to call, who to trust.

He opened the restroom door and shoved Stan inside. "Get it done!" he yelled after him.

He stood with the door open, wanting to go and push Stan's face down into the urinal. Wanted to beat him half to death until he told him what he needed to know to keep Becca safe.

When Stan finished at the urinal and walked toward the sink, Mick grabbed him, turned on the faucet and stuck Stan's face into the water, turning his face so that the water ran up his nose.

"Mmmhgh," Stan gurgled. He struggled but Mick pushed his face right into it, doing an impromptu water boarding. He held him there as Stan tried with all his might to escape, kicking and bucking. But Mick's anger gave him the strength of ten men.

Finally, he released him. "Just be glad it wasn't into the toilet. That was my first impulse." He shoved Stan back against the hard cement block wall, his hand around his throat, pinning him in place. "Now, you ass, tell me what you know, who you know and how far up the food chain you can trace this bullshit."

Stan choked and coughed for a minute, his cheeks red from the cold water, but quickly his skin turned ashen underneath the water streaming off his face. As if even the bracing water couldn't keep back the shock of the death of his friend, and the fear he felt in the face of Mick's anger.

Mick pushed his face close to Stan's and let out a guttural order. "Tell me what you know."

Stan hesitated and Mick reached behind him and turned on the water again.

"Wait, just wait a minute. I gots to think."

"Don't think, just talk."

"Okay, okay. I'll tell you what I know but it ain't much. Rowdy never tolt me any of those guys names. I never seen them afore. They weren't from round our county." He grimaced. "Rowdy said the less I knew, the less I could testify about."

And the damn plan had worked. He believed Stan because

he didn't think the guy was capable of being all that good a liar. He turned the water off and jerked Stan along by the collar, dragging him outside and toward the SUV.

Stan's hobbled feet stumbled along as he tried to keep up with the pace Mick set.

He opened the back of the SUV, and pushed Stan in, blindfolded him, and put duct tape back on his mouth.

Becca kneeled, holding Barley close, stroking his back, her face tense, white. God, he hated what this was doing to her.

"What's going on?" she asked.

"I was just talking to our boy is all," he said, wondering how much sound had escaped the bathroom walls.

"No, I mean down at the federal building, with the truck bomb." She arched an eyebrow.

Oh, that.

"I don't know. The area around the federal building should have been crawling with cops. They should have picked up whoever was driving that truck, stopped them before they got anywhere near there."

Her face was ghost pale. Pulling her into his arms, he swore he wouldn't let her get hurt.

He'd kill the son of a bitch who tried to hurt her. He'd stand between her and any harm these sons of bitches thought they could bring to her.

Even now, she could be carrying his child. What type of a man got a woman pregnant under these circumstances? If anything happened to her . . .

Becca leaned into Mick, relishing the closeness. When she was in his arms, it seemed nothing could ever go wrong.

That as long as the two of them were safe, everything was going to be all right.

But, the reality was she'd never been less safe.

Who would have thought his return into her life would have been both the best thing to have ever happened to her and still one of the worst?

"We just have to figure out what's going on. Figure out

who can help us," she whispered.

He pulled back to look into her eyes, sending that safe little feeling shooting through her that said she was exactly where she ought to be in the world, exactly where she wanted to be.

"Right." He tilted his head. "We have to figure out who can help us." Dropping one arm from around her, he pulled out the phone and powered it up.

"Who are you calling?"

He exhaled deeply. "Luke and Weston at the APD."

"The Atlanta Police Department? Not the FBI? I thought they were running this operation."

"Are they?" He laughed harshly. "Running amuck is more like it. Nobody backed us up. It was almost like they wanted me dead."

"And me," she added.

He met her gaze for a second with an intensity that almost scared her; it was so filled with repressed rage.

"Exactly," he finally added flatly. Then, he dialed a number. "Hey Weston, it's me."

He laughed harshly at something that was said on the phone. "Yeah, 'me'."

An easy identification between old friends on the force.

Weston had been a part of Tess and Mick's APD gang, gone through the academy together and been inseparable afterward.

A spasm of grief hit Becca hard at the memories of all the good times she and Mick had shared with Tess and Weston.

Tess.

She'd never joke again with her twin, never tell her secrets, never confide in her any problems she and Mick were having.

She was so emotionally strung out from all that had happened the last few days that the memories overwhelmed her.

And what would happen after they got out of this situation?

Would there be a Becca and Mick? Or would all that would be left was the possibility of a baby, Mick's baby?

She touched her stomach. Even now was there a baby on

the way that if it were a girl would surely be named Tess? Tears began to well up. But, she pushed them back.

She couldn't think about any of that. She had to use Tess' laser intense focus. To stay alive. To keep her and Mick alive.

"What?" Mick said into the phone, with such ferocity it brought her fully back into the moment. His eyes were dark, narrowed and the lines between his eyebrows bunched together, making him look much older.

He glanced at her as if he'd forgotten she was there, then away again quickly.

She tilted her head, questioning without words.

He raised a finger to wait just a minute and continued to speak into the phone, "Yeah, this is out of control crazy. I've been undercover for months now." He laughed darkly. "Yeah, that's why I haven't been in contact. No beers or games for me. I've been in prison."

His eyes narrowed. "Yeah, Jonesville State Prison." He looked straight at Becca then back down, hiding whatever thought that had just gone through his head. Whatever reaction he'd just had to what he'd been told.

"I need your help, buddy," he said into the phone. "Hernandez was my contact in the Bureau. He was running the operation."

He sucked in a deep breath, as if needing the fortifying oxygen to divulge all that was happening. "You know that bomb that went off a couple of hours ago. Yeah, that was part of what I've been involved in. Anybody killed by the way?"

He listened to a torrent of words. Then, replied. "Yeah, well it would have been a lot worse. They wanted me and Becca dead as well."

"Those guys who escaped with me from the prison? They were involved with a militia group in north Georgia. I left one tied up there in the cabin, called Rowdy, real name Sean Jackson. John McKinney, AKA White, died in the blast and we've got Stan Ralston in the back of the SUV."

He listened a few more minutes, his expression going from

dark to storm black, tension radiating out from him like an electrical cloud, ready to explode with deadly lightning bolts.

He turned.

So she couldn't see his face?

Yeah, exactly. She stepped around so that she was looking him straight on. This was not some simple high school drama moment. This was her life, his life.

He was not going to keep anything from her.

He met her gaze, narrowed his eyes and gave a little nod as if acknowledging her message. "We've got to find out where they took him. I don't know who I can trust right now. The FBI is suspect because I don't know what the lead agent has really told people there or who might be involved. I need your help, buddy."

They talked for a few more minutes then Mick hung up. He turned away, and paced back and forth several times before pivoting back toward her.

"Okay. I've got to tell you something."

He took her by the arm and walked her to a picnic bench. Sitting down was never good. Meant a ramped up level of bad. But, she sat.

"These guys were targeting you for a reason."

She nodded, waiting for the hammer to drop.

"Cause of your father." His voice was deeper than she'd ever heard him speak before, as if weighted down into the depths of his chest.

Something really bad was coming.

She tried to slow her breathing, to concentrate on drawing air in, then pushing it back out, needing to get some control over herself, because her heart began racing, and she could feel adrenalin pouring into her bloodstream.

A three count on the inhale, then a three count on the exhale. Just breath, she coaxed herself, although every cell in her body was focused on waiting for what was coming.

"They've also kidnapped him."

"Noooo," she wailed, wheezing out the word like a balloon

deflating, feeling as if all the oxygen in her body went with the word.

"I was the bait to get him," she said. "That's why I wasn't killed."

He nodded, and tightened his hold on her hands. "Weston is going to help us. He's going to round up some more help for us from APD officers we know and trust."

"The city is on high alert cause of the bomb," he said, speaking very clearly as if her emotions might have impacted her hearing.

If anything, the information had heightened all her senses, as if she needed every bit of help she could get to save her father.

"White was the only one killed in the blast downtown," Mick said, as if he were reporting for the news, no emotion, just the facts. "That's no great loss to society, the bomber getting blown up. There were a few people cut by flying glass. But, luckily not too seriously."

"My father?" she said. No one else really mattered now except for her father.

"Since no one was killed, Weston and a couple other buddies, like Luke, will be able to help us out unofficially. They're going to work with a captain who's good about that sort of thing, tell him they have a lead. That guy won't question them too much, since he knows those guys have worked undercover so many times. Figures they have a lead they can't talk about."

She nodded.

"If there had been mass casualties, everything would have been total mayhem in town, every cop on long shifts just to keep the streets safe. Funny thing, the bomb wasn't nearly as big as you would have expected from how Rowdy, White and Stan talked."

She pulled her hands away from his, wrapping them around herself, trying to keep herself centered, trying to keep her emotions from spiraling out of control. Her father needed her to rescue him.

"Where do you think my father is?"

"I don't know. That's what we have to find out."

"Stan must know where he is." She jumped up. "He must have known all along that he'd be kidnapped. What do you think they're doing to him?" Images of torture, beatings, maybe even a bullet to the brain flooded her mind.

A scream began to form deep inside, moving toward her mouth but she pushed it back. Hysteria wouldn't save her father. She braced herself for the biggest fight of her life, for her father's life.

They wouldn't take him the way Tess had been taken.

She wouldn't give up her father. She wouldn't.

She whirled back toward Mick. "My father didn't answer his phone. Does that mean he's already dead?"

"I thought Rowdy had kidnapped you out of pure meanness and revenge. To get back at the judge who sent him to prison."

She nodded.

"Now I think you were just the enticement to get him. So they could use him to get something."

"Like what?"

He shook his head. "Not sure. But, what matters now is finding him." His face turned pure mean as he glanced back toward the car.

"Stan probably can help with that," he snarled between clenched teeth.

God, she'd never seen that look on his face before. It was terrifying. She liked it. It gave her hope of finding her father.

Mick stalked to the back of the SUV, his body emanating anger, vengeance and the need to find an outlet for it. He opened the SUV's back, yanked Stan out, not even letting him get his feet on the ground, just tossing him out of the vehicle so that he landed on his side, rolling in the dirt.

Stan yelped when he hit the ground, the sound held back by the duct tape. Then, he moaned as if something hurt.

She hoped so.

Stan had been the sweetest of the kidnappers to her, had seemed kinda decent. But, now that she knew he might know where her father had been taken, she felt no mercy at all.

Beating, torture, a bullet. All of those things could face her father. Stan needed to know those things could also happen to him.

She walked over and ripped the cloth from his eyes. Then, she kicked him in the side, hard. "Damn you, damn you." She kicked him again. "Where is my father?"

Stan's face blanched. He was all alone now, no Rowdy, no White to back him up. With no gun, he was at their mercy.

"How's it feel being on the other side of the fence?" she yelled into his face.

"There's nothing I won't do to find my father!" she yelled close to his face, spit flying onto his cheeks.

Mick leaned over and ripped the duct tape from Stan's mouth in one long tearing motion that had to hurt.

She and Mick were on the same page. All that mattered was saving her father.

Mick grabbed Stan, yanked him up then shoved him backward so that he fell onto the bench, almost rolling over it onto the ground. But he hooked his foot on the side, steadying himself.

"What's up, guys?" Stan stuttered, his eyes wide, lots of white showing around the edges.

"That fake innocent look on your face could get you killed," she yelled, inches from his face. Her blood erupted through her veins, beating out from her heart like machine gun fire, searching for a target to vent her rage upon.

"My father is what's up," she spat the words at him, grabbing him by the collar, yanking him forward. "He's been kidnapped!" she yelled into his damned, lying face, acting so sweet to her, all the while knowing her father was somewhere terrified, maybe hurt.

Maybe dead?

Stan's eyes narrowed as he tried to pretend he was hearing

this for the first time.

"You already know that, huh?" she yelled. Fury gripped her like a case of cholera, burning through her veins. She slapped him, hard. And then again. "Where is he, you son of a bitch?"

His eyes wide, his face pale, Stan whipped his head around to look at Mick as if for help.

"Oh, don't count on me, buddy. I'd have started with a bullet to the knee." He pulled his pistol from his waistband and pointed it at Stan's leg. "Hurry up and answer her." He waggled the gun in a circle around Stan's knee.

"Don't get crazy now," Stan yelped. "Let's talk this through."

"Crazy?" Mick leaned closer. "Crazy? You guys meant to blow me and Becca and God knows how many people to kingdom come."

He grabbed him by the collar, jerking him closer, tightening his grip so that the shirt began to choke Stan. He twisted the material until Stan was gurgling, the material cutting into his windpipe.

Mick yelled, "Don't talk to me about crazy. I passed crazy a long time ago. Now, I'm just plumb out of control."

He released his hold on the shirt, shoving Stan backward, knocking him off the bench. Stan scrabbled in the dirt, trying to stand. Mick walked closer, standing over him before he could get up, pointing the gun toward Stan's right knee.

So much white showed in Stan's eyes, it looked like he had some type of disorder. Foam formed around his lips and he sputtered mindless sounds, words not able to squeeze past the terror that gripped him.

## Chapter Twenty-Four

"Hold on, hold on," Stan screeched. "I think I might know where he is."

"Might know?" Mick leaned closer and tapped the side of the gun barrel against Stan's knee.

"Yeah, but you gotta believe me, I never thought they would do any of this stuff. Never believed 'em."

"Yeah." Mick laughed harshly. "All sorts of not believing going on with you."

"I didn't." His eyes darted frantically back and forth between Becca and Mick. "You gots to believe me." He looked at Becca, then seemed to decide Mick was the better hope for mercy, fastening his gaze on his face.

Becca sure wouldn't have minded putting a bullet into some part of the guy if it meant getting her father back alive.

Mick leaned closer, touching the gun to Stan's kneecap and Stan's eyes took on a crazed, wild animal look.

"Atlanta, you gots to believe me. These guys've been big talkers they's whole life. I can't be blamed cause for once they really meant it."

"Enough about you being blameless. Tell me where they took the judge." Mick menaced Stan's knee with the gun, like an orthopedic doctor with a needle for an injection.

Sweat streamed down Stan's face. He seemed to know just exactly how much damage a bullet to the knee could do. His eyes never left the gun, watching it intently, waiting for the pain, bracing for it.

"There's a cabin," he stammered out. "Rowdy built his self a cabin long ago. Kinda Unabomber style. Deep in the woods. Hardly anybody knows it's there. So, makes sense they might haul somebody there they wanted to hide." His breath came in quick panting bursts, like he was ready to hold his breath against the pain at any time.

"Where's it at?" Mick leaned closer.

"Bout twenty miles from where we was at last night."

"You got an address?" Mick waved the gun around a bit in the general direction of his knee, pulling back but still close enough that he could put a bullet in it by changing directions an inch.

"It's on Route 11. Just past the Shell station as you come out from town, you turn right." His eyes darted back and forth between the gun and Mick's face, trying to gauge if he'd given enough information to spare him immediate agony.

With a non-committal grunt, Mick stuck the gun back into his waistband, jerked Stan up and pushed him into the back of the SUV, slamming it shut just as Stan jerked his feet out of the way.

Breathing heavily, Mick turned and walked away. Curses trailed him like Barley when Mick had a pocketful of treats.

Tess had told Becca how mean Mick could turn, with a fierce side that was scarier than anything she'd ever seen before. When someone's life was at risk or they were in danger.

But, Becca had never imagined Mick could be like that. She sucked in air, trying to beat back the panic and fierce anger that gripped her, knowing only one of them could go to the crazy side at a time.

She walked up behind Mick, feeling the ferocious intensity flowing off him. "You okay?"

He turned, met her gaze and smiled darkly. "Yeah. Peachy." He pulled out his phone again, punching in Weston's number, giving him the address of the original cabin where they'd been taken, telling him to get the GBI out there to pick up Rowdy, and to investigate the dead man and the little girl at the vacation cabins.

Funny, as a FBI man, he was turning to the GBI, the Georgia Bureau of Investigation, and every other police group besides the FBI.

The GBI routinely investigated crimes in rural areas like the county where the bodies had been found, so it made sense legally.

On a separate matter, he told Weston to call their buddy, Grant, sheriff of the county where Rowdy's Unabomber cabin was located, to mobilize the SWAT team down in Gainesville, but not tell anyone where they were headed. They'd worked with Grant when he was on the APD. The man could be trusted.

They'd formed such strong bonds when they were all young officers that Grant would accept the no-details request until filled-in-on-further need.

Operating under the authority of an FBI agent as well as Grant, the multi-county SWAT team would have jurisdictional reach.

He hung up, then cursed. "This phone's getting low on battery. How's yours?"

She powered up hers and waited a second. "Not much left here, either." The flashing battery light looked like a ticking time bomb.

"Save yours," he said quietly. He seemed to get quieter the more nervous he was.

He flashed a look at Becca. Taking her measure? His eyes narrowed, but his gaze softened. "One last time, let me drop you off at some local police station?"

"Hell no." She wasn't going to even get into it with him. "Just, hell no."

"Thought not." He grabbed her, pulling her into a rough embrace that wasn't about love, affection, or even passion. None of those things had a place here and now.

If those things were waiting for them, it would be later, after her father was out of danger.

But a fierce connection flowed between them, each needing to feel a living, breathing human being, to know that for now at least, they were alive.

Because, God knows, history had shown them that could change in an instant.

But, she got that so much determination was pumping through Mick that he couldn't gentle up. Not yet, not until this was done. He held her in a tight embrace.

She loved that he was steel strong in his determination to rescue her father.

With a final squeeze, he pulled back and looked into her face. "But when I say you need to hang back, you have to listen to me." He looked at her with such intensity that his words carried a double impact. "As a police officer, not as a boyfriend. Cause I'm only going to tell you to do what will make this operation go smoothly."

He tilted his head. "Okay?"

He considered himself her "boyfriend"?

Right now, all that really mattered was saving her father. Still, her heart pumped the word throughout her entire body. *Boyfriend*. That word smacked of long-term intent.

But, she pushed back any reaction. She couldn't let emotion interfere with the strength she'd need to face these people and win.

Win the life of her father.

"Let's roll," she said the words that had become a rallying cry against terrorists and other seriously bad guys after the crash of the hijacked plane into a field on September 11th, 2001.

\*\*\*\*

She'd never seen anyone drive so fast without a blue light. No cops had appeared behind them to slow them down. If they had, Mick had said he could make a quick phone call and have the cop actually lead him as far as he wanted.

Instead, they slid into the area, directed by Stan, turning off their lights when Stan said they were about a mile from the cabin.

Mick and Becca got out of the car quietly. Then, he walked around to the back of the SUV and yanked Stan out.

"I'm going in with him as my lead guy." He shot a look toward Stan. "In case Rowdy set up any booby traps, Unabomber style."

Stan's eyes rounded, confirming what Mick had said about hidden dangers as well as the fact that Stan probably knew more than he let on.

The fear in Stan's eyes was real. She liked it. Liked that he was getting payback for the terror he'd inflicted on her father, Mick, and her dog.

If Stan had been older, he might have had a heart attack by now. The guy panted like a dog in July. His eyes darted around, searching the darkened woods for hidden dangers.

"Sit down on the ground," Mick directed him.

Then, Mick took Becca by the arm, pulling her away from the felon before he turned and looked her directly in the eye with a no-nonsense expression.

She stared back at him, waiting for what she already knew he was gonna say.

"I want you to stay here," he said in a low voice as if worried Stan might gather information to use later if things went bad. "Keep your cell phone turned on and wait for a call from me."

The cell phone battery was on its last bar. Soon, it would be useless.

"Mick." She stepped closer to him. "I should come with you."

He shook his head, a bit of tender entering his expression. "I need you here to let Grant know what's happening. He's coming with the SWAT team as fast as they can get here, but I don't want Rowdy getting away before they get here. I need you to call Grant and let him know if I don't get back to you within fifteen minutes. I want you to make the call to let him know something's up."

Her stomach clenched with fear.

"Mick," she said, the word dying off at the end, her voice losing strength. Her hand rose to her throat as if it could help her get out the protest.

His gaze softened, and he tilted his head toward her, wrapping his arm around her waist and pulling her into him. "I know," he whispered. "I know. But, just do it the way I'm asking you. As a cop, I'm calling it the way I see it."

He angled his head to look into her eyes. "Okay?" The sweetness in his expression nearly undid her, nearly brought her to tears.

But, she pushed back the tears, refusing to weaken, refusing to let emotion hold her back. She had to be strong. For her father. For Mick.

She stepped back, away from the gravitational pull of his body, that pull that made her want to hold him safely here. But she didn't break connection with his gaze. "You got it," she said, huskily, not quite keeping her voice from cracking.

That little bit of a break in her voice was all the weakness she would show. Mick needed to know she could handle this situation.

His eyes narrowed, his mouth straightened in a tight line, as if he too were holding in his emotions.

He took her hand, and, with a soft kiss to it began to back away. "Be as quiet as you can. If you haven't heard from me in fifteen minutes, call Grant who'll be in charge of the SWAT team. If for any reason you can't get hold of Grant, call Weston."

His eyes narrowed. "Then sit here and wait for them to show up."

She forced a tight little smile. "Make sure you call me in fifteen minutes," she said in a commanding tone.

He grinned at her bravado even under these circumstances. "Got it."

Then, he walked over to Stan, grabbed him by the back of the neck, pulled him to a standing position, and melted into the night.

Becca gasped as he disappeared, all comfort vanishing with him, all surety, all sense that everything would be okay.

She stifled the cry that wanted to break free, to bring him back, to make sure that at least he would survive. But, she bit down on her lip, bit down the need to protect him.

Because her father's life was at risk.

And she would do anything to save him.

Give anything?

Even Mick?

That wasn't fair. She wasn't trading one for the other. She wasn't. Mick was doing what he did, as he'd said so often. Rescuing the vulnerable, going after the bad guys.

"Come here, Barley." She whistled softly, bringing the dog back to lean against her, welcoming the comfort of a living presence.

She looked down at her cell phone, noting the time, beginning the countdown, trying to ignore the blinking battery sign. If Mick didn't contact her in fifteen minutes, and the SWAT team hadn't arrived by then?

God help her, would she be able to keep her promise to just wait?

To ignore the fact that her father and Mick could be bleeding out, somewhere out there in the dark?

# CHAPTER TWENTY-FIVE

A cool breeze blew up the mountain, rustling through the trees, blowing pine-scented air across her skin. On any other night, it would have been the perfect evening.

A perfect evening to share with Mick.

In the old days, they would have lain on the front hood of his truck, staring up at the sky, watching for shooting stars, talking about their day and plans for the future.

She squeezed her eyes shut for a quick second, pushing back the fear that they might never have those normal moments again.

Might never have their conversation disrupted by her father calling to ask if they were coming to the house on Sunday for dinner. Was she going to cook it, her dad would laughingly inquire.

A rustle in the bushes caused her to jerk her eyes back open, her hand tightening on the butt of her pistol. She peered into the moonlit woods.

Barley tensed, a low growl rumbling in his throat.

"Shhh," she whispered, barely making a sound, holding him tightly, touching his back with her gun hand, the other hand tight around his mouth, just in case he decided to bark.

She'd have left him in the SUV but was afraid he'd bark more there.

There was no good solution to the Barley problem. She'd tie him to a tree and leave him but then he would surely bark, and give her and Mick away.

So, here he was with her.

A second later, a possum waddled out, with the strange side-to-side walk that only a possum could carry off. Its little gray body reflected in the moonlight and it stopped to peer at her and Barley for a long moment, with deep black eyes, before waddling away again, a ghostly gray in the nighttime.

She released the breath she'd been holding, letting it whoosh out. What sort of a lookout did she make if a possum could so easily sneak up on her?

She squatted down further in the bushes, scanning from side to side, and occasionally behind her, just in case anyone tried to sneak up from that direction.

She listened so hard that she finally couldn't discern the noises within her own body from those in the woods, the pumping blood in her neck sounding like someone walking through the woods. It was difficult to know if she imagined a noise or actually heard one.

It felt like she was going insane, with sensory deprivation or overload, she couldn't tell which, every sense so heightened that it was overwhelming.

"Calm down," she coaxed herself as if she were one of her students.

Barley looked up at her. She rubbed his back, as much for her own comfort as to reassure him.

Time seemed hard to measure, with each heartbeat feeling like a thousand ticks of a clock. She hit her cell phone button, causing the face to come to life, glowing in the night like a lighthouse beacon.

Ten minutes had passed. Damn it. Where was he?

She stood up, breathing heavily. He should have been back or called her. The phone was on vibrate, so she checked it again. No missed calls. No text messages.

Nothing.

Except the blinking button that said the cell phone was almost out of battery.

"God, no, please hold on," she prayed. Let the damn battery

last just a bit more.

She couldn't call Mick, taking a chance that the phone would light up or something at just the wrong moment, even though he had put it on silent.

She waited a couple more minutes, hoping for a text. Then, the phone made that horrible sound that signaled the battery was really about to give out, that last gasping croak it made before it would suddenly go dead.

Her heart rate accelerated as if she'd been running hard for the last fifteen minutes.

She dialed Weston.

"Weston." Her voice quivered, even though she'd tried to keep it strong. "My cell phone's about to die. I haven't heard from Mick. Have you?"

"Nnnuhh," he gave a negative growl. "It's okay though, sugar, I'm not far away now. You okay?"

"I'm okay. I'm out here in the woods waiting with Barley. So, don't shoot me when you get here if my phone dies and I can't contact you." She tried a little laugh but it came out as something closer to a sob, her voice breaking on the last word.

"Hold strong, sweetie. Mick will be fine. You need to worry about the guy or guys he's going after."

She laughed just a bit. Weston's tone of voice could make you laugh even if he were talking about the most inane thing.

"Hurry and get here," she said.

Before she could hang up, he said, "Becca?"

His tone told her something bad was coming.

She held her breath, bad news starting to become as natural as the new moon above her.

"The GBI didn't find Rowdy tied up at the cabin like you said."

"Oh, God." Her temples began pulsing. "So, that means the group is wise to what's been going on. Rowdy would have told them. They could figure the rest out. Rowdy could be with my dad at this cabin, with a real bone to pick with me and Mick. That could be who's waiting for Mick in there. This has to be a trap."

She sucked in air. "Do you think they've figured out the connection between me and Mick, and used my dad to lure us back in?"

"Don't know, sweetie." He hesitated. "I think we have to figure anything could be on the table. We don't really know what the hell is going on. But, listen Becca, I'm coming in to help. Grant will be there real soon with his SWAT team if Forrester and I don't beat him there. Be strong."

She could barely speak but forced out, "Okay. Get here quick." She pushed the disconnect button, knowing he could drive faster without the distraction of her on the phone.

How far away was the SWAT team? Mick had said Grant was gathering them together as fast as he could. But, what did that mean?

She felt so useless here in the woods, waiting.

Things could go so wrong, so fast. And then her dad or Mick could bleed out in seconds, with no one to help them.

She began panting, short quick breaths that never seemed to get oxygen to her brain. She hit the button to light up her phone so she could see the time. It seemed like so much more time had passed than fifteen minutes.

She hit the power button on her phone but nothing happened. It was completely dead.

A sick feeling swirled in her stomach.

Surely, she would have heard shots if something had gone wrong.

Unless someone had sneaked up on Mick, waiting in the woods for him. He and her dad could be tied up, just waiting to be killed.

Would Rowdy kill them quickly because he knew others must be coming after him and he needed to get away?

The evil that was Rowdy demanded her presence, demanded that she back up Mick no matter what she'd promised.

She couldn't wait here, helplessly. She had to go in and help her father, help Mick.

Not sit here and let them die.

She stood up. What should she do about Barley? Finally, she just let him trail behind her. "Ssh," she said to him. "No barking."

Thank goodness, she'd used those same words to him so many times over the years that he knew what they meant. On walks, she'd used those words when they encountered a strange dog that made Barley want to bark.

And the command had become so engrained in him that a quiet, simple *Ssh* was usually enough to silence him.

Though it hadn't worked when Mick had gone back in to the militia cabin. Barley's protective instincts were so strong that he'd charged in to help Mick.

But the shush order had to work tonight.

Because she was going in.

With her gun gripped in both hands, her eyes scanning constantly in front of her and from side to side, she advanced in the direction Mick had gone.

Her sense of direction was good, something Mick and Tess had always remarked about, laughing at how good she was in keeping her sense of north and south.

Mick had said that if he walked through the woods, keeping the road to his left that he would reach the cabin pretty quickly.

So, if she got lost, then she just needed to move to her left until she found the dirt road as a marker.

As silently as possible, she crept through the dark woods, cringing at every crunch beneath her feet. Thank goodness for the rain the night before because the leaves were soggy and matted, with only an occasional twig cracking beneath them.

As if nature wanted her and Mick to succeed in their mission to rescue her father.

If anything happened to her father, she didn't think she could stand it. The man who'd always been so kind to everyone, in the hands of the most ruthless man she'd ever met.

Mean for the sake of mean, seemed to be Rowdy's motto.

Mean cause why not?

Had someone mistreated him as a little boy to make him so

mean?

Her hand gripped the gun tighter. It didn't matter anymore what had made him that way, it just mattered that he was that way.

And the quicker her father was out of his grasp, the sooner her heart rate could return to normal.

Then, she saw it. A dark mass in the woods.

She peered at it, willing its shape to make sense.

Finally, the lines began to solidify and separate from the bushes surrounding it.

He'd built a tiny cabin that couldn't be more than one room, with windows that seemed blacked out. The tiniest glow escaped a few cracks so that she felt certain someone was inside.

An SUV was parked not too far from it. She could barely make out its shape off the road that was separated from the cabin by some distance, almost as if to hide the cabin from view if someone happened to casually drive up the rutted dirt road.

Then the lights that had shone from a few cracks suddenly went black.

What did that mean? Did he know they were out there in the woods, darkening the cabin completely so they wouldn't be able to get their bearings on the place?

Where was Mick? He had to be out there somewhere.

Unless he was hurt, perhaps stabbed, bleeding out onto the cold, unforgiving ground.

She tried to still her breathing, quiet the noise in her head, so she could listen for moans, for a call for help.

Nothing. An owl hooted and she jumped. Then, she took a long steadying breath.

She would not fail on this mission to help her father and Mick. She wouldn't.

A thousand night noises filled the air, crickets, bushes waving in the breeze, wind whistling through the treetops.

But, nothing man-made.

Then, a creaking in the direction of the cabin sounded

loudly. Different from all the natural sounds.

As if Rowdy had been waiting for her arrival, the front door opened and two figures emerged. One pushed the other before him.

The slight light from the new moon bounced through the trees and illuminated her father's face.

She sucked in her breath, tightening her lips against the scream that threatened to rip from her throat. Touching Barley slightly, then pulling him in against her left leg, she silently reassured him, praying he didn't bark.

Rowdy's face also emerged from the shadows and light bounced off the gun in his hand. With his other hand, he shoved her father toward the SUV.

Her father almost fell under the force of the blow but Rowdy yanked him up by the back of his jacket. "Don't even try that, old man," he snarled.

A fierce, ripping anger gripped Becca. How dare he talk to her father that way, treat him this way.

A killing urge pulsed through her. For the first time in her life, she knew she could kill a man.

Specifically, the man who treated her father with such disregard and held a gun on him so casually, making it clear he would use it on him without a second thought.

A crack in the bushes alerted her and Rowdy at the same time. He swung her father around so he served as a barrier between himself and whatever was coming his way.

"Stop right there, Atlanta. I know it's you." Rowdy's ugly tone rang through the night. "I'll kill the old man. Believe me, I'll do it."

Becca didn't doubt it for a second.

Blood began to pump through her, begging for Rowdy's blood, howling like a wolf that wanted to rip his flesh.

She wanted to spill his blood on the forest floor, fertilize this ancient earth, before Rowdy could do that to her father or to Mick.

# Chapter Twenty-Six

She began to creep closer. But, before she could do anything, Barley charged at Rowdy, with a vicious wild dog growl, like something that had emerged from the woods, with his own need for flesh.

"What the . . ." Rowdy turned to fire a shot toward Barley. But, it seemed like her father shoved into him, causing Rowdy to lose his balance and stumble backward, his arm swinging up wildly as he fired.

Barley yelped as if he'd been hit anyway.

"No!" Becca screamed. She stepped out halfway from behind the tree she'd used as protection and aimed toward Rowdy. "Shoot again and I'll kill you, Rowdy!" she yelled.

Maybe if she caught his attention, he'd be distracted so Mick could get to him.

It worked. Rowdy's head jerked toward her, his gun swerving up in her direction. Again, her father shoved into Rowdy, knocking him sideways.

At the same time, Mick charged forward, bursting from the nearby bushes, grabbing Rowdy's gun hand. Rowdy fought with Mick, her father getting knocked down as the other men struggled over the weapon. Two shots fired off. Any one of them could kill her father, Mick, or Barley.

Mick twirled him around so that he faced the other way, as if he'd thought the same thing. Another shot fired off into the woods.

Becca rushed forward but caught her foot on something and fell, her gun flying off into the bushes. She looked for it but in the dark had no idea where it had gone. So, she jumped up and grabbed Rowdy's head, jerking him backward. Mick pushed Rowdy's gun up into the air.

Her father regained his footing, turned and charged Rowdy, butting him full force in the stomach, using his head as a battering ram.

"Eghhh." Rowdy grabbed at his stomach with his one free hand but Becca held his head back preventing him from doubling over in pain. Rowdy reached for Becca with the hand that was free of Mick.

But, the judge grabbed onto Rowdy's other hand with his mouth, biting. Hard, apparently, because Rowdy screamed in agony.

With one final wrench, Mick freed the gun from Rowdy's grasp, tossing it away, but Rowdy continued struggling.

"Son of a bitch, stop fighting," Mick growled at him.

Becca's father butted Rowdy in the stomach again. "Old man, my eye."

Mick brought his gun to Rowdy's head, which brought a quick end to the fight. "Are you handcuffed, Judge?"

"No. The punk's got me zip tied."

Mick laughed, and nervous laughter broke free from Becca as well. The adrenaline had her so jacked up that she could have moved a car if she'd needed to. And now her body was letting off steam with laughter.

"Get my knife and cut his hands free, Becca. It's on my hip."

Becca reached for the knife and quickly cut through the little plastic ties that secured her father's hands.

"Take him, Judge, while I go and check there's no one else in that cabin."

The judge took Rowdy's other arm and twisted it behind his back, into a hold designed to prevent Rowdy from moving unless he wanted to endure a wrenching pain.

211

"Aagggh, let go of me." Rowdy's face twisted in distress.

For almost a second, Becca enjoyed it, enjoyed seeing pain in the eyes of the man who'd held a gun on her father. And planned to do God knows what to him. He'd treated her dog like garbage, not caring if he'd killed him.

He had planned to kill her and Mick, she felt sure.

So, for just a second, she took an evil pleasure in his discomfort.

Then, she remembered Barley.

"Barley!" she yelled. "Barley, where are you?"

A growling filtered through the chaos in her brain, and she looked down to see Barley with Rowdy's pants leg in his mouth, ripping at it.

Barley released his hold on the fabric and went after Rowdy's ankle.

"Get the dog off'a me, get him off'a me!" Rowdy howled.

Barely took revenge on the man who'd swung him in the air by the skin of his neck, flung him through the SUV and kicked him without mercy. She hated to end it, but finally, reluctantly, she called to him. "Barley, Barley, that's enough. Heel, Barley."

The dog released his bite on Rowdy, and looked up to her, then he ran around and jumped on her dad's leg, pawing at his knee.

"Good boy, Barley," her dad said, still holding onto Rowdy's arm. "Good boy. Way to get a scumbag."

"I'm the scumbag? I'm the scumbag?" Rowdy spit out. "You sit up there on that bench, thinking you so high and mighty, thinking nobody can touch you."

Her father pushed up on Rowdy's arm until Rowdy howled with pain.

"Never antagonize the man who's got the immediate power to hurt you, boy," her father said with a vicious bite she'd never thought possible.

He'd always been known as the man to give wisdom from the bench and kind words of hope for the people to whom he felt forced to mete out justice.

Known for giving people as much of a second chance as he could.

But, this was different. Her father had feared for his daughter for days and now had justice in his hands, in a real, physical manner.

She sensed her father wasn't entirely in charge of his own emotions right now.

Mick came out of the cabin, and seemed to realize just how close to the edge her father had been pushed.

"I got him, Judge," Mick said, taking hold of the arm the judge had pushed way up Rowdy's back. "I got him."

Slowly, reluctantly it seemed, her father took his hands off Rowdy. He drew in a long, shaky breath, then shook his head as if trying to slough off the rage that gripped him.

"Now," her dad said. "I understand how hard it is for cops not to kill someone like him, once and for all, when they have the chance to finally rid the world of such an evil force."

The seriousness of Mick's face told her how truthful the judge's words rang.

"Like you've told me countless times, Judge." Mick looked directly into her father's face. "A cold, lonely cell with the bars clanging shut for the rest of his life will be so much harder to take than a quick death."

Her father nodded his head firmly. "Don't give him a martyr's death his buddies can glorify. Let him sit in a stinking prison cell for the rest of his days."

Rowdy struggled, trying to get out of Mick's grasp. Mick just pushed his arm further up his back.

"Stop it," Rowdy howled.

"I'll stop," Mick growled close to his ear. "Because I follow the law. If I were like you, I'd finish you off right now. But, I'd rather think about you going to jail for the rest of your life. Then, once you're sentenced, I won't think of you anymore."

"Old man, my ass," her dad said, with a laugh. "I'll show him old man."

He laughed heartily and Becca went to him, wrapping her arms around him as he pulled her close.

"I guess he didn't know you work out, huh Daddy?"

"Guess not, sugar cake." He held her close, enveloping her with his daddy smell, that cologne they'd given him every Father's Day still lingering on him.

"Guess he didn't know how tough both of us are." He kissed her on the cheek.

She pulled back to look him in the eye, saw Mick looking at them both with an affectionate expression, and said, "He didn't know who he was messing with, you, me or Mick."

"Mick, huh?" Rowdy said, his lip curling up. "Guess our ladies man told you his real name."

"Did he tell you what his real job is, Rowdy?" She glanced at Mick who didn't motion for her to be quiet, then looked at Rowdy with a smile. "He's a cop, a former Atlanta Police officer, currently an FBI agent."

The change in Rowdy's expression paid her back for all the fear, the physical hardship, everything she'd gone through the last few days.

"Yeah, that's what I'm talking about," she said with a smile.

Then, another thought took the smile off her face.

If Rowdy didn't know, why had he set Mick up as the guy to get blown up when they'd met the truck bomb in downtown Atlanta?

Had someone else among the militia group known? And if so, how?

Who had set Mick up to die?

## CHAPTER TWENTY-SEVEN

Mick paced the floor, going from window to window of a lake house owned by a judge friend of Becca's father. Being cooped up, a passive player, was tough, not his style.

But, he couldn't trust anyone else to keep Becca and the judge safe, not until he'd figured this thing out.

Thank goodness for the small group of Atlanta Police officers, all friends of Mick, Weston and Luke, who were helping out, guarding the exterior of the house and property.

He'd called the FBI's Special Agent in Charge of the Atlanta division directly, and he'd taken over the investigation because of so many holes in this operation.

Mick had made the call to the bureau chief because he no longer felt safe under the direction of Hernandez.

Right now, the bureau chief was trying to find out exactly where Hernandez was and how he fit into this whole deal.

Was Hernandez dead? Kidnapped by the people who'd taken Becca and the judge? Had he been acting under duress when he'd taken Mick's phone calls? The same as Becca had when she'd phoned her dad?

There were too many unanswered questions. And that could get somebody killed. It wasn't gonna be Becca or the judge.

Mick's phone vibrated on his hip and he answered. "Hey, Weston."

"Hey, Mick. Me and Roberto are coming in."

"Great." Roberto, his partner from the FBI, the guy he'd

worked with for the last year would be a welcome sight. He needed someone in the FBI he could brainstorm with, someone he could trust.

Minutes later, he opened the door to his former good friend on the Atlanta Police force and his new best friend from the FBI.

Weston gave him a fist bump. "I'll be inside in just a minute." He turned to talk to Reggie, another of their Mick's old buddies from APD.

Mick and Roberto shook hands, coming in for a guy hug, one hand going around the other to pat him on the back.

Roberto pulled back and looked him in the eye with disbelief. "Man, I don't know how this got so out of hand."

"Yeah, it's crazy." Mick rolled his eyes. "I'd liked to have had you on the job, backing me up, someone I could trust."

You could get tight with someone when you worked that closely on a day-to-day basis, listening to the other's ideas on a case, talking evidence through and coming up with theories.

Roberto's eyes narrowed into a furious glare at some imaginary person to the left of Mick. Hernandez, Mick suspected. "This is why Hernandez wouldn't let me be involved in the operation," Roberto said, anger melting over the words.

It was good to see the righteous fire in Roberto's eyes. You couldn't fake that.

"This is an abuse of power and a level of criminality that is unbelievable," Roberto added vehemently, like any law officer would if he believed what Roberto did. Roberto had immediately gone to his default position about Hernandez. He'd never liked the guy.

"We don't know what's going on for sure," Mick said, not quite pulling off the "let's be non-biased" expression. "I want to be fair, give him the benefit of the doubt."

"Come on, don't we know?" Roberto widened his eyes. "I've always had a funny feeling about that guy."

"Let's talk in the kitchen." Mick hadn't confirmed to the guys what he'd begun to think about Hernandez. He wanted to hear their opinions and let them draw their own conclusions.

He waved Roberto back toward the kitchen, which had become home base for everything. The judge sat at the table.

Becca stood at the stove. She glanced over her shoulder, with a polite smile at Roberto.

Roberto smiled back, with his trademark warmth. That smile had opened countless doors, opened the minds of witnesses and brought them so many new pieces of information they might never have gotten, except for that smile.

Becca's eyes crinkled in response. She turned toward him. "Mick said you were coming. Thought it was great, and that you were the only guy at the FBI he really trusted right now."

Roberto's smile turned soft, a real smile from the heart, not his "best cop smile".

"I've got his back. Wish I'd been there all along. Hernandez wouldn't let me, though, said he had another project that needed just my touch." He shook his head. "That was bull. A novice could have handled that case. Mick could have handled it."

Mick laughed at the needling, because he'd been the novice two years ago when he'd joined the agency.

Roberto had called him that for the first month they'd worked together. "Let the novice do that," he'd say, sore they'd moved his partner on to another office.

Roberto had missed his partner. Mick understood that, the memory of Tess one of the reasons he had to leave the Atlanta Police force.

Her memory had walked every hall he'd turned down, every street of their old zone.

So, he'd simply let Roberto get past the loss of his partner, and known that, one day, he'd have that same loyalty at his back that Roberto had shown for his old partner.

"This is Becca," Mick made the formal introduction and Roberto stepped forward, taking her hand in his, with a gentleness he'd only seen Roberto show to crime victims. And his mama, at a family picnic Mick had been invited to join.

Roberto had laughed at how his mother had taken to Mick,

pushing food on him, telling him she had a niece who needed a nice boyfriend.

Roberto had pulled him away then, laughing. "Don't get me wrong, bro. I like you," he'd said. "But, stay away from my cousins." He'd clapped him hard on the back, almost knocking his breath out.

"No problem," Mick had said, knowing it would be a long time before he'd be in any shape for another relationship, since the ghost of Becca had haunted his every night, dreams of her often disrupted by the sounds of shots fired, then Tess' yell as she was hit.

He looked away, out the window to the lake that glowed blue in the midday sun, willing himself out of the past, and into the present.

Mick looked back to see Roberto giving him that sideways look he'd always given him when he'd realized Mick had drifted away into his own thoughts.

Mick would come out of his thoughts, out of some painful memory, to find Roberto looking at him that way, not saying anything, leaving Mick to wonder what he'd just missed, how long he'd had a vacant look in his eyes.

Mick gestured toward the table and Roberto turned. "This is Judge Lawton Jefferson," Mick said.

"Call me Lawton." The judge stood up, extending his hand. "I try to get Mick to call me that but he always calls me 'Judge' or sir." He smiled wryly at Mick.

"The Honorable Judge Lawton Jefferson." Roberto took the judge's hand. "I've read your judgments. Gotta respect a judge who's as hard on the career criminals as he is soft on the little guys who just need a second chance."

The judge's eyes crinkled. "The thing is recognizing the difference."

Like he'd done with Mick as a teen, making all the difference in the world to a teenager who'd had nobody who had his back.

"Roberto Gonzales." Roberto eyed the judge with a trace of

awe in his expression. When had Roberto read rulings by the judge?

Weston came through the door then, his shoulders entering the room before any other part of him had. The guy was built for police work, big, smart. And funny.

First guy you wanted to call to meet you for a beer.

Weston pulled Becca in for a hug. "Heard 'bout what you went through, girl. Wish I'd known, I'd 'a kicked those guys' asses."

Becca leaned her face against Weston's shoulder for just a minute, then pulled back, and gestured toward her dad. "Daddy went through the same thing."

"Ahh, I'm all right," her father said with a laugh. "Takes more than a couple of scum buckets to ruin my day."

Weston walked around to guy hug the judge. Then, he turned toward the table, pulling out a chair, turning it around, then straddling it. "So, let's brainstorm." His tone of voice was as if they had to fix a roof, or a leaky faucet, find a plumbing problem.

Not like they were dealing with a couple of loose terrorists or an information leak.

"So, what did Hernandez have to do with all of this and why is he nowhere to be found?"

Roberto pulled back a chair and sat. Mick walked around to sit by the judge.

"Coffee?" Becca raised the coffee pot.

"Great," Weston and Roberto answered.

With coffee mugs in hand a minute later, they all looked at each other. Becca sat down at the table silently.

"Nobody's heard from Hernandez," Roberto started. "You're thinking he's dead?"

Mick shrugged. "Could be. This group has gone after a judge. And they hate federal government types. Why not an FBI agent?"

Weston nodded. "That's a possibility. They maybe had him the whole time, and Hernandez was taking your calls with a gun to his head."

"But," Mick said, looking off into the distance toward the lake. "Something feels funny."

Roberto cocked an eyebrow. "Ya think?" he said with a smartass tone.

Mick looked him in the eye. They'd always had this thing of feeding off each other's ideas. "He chose me for this assignment."

"Yeah, even though with the time you'd been with the bureau, you never should have done something like this." Roberto tapped the table hard with one finger. "But, Hernandez said you were perfect for it."

"Even when you said it wasn't a good idea," Mick finished his thought. "Sending me down to that prison in the very county where I grew up."

"Yeah." Roberto laughed. "How wrong was that?"

"Almost like the guy was trying to get me killed," Mick said what he knew Roberto was thinking.

"Guess he decided to take advantage of that death wish you were so famous for after Tess got shot," Weston chimed in.

Becca gasped and Weston's face fell. He turned to Becca, guilt painted in the lines around his eyes.

"I'm sorry, Becca," he said, his voice soft and gentle.

"Don't be." She leaned over and patted his hand. "We have to talk straight. This is no time to be sensitive to people's feelings."

She stood, turned toward the refrigerator, pulling the door open, looking inside.

"You got any orange juice in there?" Mick stood up, walking to stand behind her, putting his hand on her shoulder.

She glanced sideways at him and smiled, then laid her head on his shoulder. They stood there for a second, pretending to look at the contents of the fridge.

But, they both knew they only wanted the comfort of the other's presence. Becca pulled away first.

"Here it is." She pulled out a carton of OJ. "Anybody else

want any?" She moved over to the cabinets, taking out a couple of glasses.

"I'll take some," her dad said, his deep, rumbling voice sounding like the old days when Mick had spent so much time at their house that they'd already seemed like family.

She poured half a glass of orange juice into three glasses, took a surreptitious swipe at her eyes, then filled each glass with water and turned back to Mick, handing two to him since he stood by the fridge.

He pushed them under the fridge's ice maker, dropping a couple of pieces of ice in each, then handed one back to her, did the same with another she handed him, and took it to the judge. They all took their OJ the same way. Mick had gotten accustomed to it that way at their house.

Little moments like that reminded him of just how much they'd all become a family, melding their habits.

"So, this Hernandez guy feels funny?" Becca said, taking her seat at the table again, as if the emotional moment had never happened.

"Why would he be involved in this?" Mick looked across at Roberto.

"There's always been something weird about him in regards to you." Roberto stared off into space, drumming his fingers on the table.

"The way he micromanaged me," Mick acknowledged.

Roberto's gaze snapped back to meet Mick's. "I know, right? He'd come around and look over your shoulder to see what you were working on. How he said you didn't need to be looking into things that weren't on your case load."

"That drug cartel investigation." Mick nodded.

The judge met Mick's gaze. "And those boys who busted out of jail with you were picked up on drugs."

Mick looked at the judge for a second before Becca cut in. "You think this might actually be all about drugs and not about domestic terrorism?"

"Bingo," Roberto said. "I've been thinking about this ever

since you went undercover at the prison, that there was something hinky about the whole thing."

"Hinky?" Mick said.

"Isn't that how you gringos say it?" Roberto said with a grin. He'd started calling Mick a gringo when Mick couldn't take the hot sauce at the family picnic.

He was right. Their hot sauce had almost blown Mick's head off.

The thought that Hernandez could have allowed Becca and the judge to be hurt blasted through him, with an anger that was hotter than the pepper-filled sauce Roberto's family had ladled onto everything.

Had Hernandez wanted Becca and the judge to be killed?

For what purpose?

He pushed back his chair with such force, that when he stood, it almost fell over. Righting it to a wobbling stand, he walked into the other room, where they'd positioned Stan in a separate room from Rowdy so he couldn't be intimidated.

Rowdy and Stan had been officially read their rights, but neither had asked for an attorney. It was almost as if they were afraid to ask for one.

What was worse than going to jail? Torture, murder. Who were they afraid of?

Roberto followed Mick into the room, Weston close behind him.

"Stanley." Mick pulled a straight chair across from the chair Stan was handcuffed to and sat down backward, straddling the chair, looking Stan in the eye.

"Boss," Stan said. He'd so easily adjusted his frame of mind, to one where Mick was now calling the shots instead of Rowdy. The guy was malleable all right.

Roberto smiled his most winning smile at Stan, and Stan beamed back. Stan was gonna be a big asset in this whole investigation, into Hernandez and into the militia.

Roberto pulled out his smart phone and scrolled through the FBI's internal site until he found the staff photo of Hernandez.

He enlarged it until nothing showed but the head shot of Hernandez.

"Have you ever seen this guy?"

Stan looked at it. "Well, yeah. He's the big shot downtown who helps us fund all our militia stuff. I'm not supposed to be knowing that. But, I saw him one time and White said that was right, that's who he was. Said he helps us keep the drugs flowing so we can fund the militia activities."

Stan shook his head. "I never wanted to get involved in this drug running stuff. Rowdy said it was the only way, said the Mexican said we had to do it, for the money to fund the militia."

Roberto looked sideways at Mick, that glance that told him they'd gotten what they needed.

"Do you know where he might be?"

"Emm, he has a place up north of Helen. Seems like all these militia guys have a 'place.'" Stan laughed half-heartedly. "If I'd had a 'place', I'd a stayed there and never gotten involved in all this stuff." He shook his head, saying without words that he knew his life as he'd known it was over, a life with any sort of freedom.

He was right. Many people might have died if Rowdy's plan had gone off as planned. Actually, he and Rowdy were guilty of homicide because of White's death. Didn't matter that White was a bad guy, too.

Roberto got up and Mick followed him out. They went back to sit at the table.

"It's him, all right. Hernandez is the boss of this drug running ring," Mick said to the judge and Becca. "Or at least a big player."

"You're kidding me?" The judge's eyes narrowed. "An FBI guy doing this?"

"Yeah, this whole thing is all about the drugs," Mick chewed off the words. "The son of a . . ." He stopped himself before the curse word slipped out that had been the best one to describe someone like Hernandez. He'd never cussed in front of the judge, never would.

Roberto raised a hand. "I've had a funny feeling for a while now about this operation. That's why I sent a crew of the only guys I thought I could trust to watch his house. They said he, his wife, and the kids haven't been around since they've been there."

The guy was good. Ducking-even-before-the-sound-of-a-gunshot good.

Mick turned to meet his eyes. "Stan said he had a place up north of Helen. The thing is figuring out where that place is." He shook his head, silently using every curse word he could think of about Hernandez. Where the hell was that place Stan had mentioned?

"I think I know." Roberto stood suddenly, pushing back his chair with a violent start, and began pacing around the kitchen. "My old partner caught him looking at some pamphlets, with photos of houses, views of the mountains. Hernandez yelled at him, told him he shouldn't be sneaking around people. Bob told me he saw some other papers lying on the desk later, related to a real estate sale. Said it was pretty clear Hernandez had bought a big, hunking piece of land with a monstrous house on it. Said he didn't know where the guy got that kind of money, since he already had a home that was way above his pay grade."

"I checked tax records on it later and he'd put it in his wife's name, her maiden name. So it couldn't be traced so easily to him, I figure."

Mick looked at Roberto, things registering. "He wouldn't ever let anybody drop by his city house if they needed something signed after hours, made people meet him at a coffee shop near his neighborhood."

"Said he didn't want his wife getting mad at him doing business after hours," Roberto guffawed.

"Do you remember where that second home was?" Mick looked at Roberto, who was already pulling up something on his smart phone. The guy was great with that thing and computers.

"Yeah, here it is. I actually earth googled it and used my GPS at the time to check out its location, because me and my old partner thought it was so laughable, that he would have that kind of money. Said the guy was gonna end up in debtor's prison trying to keep that pretty young wife of his happy."

"You sure she didn't have the big bucks? Or maybe get the money from her parents or something?" Becca looked around the table at Roberto and Mick.

"I don't think so. I met her once when she first got here. Didn't look like she came from money." Roberto shook his head. "She didn't speak English, was straight out of Mexico and nothing about her was polished. No fancy haircut or manicured nails."

He and Mick's gaze instantly locked onto each other's, both thinking the same thing. The wife fresh out of Mexico. Another connection to the old country where Hernandez' father had emigrated from.

Connections for bringing in drugs?

"The few times I met his wife, I had to speak Spanish to her," Roberto added. "Hernandez spirited her away from me real quick." He tilted his head. "Kinda like he didn't want her telling me too much about her family or stuff like that."

"Paraded her out at the picnic," Mick added. "But then freaked out when he remembered that you and a few of the other guys could speak Spanish and could actually talk to her rather than just look at her, like me and the other guys had to do."

Becca raised an eyebrow at him.

Roberto tsked tsked. "Don't be judging him, girl. You would have looked too. She was something else. Can't blame any guy for looking at her. But, your boy here never had eyes for any woman." He smiled at her. "I can see why now, because you had pretty much taken up any space thinking about women can occupy in a guy's brain."

Becca smiled at him, with an expression that said he was in her good graces for life.

Mick gave Roberto a dirty look, talking out of school. Mick was the only man allowed to charm Becca and flirt with her. At least while Mick was in the room. "Back to business, eh?"

Roberto chuckled. Then, his face turned deadly serious. "There's something else that makes sense now. Hernandez was monitoring e-mails between you and Lawton here."

Mick tilted his head. "What do you mean?"

"I saw an e-mail from Lawton to you open on Hernandez' computer once. That's why I got interested in the judge, started reading his rulings and any article I could find about him."

Shock rocketed through Mick. "The e-mails about how we were going after these drug runners?"

Roberto nodded slowly. "I thought maybe you had forwarded them to Hernandez."

Mick slowly shook his head no.

"Chingao! Guys like him tick me off." Roberto's jaw almost locked it was so tight. "Reflects poorly on all my people."

"What?" Mick said seriously. "Cuz, we think you're all alike? That's like saying all Anglos say the word hinky."

Roberto's jaw relaxed. "Is hinky some sort of racial code word to white guys? A dog whistle?"

Roberto half smiled at Mick then his expression turned grim again. "We know what's going on here." He tapped the table with two fingers. "Let's go get this guy."

"Oh, yeah." Mick wanted to slap the handcuffs on that guy himself. He had payback coming.

"Let's ride," Weston said, hate filling his eyes. He spent so much time undercover, having to suck up his feelings about the scum he surrounded himself with, that when he got to personally take down some guy, he loved it.

Mick felt a surge of pleasure at the thought of locking up the man who'd organized the terrorization of Becca, the judge, and even little Barley.

Becca and the Judge. He couldn't leave them alone. "I'm staying here with these guys."

The judge's eyes narrowed. "We need to get this guy before he realizes we know everything and runs."

Roberto grimaced. "Most of the guys I trust not to get info back to Hernandez are down in Atlanta, waiting to see if he comes home." He shook his head slowly. "I need you backing me up, partner."

Mick looked back at the judge and Becca. He couldn't let anything happen to them. "I can't."

The judge leaned across the table. "I'm here to take care of Becca. You got those other APD officers outside. He won't get the jump on us again."

Becca nodded. "We both have guns now. You know I'm a better shot than you, anyhow." She grinned at Mick, with a challenging expression, daring him to deny that the last time they'd shot together she'd bested his score.

A slow grin spread across his face. "Uppity broad."

The judge laughed. "Always has been, always will be."

"You've got to go, Mick," Becca said, her face turning serious. "You have got to get this guy." She hesitated for a long enough moment that he knew what was coming.

"You have to get him for Tess."

# CHAPTER TWENTY-EIGHT

Four cars of police and FBI agents sped up the road toward Hernandez' North Georgia mountain getaway. Mick had Weston, and Luke, another of their good cop buddies, in the backseat of his car and Roberto in the front passenger seat.

Mick was driving Roberto's official bureau car. Roberto had gladly tossed him the keys, probably cause he didn't want to keep hearing Mick tell him to put his foot down on the gas.

"This 'cabin' sounds way too rich for any average FBI agent," Weston said and looked at Mick in the rearview mirror.

"A mountain place, a high-priced home in Atlanta, and expensive cars," Roberto chimed in. "Sounds more like a drug cartel associate than any mid-range governmental employee."

They all snorted agreement.

"Those cars in his garage," Mick blurted out in disgust, shooting Luke and Weston a look in the rearview mirror. "Roberto and I went by his place. We couldn't reach him on the phone ahead of time."

"Yeah," Roberto said. "You should have seen the looks me and Mick gave each other when we saw those vehicles. I joked, 'Got to get me one of those management positions.'"

"Yeah. I think he got some cars from Jay Leno's car collection. All of them had little circle insignias on the front, and windows that opened upward, like gull wings." Mick remembered the lineup in the guy's garage, with barely enough room for all of them. "It didn't add up even then. But, my radar hadn't been on the guy."

"An agent definitely wouldn't have so many toys." Weston laughed harshly and Luke nodded his agreement.

"What'd the inside of the house look like?" Luke asked with a half laugh. "Maybe it was totally empty. No furniture, just a big, old empty Mcmansion."

Weston laughed heartily at the image.

But, not Roberto. He grimaced as he pointed excitedly in the air with his index finger, turning to look back at Luke and Weston. "He didn't invite us in, and the garage door closed before he even came out, like it had been left open accidentally. We had to talk to Hernandez on the front porch, like some door-to-door salesmen. We needed the go ahead for an operation that came up quickly."

Luke and Weston were listening avidly. They both liked to know the type of person they were going after, to know just how much this guy stood to lose.

Thus, how dangerous he was. It was sounding like Hernandez had a lot to live for, a lot to kill for.

"We gave him the benefit of the doubt that Hernandez was a private person. Wanted to keep his work and family life separate. He is definitely not a talkative, friendly Latino, and now we know why. He's hiding something," Roberto said.

"Those guys still back there?" Mick looked in the rearview mirror, making sure they hadn't lost the other two cars. FBI agents that Roberto had picked personally and a couple of Atlanta Police officers authorized to assist in the operation, all personal friends of Luke, Weston and Mick, followed in other cars.

Mick drove fast, keeping up with the pace set by the lead car. But, something bothered him, flitting around at the edges of his mind.

The way it had bothered him since the night Tess had been gunned down. It was something that didn't let him sleep, weighed on his mind at odd moments, had him searching the Internet for answers.

Something just below the surface of conscious thought so

that when he awoke on certain mornings, he felt he almost knew what it was.

What was he missing?

What had he been missing for the last two years?

Suddenly, with no reason, his mind replayed, like a full-fledged movie scene, the last police picnic Tess had been alive.

A car had pulled up, with darkened windows, an Escalade, which is what had caught his attention. Marcos Ramirez, the Atlanta police officer who'd shown up to finally take down the drug dealer who'd killed Tess and put a bullet into Mick, had walked up to the driver's window, speaking for a few moments, then turned and walked back toward the picnic.

Tess had caught up to Marcos before he'd had a chance to get back to the group and they'd spoken heatedly.

When Mick had asked Tess what it was about, she'd shrugged and said Marcos was acting weird.

Suddenly, like a camera coming into focus, the face he'd seen in the window of the car materialized. It was Hernandez' face.

Marcos and Hernandez knew each other?

The night of Tess' shooting floated into the mix, and suddenly he realized what had bothered him so much for so long.

The answer to Tess' murder had been waiting in his subconscious.

Suddenly, everything seemed related, in clear focus.

"Son of a bitch!" Mick's heart lurched and he drove onto the side of the road, dust flying, skidding to a stop. The two following vehicles passed them, and he accelerated, whirling the SUV in a sharp U-turn back in the direction of the lake house.

Roberto grabbed onto the side handle grips and held on. No one spoke until they'd made it back onto the roadway and were speeding south.

"What's going on?" Roberto said.

"Marcos is back guarding Becca and the judge."

"Yeah. He's a good cop," Weston said. "Got top marks at the gun range this year."

"I saw him talking to Hernandez at the Atlanta Police picnic, the weekend before Tess was shot."

"You saw Hernandez at the police picnic?" Luke tilted his head, his eyes squinting at Mick in the rearview mirror, as if trying to envision it.

"Yeah, he pulled up in an Escalade, which definitely caught my eye around a bunch of cops," Mick said.

Luke nodded. "I remember that car. Me and Weston were arguing about the price. I said that's at least an $80,000 car."

"I remember," Weston snarled.

"Marcos talked to Hernandez real quick like and handed him an envelope. I could hardly see the driver's face, but now I realize what's been bothering me all this time. It was Hernandez."

Weston, Luke and Roberto all growled knowingly. "What was an FBI guy doing at an APD picnic?" Luke added. "It's not like the FBI travels in the same circles as us. And then, he didn't even get out and eat something?"

"When Marcos walked away, Tess walked up to him, in total cop mode, almost chest bumping him." Mick shook his head. "They had words, let's just say."

"Then she got shot." Weston groaned. "Marcos was at the scene. And happened to not save her life." He leaned forward, gripping the top of Mick's seat with both hands, shaking it hard enough that Mick felt the frustration rolling through him "And let's you get shot, Mick. Conveniently, almost taking both of you out."

"I wonder what she accused Marcos of," Luke said. "You know how she just put it all out there, sometimes, whatever she thought."

"Marcos was there awful fast that night she died, showing up like that," Mick said with the growing conviction that Tess' death had been an arranged hit.

"Damn, man." Luke met Mick's eyes in the rearview mirror.

"That night," Mick said. "I heard shots and ran back toward Tess. As I came around the corner, the drug dealer shot at me. I was hit."

It was almost too much, the memory coming forth full force, with all the emotions he'd felt that night. He sucked in a deep breath, then continued. "Marcos stepped from an alley and shot the drug dealer dead."

He shook his head. "But, it was almost like the drug dealer had seen Marcos and kept shooting at me. And he seemed shocked when Marcos shot him. Like they knew each other."

"Damn," Weston said. "That drug investigation Tess couldn't let go of. Said she thought it had connections to a cartel out of Mexico."

Mick swore fiercely. "Marcos was helping Hernandez. A dirty cop with a dirty FBI agent. They had Tess killed because she was getting too close to them. Maybe even actually accused Marcos to his face?"

"And the judge?" The intensity on Weston's face said he was buying it. "Perhaps," he conjectured, "they were just tired of him sentencing their people to such long sentences?"

"Or did they pick up on how closely he and Mick have been working?" Roberto half turned in his seat. "When Hernandez tapped into Mick's e-mail account, saw all he and the judge were doing, I think it scared the hell out of him."

"Son of a bitch!" Luke swore loudly from the backseat.

"Yeah," Roberto said. "Hernandez was on the phone, talking to someone about a judge when he had that e-mail up. He was speaking Spanish, as if no one could understand him. The guy was living in the past. Didn't used to be that many bilingual people in Atlanta. Now we work with several so I don't know what he was thinking." He laughed harshly.

"He was afraid of Mick and the judge. Saw they were on a mission to find the people responsible for Tess' death, to find the drug cartel members, local and abroad. Hernandez was scared if he didn't stop them, eventually they would find his connections. Or," Roberto raised his hand in the air like he'd just found a huge piece of evidence, "had found them already. Maybe he thought that's why Mick was there in the Bureau."

"Maybe they thought Tess had told them something concrete about Hernandez and Marcos," Weston said, like it was a foregone conclusion that Hernandez had come after Mick and the judge, not just a possibility.

"That bomb," Weston added, his voice darkening. "It didn't have near enough explosives to take down any buildings. No self-respecting terrorist organization would fuck up a chance that way. Probably just meant to kill you, Mick, get you out of the way."

"This has always been about getting me and the judge dead," Mick growled, "without pointing a finger at Hernandez. He didn't want to kill one of us at a time cause he was using the homeboys Rowdy, White, and Stan to get the job done. Then, they would have been the next to get dead."

"The mountain boys were a liability leading back to Hernandez once they got caught on the drug charges," Roberto said. "That high-priced lawyer that represented them, he could have easily given Rowdy all the directions Hernandez and his cartel needed them to know. Funny how some drug runners have these real expensive lawyers show up to get them an easy deal."

"You better call the agents going to his mountain home. I've got a feeling there might be a surprise waiting there for them. A bomb maybe?"

Then, the reality of just how dangerous Marcos was hit him. He had stayed behind, purposefully, to take out the judge."

Mick's blood practically exploded into his head, with a raging need to get back to Becca and the judge. He had to save them from this man who would stop at nothing to keep the drugs flowing, with all the money that poured into his pockets.

He had to stop Hernandez, Marcos and all the other murderous sons of bitches that were working with him.

The judge and Becca were being guarded by Marcos and two other cops. Marcos only had to kill the judge to cover his ass. He probably thought no one would connect him to Hernandez.

"Call the other cars and tell them what we're doing," he barked to Roberto. "Tell them to keep on toward the mountain house in case Hernandez is there. We don't want Hernandez getting away while we're concentrating on Marcos. Want to get the head of the snake."

Pulling out his own phone, Mick dialed Becca's phone, praying he wasn't too late. Praying he'd realized the truth, put the facts together in time to save her and the judge's life.

It rang into a vacuum, not connecting.

Damn it. His subconscious had known all this time. That's what had been eating at him.

He might not have been responsible for Tess' death.

But, if anything happened to the judge and Becca, it definitely would be because he hadn't put the pieces in his mind together.

It had all been waiting there in his head for him to solve. And, it had taken him this damn long.

He pushed the car to its limits. He had to reach the lake house before Marcos could silence Becca's sweet voice forever. And the righteous man who was her father.

And the closest thing to a real father Mick had ever had.

****

"Good idea, sneaking out like this, Dad." Becca grinned back at her father, conspiratorially.

The lake spread out before them like a glass plate, shimmering with sparkles of reflected sunlight.

They'd had to slip out for their walk, knowing it would grate against the cop side of Marcos and John, both by-the-book cops.

She'd known the two cops that didn't know her so well wouldn't have approved. But, Reggie, the cop at the back door who'd been a little sweet on Tess, had taken the time to get to know Becca at police events.

He'd smiled and said it was okay when they'd slipped out his door. Said there was no danger anyway, since only cops knew where they were.

The guns she and her dad stuck in their waistbands provided an extra sense of security. They needed to walk in the woods, put some distance between them and all that had happened, and have a father-daughter talk.

To process the last few days, she needed to hear everything her dad had experienced while they had both been kidnapped.

Barley cavorted nearby, nosing into leaves, then chasing the scent of something, as if he were just inches away from the animal that had left it.

"He's in high cotton, isn't he?" Her dad laughed at Barley, then threw his arm around Becca, pulling her into his side.

A deep sense of love flowed through her. Thank God, he hadn't been hurt.

"I'm okay, sweetie." He smiled, reading her mind, like always. "Now, tell me everything."

And she did. Almost everything.

She didn't tell him about her and Mick's night together. How even now she might be carrying Mick's child.

Life was so short and precarious that she wanted to grab it, start a new life, have the baby of the man she'd loved nearly all her life. No matter what else the future held.

They'd put marriage and family off so long.

Mick had wanted everything to be right, said they needed to concentrate on their careers. That everything else would come later.

Now, she was grabbing what she wanted, regardless of Mick's ideas of timelines.

She and her father turned toward the lake. They'd hiked to the other side of the lake before taking a break.

Pine-scented air ladled out contentment as the lake's surface rippled in the wind. A sense of peacefulness filled her, after all the turmoil of the last couple of days.

She felt so happy with her dad's arm around her, a place

that had always been safe.

"What time is it?" her father looked down at her. "How long do you figure till we hear something about whether they've got Hernandez yet?"

Becca pulled out her phone. Thank goodness one of the guy's cell phone chargers had been compatible with hers so she had been able to recharge her phone.

"Oh, wow, I got a text. I didn't even hear a ding or anything. It came in a while ago."

She read the message to her father, "This is Roberto. Mick wanted me to check in on you."

She texted back: *Everything okay, keep safe, tell Mick not to be too much of a hero.*

"They texted me at least twenty minutes ago." She looked toward the north in the direction of Hernandez' cabin. "I wonder where they are now."

A nervous shimmer ran through her. God, please don't let Mick, Luke, Weston, or Roberto get hurt. Don't let any of the cops get hurt, she prayed silently.

"Look." Her father peered out across the lake, pointing at something by the house.

"What the hell?" he said quietly, pulling Becca backward into the obscurity of the trees.

Marcos stalked around the side of the building, gun extended in front of him.

"What's going on?" Becca whispered.

"Don't know," her dad said quietly. "Maybe he thinks someone's around the house or something. I didn't see anybody drive up. Someone could have sneaked up on them."

He backed them further into the overgrown bushes, until they couldn't possibly be seen from the house.

"Come here, Barley," Becca called, kneeling and gathering Barley close to her side, putting her hand over his muzzle in case he decided to bark at a squirrel.

Her father narrowed his eyes and pulled his pistol from his waistband, checking it quickly. Becca followed suit and checked hers.

Her heart accelerated, her pulse beating in her ears as she peered determinedly at the house. "We need to go help them."

"There are three cops up there. We'd just confuse things. Maybe get caught in the crossfire." Lawton squeezed her shoulder.

Marcos continued around the corner and pointed his gun at Reggie. Reggie glanced at Marcos, then looked behind him into the woods, as if wondering what Marcos saw. He reached for his gun.

A shot rang through the clear country air. And Reggie fell. An electrical shock surged through Becca's body, almost as if the bullet had pierced her flesh.

Her father jumped too. "Jesus."

"Oh, Reggie, no," she whispered. "God, please don't let him die."

Her father drew in several shaky breaths, then took her by the arm. "Come on," he whispered, pulling her to her feet. "We've got to get out of here."

"The other officer," she said.

"We don't have time to get there. Hopefully, he heard the shot and will protect himself."

"Run," her father ordered in a harsh voice. The tendons in his neck strained, his jaw tightened and red blotches sprang out on his neck. "We need to get as far away from that house as we can."

Her sense of self-preservation kicked in and she complied, not because he was her father but because he was right. Barley took off in a spurt after her father, as if he felt their panic.

Her father ran and she had to push herself to keep up with him. He ran fast for an old guy.

Branches tore at her arms as she fled through the trees. But, adrenalin surged through her, obscuring the pain.

She reached for her cell phone to call Mick. Where was it? She stopped. It wasn't in her back pocket where she always stuck it. She patted every pocket. It was gone.

"We have to go back," she called to her father's retreating

form. "I dropped my cell phone."

Her father jerked to a stop, whirling to look at her. She'd never seen such determination on his face. "We're not going back for anything. We need to get as far from here as possible."

Her father's cell phone had been lost when he was kidnapped. With no cell phones, they were on their own, no contact with the outside world. They'd have to save themselves.

A fierce anger pulsed through her. She wasn't going down easily, wouldn't let them hurt her father.

Her father's body radiated steel, determination and defiance rolling off him. Together, they'd be a tough pair to break.

"Come on." Her father jack-rabbited into a sprint, with a glance over his shoulder to be sure she was following. She ran, pushing herself, closing in on him until she ran just behind him. "Why did he shoot Reggie?" she whispered breathlessly.

He shot her a look that said she knew why. "Save your breath for running," he ordered, his own words catching, as if rasping over exhausted lungs.

Marcos had to be connected with the people who had kidnapped her and her father. Dirty FBI agents connected to dirty Atlanta Police officers? A snarl of evil spreading across lawmen of Atlanta and the North Georgia Mountains?

A network of dirty connections?

It boggled the imagination.

Marcos had been there the night of her sister's shooting, the one who'd shot the drug dealer who shot her sister and Mick.

Instantly, the situation became crystal clear.

Marcos could have saved her sister, but, he'd let her die because she'd been so avid in her search for the drug dealers who haunted her police zone. Tess had searched for people like Marcos, wanted to root them out like the demons they were.

So, Marcos had let her die, maybe even arranged her death.

The need to avenge her sister's murder roared through her.

This guy and the people he was associated with had already taken out so many people, better trained and more professional people at fighting than her and her dad.

That didn't matter. The rage inside of her would equalize the fight. The responsible parties would pay for the loss of her sister's life. She would be the one to make them pay.

Marcos would be a good place to start.

\*\*\*\*

Mick barely held the SUV on the road as they careened around a particularly tight curve. But no one said to slow down, instead, they held on, their faces strained as tight as his hands on the steering wheel.

"Text Becca for me. Ask her to call me," Mick ground out. Roberto picked up Mick's phone.

Long minutes passed before Roberto hit a button to view Becca's return text. "Everything okay. Take care of yourself," he read off the phone.

"Why didn't she call like I asked?" He pushed his foot down on the accelerator. "Text her to ask Lawton how he's holding up. Say *Lawton*. Use his name, *Lawton*."

A second later, Roberto read back, "Dad says he's fine."

"That's not her sending texts," Mick said.

A running joke with them for years, because in person, he always referred to her father as the judge. But, as Lawton in texts. And she always answered back, *He's "The Judge" to you* or *The Judge is fine.*

Roberto started dialing even before Mick could say the words. Roberto grimaced a second later. "Went straight to voice mail." His eyes darkened, as if thinking the same horrible thoughts as Mick.

Weston clicked his phone shut. "Nobody's answering on any of the officers' phones. What the hell is going on back there?" His voice was rigid, biting, ready to chew nails and spit them back out.

"Call Grant, tell him to get his SWAT team activated, tell them exactly what is happening. This is all-out war. We know who the opposition is. It's Hernandez, Marcos and whoever else they have involved.

But, at least those two. Make sure Grant understands. We can figure out who else is with them after the shooting dies down. Tell Grant not to take anyone in with him that he's not absolutely sure of, that he's certain isn't dirty."

Weston dialed Grant as Roberto dialed the Southeastern Director of the FBI and filled him in.

When he hung up, Mick said what they all were thinking, "Everybody needs to know what this is about. Who would have thought there'd be a connection stretching all the way between an agent of the FBI and a police officer of the Atlanta Police Department?"

"No one." Roberto grimaced. "But, now that I do know, I am ready to shoot to kill these cabrones. No one else will be dead at the hands of these self-serving cabrones."

"Drug dealers posing as cops." Weston's face in the rearview mirror shone with hatred. "People ought to be able to call the police and know the good guys will show up. Not just the same victimizers who've hurt them but are wearing a uniform and a badge, with the courts ready to believe whatever version of the facts they testify to."

Mick knew something about Weston's family history and that he had a personal ax to grind with these guys as much as Mick did. That was good, cause they needed all the hatred and vitriol they could get on their side, motivating them as strongly as Hernandez and Marcos' desire to survive would make them.

Mick's gut churned. His subconscious had known the drug dealer that had been gunned down in that alley could have been stopped before he killed Tess.

Underneath his grief, he'd known he hadn't picked up on all the clues, all the bits of information that had pointed to Marcos, Hernandez and the drug cartel.

Damn Marcos. Damn Hernandez. Damn everything they stood for.

He would make these people pay for all they'd done, killing Tess and what they'd put the judge and Becca through. Then, he'd make them pay for dirtying the names of the Atlanta Police Department and the FBI.

They'd pay for it in time spent in jail for the rest of their lives. If they survived the next couple of hours.

Please God, don't let him be too late. He couldn't find the bodies of the two people he loved most in the world laying in a pool of their own blood, the way he'd found Tess.

Becca and the judge didn't deserve to die.

He hadn't prayed since the night he'd held onto Tess as she lay dying in a dirty Atlanta alley. Because he'd felt God had let him down.

But, God had kept talking to him, niggling at him until he realized what he needed to know.

He'd never prayed so hard as right now. Hopefully, God was still taking his calls.

# Chapter Twenty-Nine

A briar caught on Becca's arm, with a fierce clawing pain, releasing long, bloody rivulets that stung almost instantly as her sweat ran into the scratch. Dirt and blood and sweat covered every inch of her skin.

She wiped sweat from her eyes, the stinging begging for tears to rinse away the discomfort. They'd pushed through briar-filled bushes for almost an hour, trying to circle the lake.

Barley looked up at her, his little pink tongue curling out of his mouth as he panted. Even Barley was feeling the effort.

"It's going to be okay," her dad whispered.

"I know. I know. We're going to be fine," she lied back to him.

She pushed through a thick set of bushes and glimpsed a flicker of white. "The house," she whispered and pointed to her dad. "There's the driveway."

The bushes just in front of them were a final cover between them and the driveway.

"We've got him outnumbered, two of us against one of him," Becca whispered. "Though, he's probably untied Stan and Rowdy, increasing the odds in his favor." She turned to look at her father. "I wonder where they are."

He shrugged. "Could have gone into the woods looking for us, or someone could be waiting up there." He tilted his head toward the house.

The indecision was maddening. Go to the house and get

shot. Run up the driveway to the road and maybe get shot doing that. Stay where they were and have him circle round behind them.

Nothing was assured. There was no telling where the guy was now.

"Do you think we should head out the driveway, hope to find help, or is that what he'd expect us to do?" Becca peered at the house.

Lawton shrugged. "It's a toss up either way." He looked down the driveway toward the house, and then back up the driveway leading to the main road. Then, a quick glance over his shoulder into the woods they'd come through.

"We should go and see if any of the cops are alive and can still be helped," she said.

Her dad tilted his head, an indecisive look on his face. "If we go up there, we can see if we can help those guys. Maybe make a phone call. If this guy hasn't cut the lines."

Something told her Marcos would have thought of it. These guys seemed to think of everything and to have an awful lot of luck.

God, if only Mick would finish up his business with Hernandez and hurry back here.

"No," her father said. "Those guys are probably already dead. Even if they're not, our best bet is going for help for them and for us. It's not gonna help anybody if we get killed too. We need to put as much distance between us and this area as we can. Go to the road, see if we can wave a car down, call 911."

The idea of just leaving those police officers ate at her. But, her father was right. They needed to go for help.

Her dad nodded then took her by the arm. "Listen, Becca." His eyes narrowed. "If it comes down to you getting away, or trying to save me, I want you to run like hell. Run like hell and don't look back. I can take care of myself."

She opened her mouth in protest but he tightened his grip on her arm. "I've had my life. Yours is still ahead of you. I want you to live it."

He moved his hand to her shoulder bringing her in closer, looking her in the eye. "Promise me?"

Becca met his gaze, tears struggling to get out. She sucked in a long breath, and gave a promise she would never keep.

"I'll save myself at the expense of my father," she said wryly.

She would never do that, run for her life, leaving her father, the man who'd always been there for everyone else, the man who'd been mother and father to her, Tess and Mick, to face death at the hands of that bastard Marcos.

A man who turned on his own brothers and sisters in blue was a man who needed killing.

She'd be happy to do the deed. Another member of her family would not die because of him.

A steely strength flowed through her, giving her the determination needed to survive this man.

"Let's go," she said, like they were going out to get a bite to eat. Her dad gave her a grim smile, as if he'd read everything that had just run through her head.

Just then, Barley's little ears perked up as he swiveled to look down the driveway toward the road. Becca grabbed Barley, putting her hand over his mouth.

A rustling in the bushes sounded like a large figure, like Marcos coming for them.

"Toward the house," her father whispered. The decision was made for them. "Be quiet, Barley." Her dad pointed a finger at Barley and the dog almost nodded. Barley and her dad had an understanding, always had. He'd been the one who'd pointed the dog out at the shelter.

He'd been the one who'd saved Barley, and Barley always acted like he got that.

Like a father-daughter strike team, they sidled through the woods, heading toward the house, guns ready, looking ahead, behind and to the side of them as they went.

Then Barley yelped and took off down the driveway in the opposite direction of the house. He was a dog, after all.

"Go," her father whispered imperatively. "Go."

They took off running toward the house, branches slapping at them, the undergrowth suddenly becoming thicker as if just to spite them.

Becca twisted her head to get a quick look behind them, to see how close Marcos was to them, or to see if he had a co-conspirator.

But, only a deer ran up the driveway, Barley close behind.

"Dad." She grabbed his sleeve, pulling him to a stop. "It's only a deer."

He whirled to look just as Barley and the deer disappeared into the woods on the other side of the driveway.

"That doesn't change anything. Anyone coming after us knows exactly where we are now."

A quick flash of skin shone in the greenery to her left. She whirled and began firing.

Marcos shot back, his bullets kicking up dirt and gravel near her feet. She jumped behind a tree but kept firing off rounds.

Shot after shot after shot from her gun as well as her father's gun pelted the trees around Marcos, until he fell back into the woods, melting into the undergrowth.

A low moan sounded behind her. Oh God, her worse nightmare. Her father leaned against a tree, holding his side.

Pivoting, while still keeping her gun extended, Becca slid an arm around her dad's waist. He put one around her shoulders so that she helped support his weight. She didn't even bother checking out his injury. Because they both could so quickly be dead if Marcos came out firing.

"Run, Dad, run," she begged. And he did. Stumbling, his gait unsteady, he ran with her toward the safety of the house.

Becca fired backward, aiming at the trees Marcos had dove into, firing again, and again, hoping to keep him from getting another lucky shot off.

When her gun was exhausted of bullets, she grabbed her father's gun and kept firing.

\*\*\*\*

Mick and Weston jogged up the long driveway, their guns at the ready. They'd dropped Roberto and Luke off before they'd turned into the drive, so they could come in through the woods toward the back of the house.

Mick had parked the car near the road so Marcos wouldn't hear them driving in.

What would they find when they got to the house?

The house was still around several bends in the driveway when shots rang out.

Mick broke into a run, a flat out, gonna-get-there-before-anybody-dies run.

He left Weston behind as panic and adrenalin drove him in a raging fury.

He wanted to yell, needed to know if Becca was safe. But, he couldn't, had to keep running, wondering what he would find at the house.

Loud voices stopped him at the last curve in the driveway before the house. He moved forward, slowly, listening, trying to discern the words.

Finally, he darted around a tree and he could hear clearly. He couldn't see the people involved. But, he didn't need to see them to know exactly who they were.

Hernandez and Marcos.

"What an idiot you are! I can't believe I ever trusted you to do this."

That was Hernandez.

"Hey, I'm your cousin, your primo, you know I'll always be there for you. No one has your back like family," Marcos answered loudly. Sounding self-righteous, as if he weren't a murderer.

"These local rednecks were supposed to take care of all of them at the same time," Hernandez growled. "Make it look like homegrown terrorism. This is too screwed up now. No one will buy that we're not involved."

"Yeah, they will. We just gotta kill the judge and his kid, then we shoot the two crackers in there, put a gun in their hands, shoot it off a couple of times so they have gunpowder on their hands, and kaboom, a murder by escaped felons and I'm a hero, coming in and taking them out."

"You're a hero. What about me? I've run a completely screwed operation. They will look long and hard at me." Hernandez cursed loudly, frustration blowing out of his mouth with every syllable.

"So, just don't go back, primo," Marcos said, like it was clear to understand.

Mick angled for a shot around the tree. He looked behind him. Where was Weston, somewhere in the trees behind him, or angling to the left to get a bead on these guys?

"I need to get to my plane and get the hell out of the country till things quiet down. You need to come with me," Hernandez ordered like he was still in charge, still calling the shots. "The network's in place. It will just about run itself."

"I ain't going back to Mexico ever." Marcos' tone turned ugly. "The cartels down there are gunning for me. I'll be a dead man. If everybody who can rat us out around here is dead, then we'll be okay. Let's just go in and finish off that judge and the girl. Then, we can figure out what damage control we need to do."

"You'll be okay, you mean. You'll be a hero. It would take a genetic engineer to figure out how we're related, with the different family names and all." A growl of disgust from Hernandez said more than any words could express.

Marcos took off running for the house before Mick could get into position to take a shot. Hernandez also started running, but Mick yelled, "Stop!" To slow him down more than anything, since he didn't really feel the need to warn the guy at this point, to give him time to give himself up. Cause, it was apparent this guy wasn't going down easily.

Hernandez pivoted, his gun pointed toward Mick. Mick quickly noted the outline of a bulletproof vest under Hernandez' shirt and fired, hitting him in the hip.

Hernandez howled and rolled on the ground, but came up running, stumbling closer to the house, into the cover of a group of trees.

Mick tried to get a fix on Marcos as he headed toward the house but lost sight of him as he ducked into the tree line.

Then, he saw Hernandez dart out of the trees and run toward the house, faster than anyone who'd just taken a bullet in the hip should be able to travel.

Adrenaline. The drug of choice in shootouts.

"Stop!" Mick yelled again.

Hernandez swiveled, pointing his gun. Mick ducked behind a tree as Hernandez fired round after round, wild bullets pinging everywhere.

Mick waited until Hernandez had exhausted his clip. Then, Mick stepped out and trained his gun on Hernandez. "Stop!" he ordered. He'd rather the guy spent a long time suffering in a cell than get off quickly by dying.

But, Hernandez wasn't giving up. Mick trained his gun on Hernandez' forehead as Hernandez jammed a new clip in his gun and raised it. Before he could get it level, Mick fired.

A killing shot sent a bullet straight into Hernandez' head. He crumpled and didn't get up.

Warily, Mick ran toward him, watching for Marcos, expecting at any moment he would turn to protect or at least try to aid his cousin.

But, he caught a glimpse of Marcos running on toward the house, leaving his cousin to die in the dirt, alone.

Mick leaned over and checked for a pulse.

Dead.

One threat down.

He darted to the last tree before the house, looked to his left and saw Weston behind another tree, taking out his phone. Weston pointed toward the back of the house, indicating he'd call Roberto and Luke, telling them Hernandez was taken out but that Marcos was at the house.

Mick surveyed the house, watching for Marcos.

Was he killing Becca and the judge right now?

He broke and began running toward the house with fierce, pumping legs that took him closer and closer. He had to be in time. He had to.

A shot rang in the air and he fell to the ground, rolling, ending up with his gun pointed toward the house. Two more shots fired.

They weren't firing at him. He jumped up and charged toward the house.

Running as fast as possible, he reached the porch and headed toward the other side of the house. Slowing as he reached the corner, he stuck his head around for a quick look.

Marcos lay on the porch, flat on his back, blood and shattered glass covering him. A shot out window said he'd been shot from inside the house.

Becca peered around the doorway, gun in hand. She made eye contact with Mick. "It's me, Becca," he said before he came out from behind the side of the building.

She nodded, stepped outside and pushed Marcos with her foot. He didn't move, his eyes staring lifelessly.

Mick raced forward, checking Marcos for a pulse. Dead. He picked up Marcos' gun, shoving it in his waistband.

"Are there any more of them that you know about?" He grabbed Becca by the arm. He needed to touch her, reassure himself that she was alive.

A pulse of relief shot through him at the feel of her living, warm flesh under his hand.

"No. Stan and Rowdy are still inside, tied up. But, my dad's shot. We need an ambulance." She swiveled away from him and raced inside.

He followed her to a closet on the first floor.

She opened it. Blood was the first thing Mick saw. Lots of blood. His stomach clenched at the sight of the judge's blood.

The judge's face was pale, one hand pressed to his side. Blood seeped down his shirt.

Mick stepped in and leaned over to put an arm under his arm, lifting him to his feet, then to an armchair.

"I'll get some towels to use for pressure," Becca said, then fled toward the bathroom. The pressure would stop the blood loss.

It had to, or the judge was done for.

"I'll have to have this place cleaned for my judge buddy." The judge grinned weakly.

"A bullet in you and you're still kidding around?" Mick said, hoping to keep him talking, keep him from going into shock.

"When better to joke? If you're going out, leave your family with a smile on their lips." Then, he shook his head. "But, I'm not going out. I refuse to let some scumbag, drug-dealing, dirty cops kill me."

Mick couldn't help the grin that spread across his mouth.

Becca returned with several towels, and placed one against her father's side, then pushed into it.

"Emph," her father gave a reactionary groan.

"Sorry," she said.

"S'alright," he mumbled, his mouth tight, obviously trying not to show weakness to his daughter.

Mick looked down at this man who would go with dignity, even if it were from a bullet from a scum-sucking dirt bag.

A knifing shard of pain stabbed him, almost making it impossible to breathe. Was he watching the man he loved more than any other man in the world die?

He turned away so neither the judge nor Becca could read his face "I gotta be sure an ambulance's on the way." Mick pulled out his phone and began punching in some numbers.

Just then, Weston came into the room, gun extended, scanning for any further threat. "Any more of them?" He eyed Mick and Becca.

"Not that I know of," Becca said. "But, then I didn't know any of these guys were dangerous until they started shooting at cops, then at us."

"How's Reggie and Phil?" she asked.

Weston looked away and didn't answer. That was answer enough.

"Oh no," she moaned softly.

Weston walked over to take over the job of applying pressure to the wound on the judge's side, and Mick put an arm around Becca, pulling her into his chest for just the brief moment that she let him hold her, then she pulled away, leaning down to check on her father.

"Looks like it's just the one wound," Weston said.

The judge nodded. "Just the one lucky shot."

He wasn't giving anything to those guys. Not acknowledging in any way that they'd gotten one over on him.

"You're going to be okay, Dad." Becca patted him on the arm.

"Damn straight I am," he growled. "No scumbag, drug-dealing, dirty cops are gonna get the best of me."

Mick laughed harshly. "Their full names, Scumbag, Drug-dealing, Dirty Cops." He tilted his head at the judge. "Add dead to that list."

"Only fitting," the judge forced out through tight lips.

"That just leaves Stan and Rowdy that we know of. They'll be going away for the rest of their lives," Mick kept talking, wanting to keep the judge engaged, awake, diverted from the pain he had to be feeling.

"Or get the death penalty," Lawton said. "They can be charged with Reggie's and Phil's death. Not to mention their buddy's in that bomb downtown."

Mick nodded his head fiercely. "Damn straight. And Hernandez and Marcos as well."

Becca met Mick's gaze over her father's head. Mixed with concern, a bit of humor glittered in her eyes. Because even shot, her father didn't seem to be slowing down in his thirst for justice.

Mick looked into her beautiful eyes. After all this was over, would there be a chance for them?

Could he forgive himself enough to move forward with Becca for a lifetime? Could she forgive him and move forward with him, even though she said she had nothing to forgive him for?

Underneath it all, she had to realize just how he'd failed.

He should have listened closer to Tess' theories, believed her conspiracy talk, put two and two together before it came to her death and to Becca and her father being put into so much danger, her father shot.

How could she ever trust him to keep her safe?

And now, possibly a baby? What a damn fool he was to risk starting a new, little life under those circumstances?

With him living as a cop, Becca would always wonder if he would come home to her and their baby at night. She deserved a better life.

# CHAPTER THIRTY

Becca sat by her father's hospital bed. Just outside the door, Mick paced continually. His footsteps blended with the hospital noises, like just another mechanical, monitoring device, his shoes clicking along the tile floor, with his nonstop back and forth.

Something boiled inside of him, the building pressure powering his pacing.

Earlier, they'd stood in the hallway, clasping each other's hands while the doctor checked her father after his initial treatment. When the doctor had finally come to tell them her father was out of danger, Mick had told Becca he'd sit with her father while she went to fill out some paperwork the doctor needed.

As she'd walked away, she'd looked back. Mick was at her dad's bedside, speaking to him. Her father's eyes had been fixed on Mick, intently listening to every word Mick said.

What had Mick said to her father?

When she'd returned, questions inside of her waiting to be answered, Mick had walked outside, taking up his position, pacing the hallway, while she sat bedside until her father had fallen asleep.

The quiet snores of her father sounded normal, asleep after any ordinary day. She listened for a long time, reassuring herself that he was going to have many more ordinary days to come.

Then, it was time.

She pulled her hand out of her father's sleeping grasp and tiptoed outside to face whatever was coming.

Because it was obvious Mick was just waiting until the crisis had passed. Something was coming, and she might as well face it.

"Hey," she said, meeting his gaze, making the connection that still shook her to her core every time she looked into those eyes.

Fourteen years old or eighty-four years old, she knew his effect on her would always be the same.

"Hey." His voice was calm but his hand shook, giving his nervousness away, hinting at the emotion boiling inside of him. Confrontation with her wasn't his style.

She'd always been the one who had to get in his face when they had a problem. Cause "talking bout it" just wasn't his thing.

He held up one finger, then hit a few buttons on his phone. "Hey, you want to come up and keep an eye on the judge for me?" Hanging up, he waited until Weston got off the elevator and went into the judge's room.

Mick gave a quick wave to Weston, sucked in a long, deep breath, then motioned her toward a quiet area at the end of the hall. Perfect for a private conversation.

A conversation that wasn't going to be good.

She knew what was coming even before he said it. Felt him pulling back, removing himself from her emotionally.

Once again.

Well, to hell with that. She wasn't losing him again. Not without an all-out fight.

His willingness to talk was at least progress. Last time, he'd just walked away.

Hope. There was hope for them. Surely, there had to be. He loved her. He'd always loved her. No matter what else had happened, that love still remained. She knew it.

"Becca." He looked at her and a wall of cold steel slid down behind his eyes.

That slamming shut on access to his emotions sent a frigid shiver through her. Chilled blood began pumping throughout her body, lowering her body temperature with a killing frost that slowed the beat of her heart.

A gray mist shimmered between them, like a fog moving over the mountains, obscuring the sharp detail of the landscape between them.

"I think you've known for a long time just how much guilt I felt over Tess' death, how responsible I felt."

She nodded, waiting for him to finish his statement.

She began to push back the fog that threatened to hide the way forward.

She'd had two years to think about what she wished she'd said to Mick.

Two years to wonder if anything she could ever say would bring him back. Or if he was just so far into his own head that she could never reach that inner bit of guilt that gnawed at him.

Nothing would obscure the clarity of her vision for them. Her vision for the future.

"I wondered." He stopped and pressed his fingertips together into a steeple, as if trying to compress his emotions into a tight box.

But, she could see them straining at the seams, fighting to break free.

"I wondered," he continued in a tightly controlled voice. "How I could ever bring you into a lifestyle where you would never know if your husband was coming home at the end of the day."

She nodded again. Where was he going with this? It was an unexpected turn. She hadn't prepared an argument for this. So, she just listened, waiting for the fog to clear, taking in his words, absorbing what he was saying.

Which mainly seemed to be leading to the fact that, once again, they couldn't be together.

His green eyes stared intently into hers, the middle yellow flecks around the iris reflecting back the afternoon light filtering through the window.

He took her hand, and her stomach compressed into a tight knot. This was it, the moment he justified walking away from her again.

Could she fight it, this new justification, that for her own good, he was going to rip out her guts, and leave her empty and hurting?

Could she continue to fight for them as a couple, against this nameless force inside of Mick that kept pulling away, saying that for whatever reason, he wasn't good enough? That she would be better off without him.

He motioned toward two armchairs against the wall, a quiet place for families to talk. Mick sat down.

She collapsed into the chair, leaning back. Her legs seemed too weak to stand under the weight of his disappointing words. She felt a headache coming on.

How many people had sat here dealing with losing someone they loved, dealing with the fact there was nothing they could do?

He leaned forward, turning toward her, taking both of her hands in his, looking into her eyes.

At least this time he was saying it, owning it, not just walking away like a wounded dog to hurt by himself, leaving her wondering was it really final.

At least this time, she would hear the words.

If this was how he felt, after all they'd been through, then maybe there was no possibility of saving them as a couple. Maybe they'd been on life support, in a coma the last two years.

They were just making it final, admitting there was no hope, pulling the plug.

The hospital smells of antiseptics and desperation wafted around her, the quiet voices of doctors and nurses formed white noise blocking out everything except the sound of Mick's voice.

She'd been prepared to fight but suddenly realized maybe she should just accept it. It wasn't healthy to hold onto someone who kept pushing you away.

If she were carrying a child, she wouldn't want that child to live that way. So, neither should she.

She looked up at him, waiting for the words, waiting for the final blow. *God*, she prayed, *please give me the strength not to beg, cry, or plead. Let me walk away with my dignity.*

Even if she were losing the one person she didn't think she could live without.

"I can't put you through what you've been through the last couple of days. Hell, every day since I became a cop. The life of a cop's wife?" He shook his head.

"Never knowing when you kiss me in the morning will it will be the last time you see me. You've lost too many loved ones." His eyes filled with emotion. Sorrow and regret played across his face. "Your mother as a young child, your twin in the line of duty. And today, almost losing your father. Hell, even your dog almost got killed."

She laughed, nervous, crazy laughter that welled up at the darkest moment of your life, off kilter, feeling disoriented at the wacky comment.

"I love you, Becca."

He loved her? What did that mean to him?

"That's why I can't ask you to live that life."

A twisting pain wrenched through her. This was it? Good-bye, no turning back?

"So, I've decided to quit law enforcement."

"What?"

He wasn't saying they were through? Shock surged through her, followed almost immediately by hope, the deadness fading, pushed away by exhilaration, excitement.

For the first time since this conversation began, she sucked in a deep breath and the huge weight on her chest lifted. Laughter bubbled up inside of her, happy, hopeful laughter just waiting to burst free. She pushed it back, not wanting to miss a single word from Mick's mouth.

"I'm going to get some type of 'regular job'. Maybe I could be a teacher." He twisted his mouth ruefully. "A coach, something where I can still make a difference in the world, be a force for good." He laughed harshly. "But, where there's less chance of bullets flying."

"Good luck with that, the way schools are anymore. Or at least what you see on the news."

He arched an eyebrow but didn't get into that whole conversation about school safety.

She met his eyes, happiness washing away all the hopelessness she'd felt only moments ago. "You love me and are willing to give up the most important thing in your life for me?"

"Second most important thing," he corrected her. "A life with you is the most important thing I could ever imagine."

She stood up and slid onto his lap. His arms wrapped her into an embrace that seemed like it could keep any danger away from them, could protect their love forever.

Snuggling into his chest, she breathed him in, that scent that was pure him, that essence of him she'd missed so much. As it filled her chest, she accepted his commitment. "You can't live without me any more than I can live without you."

A gentle light filled his eyes. "I could exist. I proved that these last two years." His mouth moved closer to hers. "But, that's all it was, existing."

She nodded. "I went through my days, enjoying teaching and mentoring, enjoyed Barley, my dad, my friends."

"But a small piece of life was missing." She snuggled closer to him. "The central piece of my life that was you, you and our love, the love that made everything right. Made life worth living." She shook her head.

"So, exactly what are you saying, Mick?" She looked into his eyes, wanting him to say the words, needing the words.

A gentle, strong, giving smile spread across his face, turning him into the most handsome man she'd ever seen. In real life, in the movies, on television or in magazines, there wasn't a more appealing man on the planet.

"I'm saying I love you," he said quietly, the words

whispering into her heart. "I want to marry you. I want to spend the rest of my life with you."

He looked into her eyes for a long moment, and she felt her heart stopping, waiting for the words.

"Will you marry me, Becca Jefferson?"

She gasped, felt her heart start beating again, and waited a moment until oxygen reached her brain and she could respond.

But, the moment wasn't quite perfect.

"Shouldn't you be on one knee?" she said with a lifted eyebrow.

He laughed softly. "You've brought me to my knees emotionally. I'm offering you all that I can bring, love, safety, security that your husband will come home every night. Marry me?" he whispered.

Their mouths were just a breath apart. The one word that would seal their lives together forever needed saying.

She looked up from his mouth to his eyes.

"No." She shook her head. "I can't."

He leaned back, confusion clouding his beautiful, green eyes. "That's not how my fantasy goes," he said with a disbelieving laugh.

She laughed low in her throat, and thought of how to frame her response. "I'm not saying no to the proposal. I'm saying I can't take you away from the work you were made for. The world needs people like you, designed to fight evil, to keep men like Hernandez, Marcos and Rowdy in check. I don't want to live in a world, bring children into a world that doesn't have good men like you fighting for their future."

She shrugged. "You were right about my resentment toward law enforcement after Tess' death. I couldn't believe you would go back, put your life at risk. I took it as a personal affront. Maybe you sensed that even if I didn't come right out and say it."

His face showed he'd gotten the message loud and clear.

"But, when someone I loved was threatened, you, Barley, my dad, I was determined not to let those evil men hurt any of you. I started to get what drives you and Tess and all those other cops out there."

His eyes warmed, the liquid yellow around the iris turning into honey, sweet and promising.

Her skin heated in response. She leaned just a bit closer, his breath brushing across her lips, and she was barely able to hold back.

But, there was more that needed saying. "I can't say yes to marrying you if it will take you away from the life you were destined to live, the work you love. A career that I respect so much."

He opened his mouth to speak but she placed one finger over it. Softly, he kissed her finger and she almost lost it, almost gave in to the physical desire he invoked. But she couldn't.

"We had to grieve, Mick. You your way, me mine. To work through all the emotions of losing Tess. That happens to people sometimes when they go through a traumatic loss, an event like you witnessed, with the loss of your partner, me with the loss of my sister, my twin."

Their eyes met with a deep sadness passing between them. Then, she shook it off, the way she'd learned to do so that she could go on living.

"Tess wouldn't want either of us to be so damaged by her death that we couldn't fulfill ourselves in life. We needed to grieve. Now, we can just be happy that we found each other again, even if it was in this crazy, horrible way."

"Crazy." He arched an eyebrow.

"We need to move on," she said softly. "Do what we were destined to do. I was made to teach." She tilted her head.

"I'm the perfect teacher, loving and molding them when they're young and malleable. You're the perfect cop, going after the ones that didn't learn, who need to be brought under control. We have to do what we're made to do. If that means I have to live with the possibility that one day you might be taken away from me, just like countless other law enforcement spouses know could happen, then that's how it has to be."

She nodded. "If you were to give your all doing what is so important to society, doing what you love." She shrugged, as if she hadn't just acknowledged a world shattering possibility.

"I'll know it was the right thing to do. I'll teach our children that people have to take that risk to make the world safe and good."

She smiled into his eyes, feeling the connection that had rocked her the first time she'd seen him at fourteen. "There are no guarantees in life, Mick. You have to live as if nothing is guaranteed. Live the way you love."

His eyes glistened with unshed tears, with gratitude. "We'll live like there is no tomorrow, grabbing every minute as if it could be our last. Every second will be precious, every moment filled with our love."

He touched her stomach. "I hope our child is on the way because it's going to be a wonderful life that he or she comes into, a wonderful home."

He moved a millimeter closer to her mouth. "Because if you're made to be a teacher, and I'm made to be a cop, then it's even more true that we're made to love each other and spend our lives together."

He looked into her eyes. "Do you take this cop to wed and love for the rest of our lives, Becca Jefferson?"

"I do," she said, just before he moved in, meeting her lips, cutting off any further comment.

No more words were necessary because everything that needed saying had been said. Because all that really mattered in life was that they would be together. Everything else was negotiable. Everything else came second.

## CHAPTER THIRTY-ONE

When Mick and Becca returned to the hospital room, Weston, Luke, Roberto and Grant were all seated around the judge's bed. The last three had slipped into the room without Becca or Mick even noticing them.

The judge's eyes were droopy but a big smile covered his face. Barley cuddled on his lap, leaning into the judge's chest, a smile of contentment on the little dog's face that mirrored what Mick was feeling through and through.

"I sneaked him up in a duffle bag," Luke said with a grin and a head tilt at the dog. "A nurse stuck her head in here. Lawton said we were cops, and she left without comment. They never question cops too much. One of the perks of the job."

"Barley's my therapy dog. He's medicinal," the judge said. "Makes me feel better."

"Nice of you guys to come check on the judge," Mick said.

"They came here for more than that," Lawton said, his expression hardening.

Weston, Roberto, Luke and Grant all exchanged knowing looks with Lawton.

"What's up?" Mick placed his hand in the middle of Becca's back, leading her closer to the bed.

"I was talking to Stan," Roberto said, tilting his head with the expression Mick had come to recognize as meaning something big was coming.

Weston nodded in agreement. "Stan was just a treasure

trove of information after you all left for the hospital."

"Yeah, he's like that," Mick said sarcastically.

"I kept wondering why Hernandez didn't just get you killed in prison, Mick, then have Lawton killed later on." Roberto rubbed his hand down his cheek, scratching thoughtfully. "Didn't make sense to me. But, Stan said he heard Rowdy talking to Hernandez on the phone in the car one day. Said he could hear everything Hernandez said billowing out of the phone. Hernandez said he had it all timed out to make it look like you, the judge and Becca were just another couple of victims."

Mick arched his eyebrow for Roberto to continue.

"Hernandez said the big guy didn't want any investigations into the judge and his daughter's disappearances leading back to him. He said it had to look like just another part of the domestic terrorism."

"Stan said some other stuff too." Roberto shot a meaningful look around the group. "I think Mick was supposed to die when he drove the truck underneath the federal building, and then called for them to bring the judge out. Hernandez knew you wouldn't be able to let the judge die. You'd do whatever was necessary to save the judge as well as the people down at the federal building."

Roberto tapped the side of his head. "He knew you'd think you could get the truck out into the Gulch once the judge had been released. Counted on you being the hero that you are." He grinned at Mick.

"But, the judge was supposed to be in the back of the truck and your phone call would activate the bomb, killing both of you. Stan, Rowdy, White and Becca were going to go to another vehicle where they thought Rowdy's cousin would be in the trunk."

"Cops found a second vehicle full of explosives near the original blast site, corroborating Stan's story," Roberto added.

"Someone had to be watching to make sure everything went off right. When Mick didn't call the phone that would ignite the blast, they did it, blowing up the truck. But, the second bomb never went off because Rowdy and his crew never showed up there."

Lawton nodded. "Hernandez had planned to wipe out any connection back to himself. Me, Becca, you." He pointed at Mick. "Even Rowdy, Stan, and White."

A huge gust of breath collectively left everyone's lungs.

Mick just nodded, trying to process all the possibilities, all the times that Becca and the judge could have died. And yeah, him too.

He looked down at Becca, who returned his look with a strength in her eyes of the type of woman who would never back down from evil. "Guess they didn't figure on Becca refusing to be a victim."

A low laugh spread around the circle. Becca smiled. "Darn straight. Never been a victim, never will be. Things happen, but you just have to surmount them."

The judge reached for her hand, giving it a squeeze. For a moment, their gazes connected, and Mick thought of all they'd surmounted in their lifetime.

Then, the judge looked back up at the group, his expression hardening. "Who is the person who was pulling the strings on Hernandez?"

"Someone who thinks they're pretty powerful," Roberto said.

"Sounds like someone who is," Mick added.

"We're going to find that out," Weston said. "We're gonna find all of these guys who bring this poison into our communities, addicting kids and adults alike, ruining so many people's lives." Weston's eyes held a fierceness that was a little bit frightening. If you were on the wrong side of it.

The judge and the others nodded, conviction embedded in the lines around their mouths and eyes.

Weston's intensity equaled anything Mick had felt in the last couple of days. The guy had an ax to grind.

"We'll find that guy who was calling the shots to

Hernandez," Roberto spoke up. "We'll find them all. Mick and I can bring all of you in under the jurisdiction of the FBI, forming a joint task force, a coalition to fight drugs and all the violence and ruin it brings into our community. We'll eat our way up the food chain, taking out little fish, bigger fish, then the sharks that run this show."

"In the name of Tess," Mick vowed to Becca and her father, looking into both of their eyes with a promise.

Becca looked around the group, satisfaction filling her face. "In the name of Tess."

"Exactly," Weston said. "And all the little girls and other innocent victims who've been led to their death by these people who don't care who they hurt."

Like Weston's sister. Mick might be the only one of the group who knew just how personal this fight was to Weston.

Mick wondered if each of these guys had a stake in this fight? Was it as personal to each of them as it had been to him, the judge and Becca?

He might not be certain of the origins of each of their passions to get the bad guys out of their community. But, he felt their drive. It showed in their faces.

Barley gave a little woof and everyone laughed, the serious mood broken.

"Keep it down, Barley," the judge said. "Want us getting labeled as lawbreakers?"

"We're rule breakers, not lawbreakers. There's a difference between a rule and a law," Mick said. "You can bend the rules for a good cause."

Becca smiled and glanced up, meeting Mick's eyes. "I have one concession I'd like to ask of all you tough law enforcers."

"Name it," Luke said.

"Can y'all take a short break from righteous endeavors for a wedding?"

"Woo hoo," Luke yelped. "About time." Luke was a happily married man and had been pushing Mick to "tie the knot" before Tess had gotten murdered.

A loud murmur of approval circled the group.

The judge looked into Mick's eyes, and Mick saw the father the man had become when Mick had needed one at fourteen smiling back at him.

He'd always need that man's love and approval. The judge and Becca were a lucky package deal.

"Soon as they let me out of this hospital bed, my schedule's clear," the judge said, his voice raspy and hoarse with emotion.

"Let's call my mother," Roberto piped up. "She can pull a wedding together in no time. Even with all her rosary-praying, she's losing hope that I'm ever gonna walk down the aisle, so this would make her very happy."

He cocked an eyebrow. "And take her focus off me for a while."

Mick looked down into Becca's eyes. "How's Saturday two weeks from today sound to you?"

"Like the happiest day of my life," she said, then rose on her toes to kiss him in front of the whole damn task force.

The End

*Read Weston's story*

# *Tempted to Kill*
A Men of the Badge Novel

The chemistry between Alisa and Weston could be as deadly as the drugs that are readily available in the dark underworld of sex and drug trafficking in Atlanta.

An undercover cop, Weston's job is to "blend in with scum," and go after the big guy in the drug ring. Protecting Alisa as she searches for her missing teen sister could jeopardize the mission as well as his and Alisa's ability to keep breathing.

*Read Forrester's story*

# *Taunted by a Killer*
## A Men of the Badge Novel

*Second time romance?*
*Or second chance at heartache?*

Will Cassie and Forrester have their second chance at love? If she survives the serial killer who sets fires around his victims, then she can face the flashfire of heat and want that sweep through her in the arms of her former love. A fire that once burned her badly.